D0494452

THE WOMAN
ON THE CLIFF

An addictive crime thriller full of twists

JANICE FROST

JOFFE
BOOKS

First published 2019
Joffe Books, London
www.joffebooks.com

This book is a work of fiction. Names, characters, businesses, organisations, places and events are either the product of the author's imagination or are used fictitiously. Any resemblance to actual persons, living or dead, events or locales is entirely coincidental. The spelling used is British English except where fidelity to the author's rendering of accent or dialect supersedes this.

Please join our mailing list for free kindle crime thriller, detective, mystery, and romance books and new releases.
http://www.joffebooks.com/contact/

©Janice Frost

ISBN: 978-1-78931-131-0

To my husband and sons.

CHAPTER ONE

Suddenly, the car is all packed. At the last minute, Izzy runs back into the house to grab Sebastian, her favourite teddy bear. I'm pleased she's decided to bring him after all. He's a cheerful, traditional sort of bear, with a red bow tie and blue-and-white striped dungarees. My mother gave him to Izzy on the day she was born. When she brought him to the hospital, he was plush, new as Izzy, his fur still soft and silky. Now he's battered by years of love and misuse.

I wait in the car. I'm in no hurry to leave, even though we have a long journey ahead of us. The next four years will be full of moments like this. Partings. Of course, there will be happy reunions too. Visits to St Andrews for me, visits home for Izzy. Long holidays and the odd long weekend. It will be different, that's all. I've told myself this over and over in the past few weeks, but I still have a lump in my throat every time I think of Izzy embarking on this new phase of her life, without me.

Not least because of Moira.

Izzy appears at the front door, tucking Sebastian under her arm as she locks up.

I catch the old bear's eye. He seems to mock: *I'm going with her, and you're not.* I don't resent him for it. He's known Izzy as long as I have.

'Just make sure you look after her,' I mouth back.

"Got him," Izzy says, tossing Sebastian carelessly onto the back seat. It seems no time at all since she spent ages carefully securing Sebastian in his own little car seat before we could set off on the shortest of journeys.

I've been thinking a lot about my own student days since my daughter was accepted to study at my old *alma mater*. I suppose it's not so surprising that she put St Andrews at the top of her list, given that she's grown up hearing stories about my time there. Not just from me, but from Elspeth and even Shona on her occasional visits.

There is one story about those days that Izzy hasn't heard. Not because it's a secret, exactly. But stories need endings, and Moira's never had one.

I start the engine. Izzy falls silent. I sneak a look at her and see that she's gazing in the side-view mirror at our house as it disappears into the distance. *This is it*, I think, with a stab of poignancy. One of those moments that you hold in your heart forever. An end, and a beginning for both of us.

CHAPTER TWO

No one realised that Moira was missing. Lucy claimed she was the first to notice, but only because she was looking to borrow Moira's hair dryer. She'd been calling up to Moira's room. When no one answered she'd gone in and, finding no one there, helped herself. Moira wouldn't have minded. She'd have been pleased to know that she'd done one last favour for her friend.

Of all of us, Shona might have been the one to wonder where Moira was hiding herself away, but Shona was on a geography field trip that weekend, somewhere in the Outer Hebrides.

So it was me who saw the police car draw up outside our house on North Street. It was Sunday. Tea-time. I was in the kitchen, scraping days-old gunk off the bottom of a pan that Lucy had abandoned on the worktop. I'd just popped a tape into my cassette player and was singing along to Bruce Springsteen when I heard the engine. I looked out of the window just as two men emerged from the car. One was in uniform, the other was dressed in a grey suit under an open raincoat, which also looked grey in the fading light of the early evening.

I'd like to say that I had an intuition that they had come about Moira. But I didn't. On catching the flash of the vehicle's orange-on-white markings, my first thought was of the little block of cannabis resin hidden in the top drawer of my bedside table. Other possibilities then flashed through my mind. By the time I opened the door and took in the grave faces of the two men outside, I'd guessed it must be bad news.

The uniformed officer was very young, not much older than me. He looked at me hesitantly and cleared his throat. His colleague stood by, fingering a packet of 'Player's No 6' and looking impatient.

"We're here about Moira Mackie. This is her address," the young PC said, in a broad Fife accent.

It didn't sound like a question. I thought of calling Elspeth down from her room, but there was no need. She was already leaning over the banister of the upstairs landing, asking what was going on.

"It's the police," I called up the stairs.

"I can see that. What do they want?"

"They're looking for Moira."

"She's not here." She was halfway down the stairs now, peering over my shoulder at the two men still waiting on the pavement.

"We know she's not here," the older man said ominously. "Look, can we come in? It's a bit of a . . . delicate matter."

Elspeth, standing directly behind me now, asked, "Is Moira in some kind of trouble?"

It was worrying to hear the hint of pleasure in her tone, given what had happened only two weeks previously. *Still*, I reasoned, *people need time to change.*

"Let's go inside first. Then I'll explain," the older man insisted. Still we made no move to let them in, so he brushed past his colleague and, with a sort of domino effect, somehow we all ended up in the sitting room.

"My name is DI John Menzies. This is PC Innes Nevin. I'm sorry, but I have some bad news about Moira Mackie."

By then, it was obvious what he was going to say. Elspeth beat him to it. "Oh God. She's dead, isn't she?"

"I'm sorry, but yes." Menzies suggested we all sit down. Elspeth and I sat together on the couch. My fingers gripped the patchwork crocheted blanket that Shona had thrown over it to hide the threadbare seat covers. The policemen looked blurry and I realised there were tears in my eyes. I glanced at Elspeth. She seemed calm enough, but she was never one for histrionics.

"I'm sorry," Menzies said again, sounding sincere enough, though this was probably routine for him. I glanced at his companion, PC Nevin. His head was bowed and his hands were tucked under his armpits. He looked troubled. Perhaps this was his first experience of being a harbinger of death.

"Are you sure?" I asked.

"Yes. Her parents have been informed."

"What happened?" Elspeth asked.

Now Menzies seemed ill at ease. Whatever happened to Moira, it must have been something very bad. He cleared his throat. "It's looking like the poor wee lassie was murdered."

After a respectful pause, during which I cried unashamedly while Elspeth patted me on the arm, Menzies asked, "Who else lives here? Just the three of you, was it?"

"Four."

"Five."

Elspeth and I spoke simultaneously. I was the one who forgot to discount Moira. Elspeth clarified. "Besides Ros and I, there's Shona and Lucy. Shona's on a field trip on the Isle of Lewis this weekend."

"Ah, archaeologist, is she?"

"No, geographer."

"When will she be back?"

"Tomorrow."

"Right. Well, we'll need to talk to all of you. Where's . . .?"

"Lucy?" Elspeth prompted. "She's at the library. She'll be back any minute."

Menzies looked around the room and, finding no clock, consulted his wristwatch. "I suppose it won't do any harm to ask some questions in the meantime. Do you two lassies feel up to it?"

I couldn't speak for Elspeth, but personally I'd never felt less like talking. I marvelled at Elspeth's calm. There'd been no love lost between her and Moira, but still . . .

"Did Moira have a boyfriend?" I'd almost forgotten PC Nevin was there until he asked the question.

"No." Elspeth.

"Yes." Me.

We answered simultaneously again.. "Well, which is it?" Menzies asked.

"Sort of both. Moira was going out with a local boy," Elspeth said.

This seemed to spike their interest. I knew what they were thinking. St Andrews isn't a big place. Chances were the name would mean something to one of them.

"His name was Stuart Brogan," Elspeth said.

A knowing nod from Menzies. "Eddie Brogan's laddie. I know his father."

"But they split up," I added.

While PC Nevin was scribbling away in his notebook, the front door banged shut. From the hallway came the tuneless sound of Lucy singing a Michael Jackson song. Her jaw dropped when she entered the room and saw us all sitting there, Elspeth and I huddled together on the couch. The two strangers. I suspect her first thought on catching sight of a police uniform was, as mine had been, of the illegal substance she had in her bedroom.

"What's going on?" she asked.

"Something's happened to Moira," Elspeth said. "Maybe you should sit down."

Lucy removed the khaki army bag she carried everywhere and slung it on the nearest chair. It slipped off and landed on the carpet with a dull thud. Menzies used the word 'murder' again, which seemed somehow indecent in the same sentence as Moira's name.

Like me, Lucy was disbelieving at first. Maybe she thought it was a hoax. But as the moments passed and no one smiled, the truth dawned on her, and she sat in a heavy silence, chewing on her knuckles, a picture of misery.

"Was it quick?" she asked at last. I felt a stab of shame for not having considered this before. Maybe it was the shock. Lucy was really asking if Moira had suffered. After the fact of her death, it was the only thing that really mattered.

"We believe so," Menzies said, but I had the impression he would have told us that whatever.

"How did she die?" Lucy pushed damp strands of mousy brown hair away from her face, revealing eyes glistening with fearful anticipation.

Menzies retreated behind stilted police speak. "Er . . . I'm not at liberty to release any details."

"Why?" Her tone was confrontational. I cringed. Lucy was in an anti-establishment phase in those days. Everything was black and white. The government was fascist, the police pigs. No doubt she saw Menzies and Nevin as the enemy. In the weeks following Moira's death, Lucy became convinced that 'they' had done away with her friend as part of some wider conspiracy.

One afternoon, irritated by her senseless paranoia, I finally challenged her. "Who are 'they' exactly, Lucy? A person killed Moira. A deranged, sick, evil *individual*. There's no 'they.'"

When she only stared at me, I added, "And just tell me, why 'they' would be interested in Moira anyway? She was a nobody. An ordinary working-class girl like you and me."

Still, Lucy was unshakeable in her beliefs. Her distress over Moira only fuelled her existing fears. Blaming some nameless and faceless entity was her way of processing her grief. It provided distance. I think it was too much for her to face the bleak truth that Moira's killer could have been someone she knew, someone who was as ordinary as the rest of us.

Now Elspeth came to Menzies's rescue. "Because if they give out too much information, it might hinder their investigation. They keep things back, so they know when people are lying to them." She looked to him for confirmation and was rewarded with a nod.

"It'll all be in the papers soon anyway, won't it?" I said. "All the grisly details. Poor Moira."

"Poor Moira's parents, you mean," Elspeth corrected. "Moira won't know anything about it."

It must have been awkward for Elspeth. She'd hated Moira from the start. I worried that she sounded unsympathetic, that the police might judge her heartless. Elspeth possessed an analytical brain and a direct way of talking that could sometimes come across as cold.

"Can you at least tell us where she was found?" I asked.

"Out on the cliff path, near the rock and spindle," Menzies said.

We all nodded. The rock and spindle was a well-known local landmark, and an interesting geological feature in its own right. A vertical pillar rising out of a circular slab, it was believed to have once formed part of a volcanic vent system. There was a black-and-white photograph pinned to the corkboard on Moira's bedroom wall, showing her leaning against the rock formation, her skin silvery in the moonlight, the sea a black abyss behind her. Andrew Kelso had taken the picture. Oh God, Andrew. Someone was going to have to tell Andrew that Moira was dead.

I glanced at Elspeth, mouthed his name. I'd been about to mention him to Menzies earlier, when he'd asked about boyfriends, but Lucy arrived and it slipped my mind. Elspeth narrowed her eyes and gave a slight shake of her head. Menzies didn't notice but Nevin, looking up from his notebook, saw the brief communication between us and frowned.

"What can you tell us about Moira?" Menzies asked.

Lucy shuddered, still too upset to gather her thoughts. Elspeth frowned. She'd never had a good word to say about Moira.

"That's too big a question," I said at last. "Can you break it down?"

"You're right," Menzies agreed. "For now, I'm just after something general."

"She was . . ." I faltered, searching for the right words. My mind went blank.

"She was a good friend. Loyal. Trustworthy. The sort of person you can depend on," Lucy said, suddenly articulate. I nodded, though I didn't necessarily associate any of those qualities with Moira. Not because she didn't possess them but because I'd never thought to define her before now.

Nervous excitement was making Lucy say whatever popped into her head. "She was bubbly. Full of life. Always up for a challenge." Some of that might be true. Menzies had asked for general, and that's what he was getting. I nodded along. Elspeth was probably just grateful that the focus wasn't on her.

PC Nevin seemed to be writing a lot in his notebook. I wondered how the scraps we were offering could possibly help in their investigation.

Menzies asked us some more questions. About Moira's friends, her comings and goings. I thought that they would leave after that and was surprised when Menzies announced that he and Nevin needed to search Moira's room. Lucy and I exchanged panicked glances.

But they weren't interested in anyone else's room. Moira's bedroom was next to mine. The walls in the house were thin and left nothing to the imagination when one of us had a boyfriend around for the night. Even so, I couldn't make out any of the hushed conversation between Menzies and Nevin while they were searching through her things.

I wondered if they'd notice the photograph of Moira at the rock and spindle and wonder who had taken it. I thought of Innes Nevin catching the look that had passed between Elspeth and me. I'd realised almost immediately that he was sharper than Menzies. He had the sort of eyes that books always describe as 'piercing.' Maybe he wasn't allowed to ask too many questions or take the lead. They probably had roles assigned by their rank.

After they had gone, Lucy said, "Do you think we should have mentioned Andrew?"

"No," Elspeth said decisively. "You know that would probably get him into trouble. He has a wife and a child, remember?"

"But . . ." Lucy's comment died on her lips. It wasn't hard to guess what she had been about to say. The police would surely regard him as a suspect.

Andrew Kelso was a lecturer in the history department at the university. He had been having an on-off affair with Moira for the best part of a year. His wife had given birth to their first child during the summer holidays, and at the end of the previous year he'd written to Moira to say that their affair had to end, but before his daughter was a month old, they'd resumed their relationship.

"Andrew is no angel, but can you really see him harming anyone?" When it came to Andrew Kelso, Elspeth could hardly be regarded as impartial. Even though she was seeing a man called Piers Thornton, a postgraduate student at Edinburgh University, she was hopelessly in love with Andrew. It was one of the reasons why she'd hated Moira.

In any case, it turned out that Andrew and Moira had not been as discreet as we, and they, had thought. The police soon found out about their relationship, and an enraged Menzies paid us another visit, demanding to know why we'd seen fit to conceal this vital piece of information from him.

Lucy hadn't thought about it until after Menzies and Nevin had gone. As for me, that glare from Elspeth had cautioned me to keep my mouth shut.

But Elspeth's attitude worried me. She gave the impression that if Andrew turned out to be Moira's killer, it would make no difference to her opinion of him at all.

CHAPTER THREE

We're not going straight to St Andrews. My old friend, Elspeth Blair, has invited us to stay the night at her house in Edinburgh.

I hate driving on motorways, so we take the scenic route to Edinburgh. It involves sticking to the A-roads, which will add a lot of time to our journey, but as I've said already, I'm not impatient for this trip to be over.

Izzy and I skipped breakfast in favour of an early start. Even so, it's going to take the best part of the day to get to Edinburgh. I don't just despise driving on motorways, I also hate driving for more than a couple of hours at a stretch. The plan is to stop at Scotch Corner for breakfast, then have another stop later for lunch, perhaps somewhere in Northumbria or the Scottish Borders. It's a drive I've done many times before, with Doug at the wheel.

Sometimes I forget that I'm a widow. My husband of ten years, Doug, was killed nine years ago in Iraq. He was a photojournalist.

There haven't been many men since Doug's death. It was a while before I fully accepted that my husband wasn't coming back, and in the meantime, working full time and raising my daughter alone kept me busy. If loneliness ever drove me to bring a man home to my bed — and that wasn't often — I would insist on him leaving while Izzy was still asleep or after she'd gone to school. Not the ideal basis for a lasting relationship.

When she was about eleven, Izzy began asking me why I didn't start dating again. Since she'd given me her approval, I joined an online dating group and met a man called Simon. We dated on and off for a couple of years, but our hearts weren't really in it and we called it a day. I've resigned myself to the idea that I may never find someone to grow old with.

Around eleven a.m., I turn into the unremarkable services at Scotch Corner. The homogeneity of these places is at once depressing and reassuring. You can't tell one from the other, but you can be pretty certain about what you'll find there.

I've had a soft spot for them since the days when Doug and I, unable to afford the train, travelled by overnight coach from London to Edinburgh to visit our families. It was an endless journey, with a single stop at a service station to relieve the monotony.

Izzy and I drink coffee and munch on bacon butties, surrounded by lorry drivers and business people, and other travellers less easy to categorise. And then it's back on the road. We don't stop again until we reach Jedburgh. I'm not hungry, but Izzy announces that she's famished again, so we choose a café that caters for both our appetites.

Elspeth won't be home from work until six, so there's no advantage in arriving early. After lunch, we take a stroll along the river and visit the beautiful ruins of Jedburgh Abbey, before beginning the final phase of our journey.

The sky is growing dusky by the time we hit the outskirts of Edinburgh. Elspeth lives in a palatial four-bedroom house in Morningside, one of the poshest areas of town. She's a successful accountant and doesn't need to worry about money.

Her life has been tumultuous at times. Briefly married and divorced twice, Elspeth describes herself as a serial spinster. She has a son, Aaron, from her first marriage, whom she seldom sees. For the past eight months, she's been in a relationship with a man called Duncan Shore, a quietly-spoken civil servant who works in the Scottish parliament. I don't hold out much hope that their relationship will endure. Elspeth isn't an easy person to get along with. You need to be able to understand why she is the way she is.

Elspeth waves from the window when we step out of the car. She's trying to tell us that Duncan is coming out to help with our bags, but there's no need. Izzy and I have it under control, balancing suitcases and boxes between us, so that when Duncan meets us at the end of the path, he's redundant.

"Here, let me take some of those," he fusses.

"If I let go of one, they'll all go flying," I laugh. "Anyway, they're not heavy, just a bit bulky."

"Mine are heavy," Izzy says. She slings a large canvas tote off her shoulder and thrusts it at Duncan, who pretends to buckle under the weight.

Elspeth is on the doorstep waiting to greet us. There are hugs, kisses, sighs and exclamations. Duncan, slightly awkward in the midst of all this female shrieking, busies himself with the bags.

"No more of that auntie stuff, Izzy. Just call me Elspeth now that you're all grown up."

"Ok, Auntie Elsp—"

Elspeth has prepared the spare room for us. Like the other rooms in the house, it is elegant and spacious, with ornate cornice work around a high ceiling, painted in white. A vase of scented lilies sits on a table top near the window. Izzy screws up her nose. She's never liked their scent. I tell her to put up with it because they look glorious there, framed in the window with its backdrop of pink sandstone buildings and, more distantly, the brooding outline of the Pentlands.

"Duncan's made a lasagne, when you're ready," Elspeth calls from the hallway, and right on cue, Izzy declares that she's ravenous.

Duncan has laid the table in the dining room, in a wide bay window. Elspeth pours chilled Pinot Grigio into cut-crystal glasses, and we eat by flickering candlelight with the blinds drawn up, so that the garden outside seems to glow and waver in the encroaching darkness.

"I miss the smell of the hops," I say, referring to the aroma — some say stink — that pervades the Edinburgh air at certain times.

"You can still smell them but it's not as pungent as it used to be. Most of the breweries have closed down," Elspeth says.

Our conversation veers randomly from topic to topic as we play catch up with each other's news. We haven't had many opportunities to meet up in the past year. Sometimes it's like that. It depends on the patterns of both our lives. That song, 'Who Knows Where the Time Goes?' is the refrain of our lives.

"Elspeth's had another promotion at work," Duncan says, his voice full of pride. *He's a keeper*, I think, and hope Elspeth can hang onto him.

"Did I tell you Aaron's off backpacking in New Zealand?" Elspeth says, her words drawing a deep sigh of envy from Izzy.

"I've told Izzy she can do that when she's thirty — and only if she's completed her Krav Maga master's training."

"I'm going. Next June to September," Izzy says. "Get used to it, Mum."

"So, why St Andrews?" Duncan asks, topping up our glasses. Izzy is already a little drunk. "Apart from the obvious, of course. English universities aren't good enough."

We laugh. Izzy was born in England. She has an English accent and has to put up with a certain amount of teasing whenever she comes north of the border.

"Well, it's Mum's and Aunt— I mean, Elspeth's fault, partly. They've always told such great stories about what they got up to when they were students there."

I glance at Elspeth. There's one story we've never told. I wonder if that's what Elspeth is thinking too.

"I like the four-year degree structure," Izzy continues. "And the fact that you can do more subjects and don't have to choose your main one until after two years."

"It has a reputation for being a bit elitist, doesn't it, St Andrews?" Duncan asks. "Didn't Prince William and Kate whatshername go there?" Elspeth and I roll our eyes.

I hadn't been aware of the elitist tag when I applied to go there back in the eighties. I'd spent a lot of happy family holidays in St Andrews with my parents when I was growing up. I associated the town with sandy beaches and boat trips, the Lammas Fair and walks on the pier. Ice cream on hot July days. That's what influenced my decision to apply.

I look at Izzy's face, flushed and glowing in the candlelight. She's only a little younger than Moira was when her life ended so abruptly, so violently. I give a shudder and Duncan, thinking I'm cold, draws down the blind against the draught from the window.

"So, Shona's in town," I say a little tentatively. Elspeth raises an eyebrow. "She flew in from Sydney earlier in the week to visit her parents."

Shona specialised in geology after she graduated. She has worked all over the world, most recently for a mining contractor in Australia. I haven't seen her for over a year.

"That's nice," Elspeth says without enthusiasm.

Elspeth and Shona were never particularly close. "Perhaps we could have a get-together on Sunday evening?" I suggest. "Before I head back to London on Monday?"

"I'll arrange it," Elspeth volunteers.

"To old friends," Duncan says, raising his glass. Elspeth and I exchange a look. There's the slightest pause before we raise ours.

"To old friends."

CHAPTER FOUR

Shona had been informed of Moira's death before she got back from Lewis. As soon as Menzies and Nevin left, I'd walked along to the phone box near our house to call her. She returned to St Andrews hell bent on finding someone to blame.

"Why did none of you wonder where she was?" she demanded as soon as the four of us were together.

"We assumed she was with Andrew," I said. Lucy merely blubbered and Elspeth didn't comment. There was no point in her angering Shona more by pointing out the obvious: that, for her, a weekend without Moira around was a cause for celebration.

"How the hell could she be with Andrew for two bloody days? He has a bloody family, remember?"

"She's been away with Andrew before. To those conferences he's forever going to. His wife doesn't usually go with him now they've got the baby," I said. "Or she and Andrew might have taken the train to Edinburgh for the weekend while his wife went to her mum's or . . . or something."

Shona was having none of it. "Moira had barely enough of her grant left to last to the end of term. How could she afford to go shopping in Edinburgh?"

No one had said anything about shopping. I was about to retort that maybe Andrew Kelso had paid for them both, but I knew Shona would only trash that theory too. She'd calm down eventually and stop irrationally blaming us.

Lucy stood by, biting her lip, while Shona raged and ranted. Like me, Lucy didn't go in much for conflict. I hoped she wouldn't start on about her conspiracy theory. That would send Shona over the edge.

"I mean, two days. I would have thought one of you might have had the gumption to realise something might be up with her . . ."

Elspeth allowed Shona to rant for a few more minutes before she intervened. "Are you quite finished, Shona?"

"No. I'm just getting started. I—"

"Shut up," Elspeth said, making Lucy and I cringe. "Just. Shut. Up."

"What did you say?" Shona's eyes blazed.

"You heard me. None of us are to blame for Moira's death. Stop trying to take the moral high ground just because you weren't here. I don't recall you missing me and coming to enquire after my health when I had the flu."

It had been a joke between them until that moment. Elspeth had come down with flu in the middle of December, and hadn't had the strength to drag herself out of bed to go down to the kitchen to make a cup of tea. The only other one in the house all weekend, Shona hadn't realised Elspeth was ill in bed until Saturday evening, when Elspeth, practically dehydrated, had crawled out of her room to ask for a glass of water.

Shona coloured. Her mouth opened and closed. Tears filled her eyes. I crossed the room and gave her a hug.

"I know. I know," I repeated over and over, until Shona, cried out, collapsed on the couch.

"It's just . . ."

"You wish you'd been here," I said.

"Yes." She looked at us all in turn. "I'm sorry."

"No need." Elspeth shrugged.

"Who would do such a thing?" Shona asked.

I glared at Lucy, hoping she wouldn't take this as an invitation to voice her crazy theories.

"The police asked about boyfriends," I said.

"And?" Shona prompted.

"Well, we mentioned Stuart but not Andrew." Unexpectedly, Shona didn't ask why not. Like the rest of us, she probably couldn't see him as a murderer. I thought guiltily of Stuart Brogan.

"Well, Andrew's a shit, but I can't believe he'd hurt anyone," Shona commented. "He's a spineless shit. What about Stuart Brogan? I mean, he did hit her that time."

"We can't just leave this to the pigs to investigate," Lucy said. "They're useless. And they're not to be trusted."

I thought of Inspector Menzies and felt some sympathy with Lucy's pronouncement. And then I thought of PC Nevin. "They aren't all rubbish. They'll be coming back to talk to us again. We should think about what we know that might help them."

Lucy snorted.

"Which of you was the last to see her?" Shona asked.

I thought back to Friday. It was my busiest day, lecture-wise — two in the morning, a tutorial group in the afternoon. In between classes, I'd spent time in the library doing research for an essay. "I saw her at breakfast on Friday morning. She'd run out of coffee and I let her have some from my jar," I remembered.

"That sounds like Moira. Always running out of something," Elspeth said.

There was a silence. I could tell that, like me, the others were remembering Moira and all her idiosyncrasies. It was true that she was forever running out of things and relying on the generosity of her housemates. She wasn't above pinching stuff either, a slice of bread here, a hunk of cheese there. It drove Elspeth crazy, but the rest of us tolerated Moira's transgressions because for the most part, she was good to be around — always cheerful, ready with a witty comment or even a helping hand if you needed one where academic work was concerned. And to be fair, although she'd borrow a spoonful of jam, at some later date she'd buy you a whole jar in return.

"I saw her on Friday afternoon," Elspeth said. "Must have been around two o'clock. I was on my way to a lecture. She was getting money out from the hole in the wall outside the Royal Bank of Scotland."

We all looked at Lucy. "I passed her later on. Between four and five? Near the students' union. She was talking to a man I didn't recognise. An older man. She seemed to know him."

"So, we don't know where she went after that?" Shona asked.

"I didn't come back here on Friday night." Coming from Lucy, that was unexpected. As far as we knew, she didn't have many other friends. "A girl in my Spanish group had a party at her flat. A lot of us crashed there for the night."

"Well, I for one didn't miss you," Elspeth declared. "Which just shows that none of us really know what the others are getting up to."

This remark, clearly for Shona's benefit, resonated with all of us. But somehow it made it worse to think of us all going about our everyday business, while Moira was . . . what? I was momentarily thankful that Menzies had held back the details of what exactly had happened to Moira.

"Lucy, you should tell Menzies and Nevin about the man you saw Moira talking with," I pointed out.

Lucy nodded. "I'll go tomorrow morning. After my nine o'clock lecture. I can give them a pretty good description, I think."

"Not much point," Elspeth commented.

I forgot to ask Lucy if she ever contacted Inspector Menzies about the man she'd seen with Moira. In any case, speculation about who murdered Moira was swiftly overtaken by events. The following day, Stuart Brogan was discovered, hanged, in his uncle's garage. In his pocket, the police found a note of confession and a ring that had belonged to Moira.

CHAPTER FIVE

Izzy wakes first and gives me no quarter. This isn't a morning for lying in bed. She pads across to the window and pulls back the heavy velour curtains, flooding the room with bright October sunshine. I scrunch up my eyes, pull the cover over my head and pretend to go back to sleep.

"Wakey, wakey, slugabed. Time to get up." Izzy bounces on the mattress until I give in, sit up, rub my bleary eyes.

"Why? What's the hurry? Is something special happening today?"

"Yeah, I'm leaving you, remember? Or, more precisely, you're leaving me."

Never in life. I look at her. My girl. She's perfect. I know I'm her mum, but I think she's beautiful. She has Doug's long, lean body, his gingery fairness and violet eyes. I'm always taken aback when people say she resembles me, because I can't see it. To me she's a female version of my late husband, a gift that keeps on giving.

Izzy pulls out of our embrace. For a moment, we're attached by long strands of static gold hair. And then she's off, a firefly darting around the room, collecting her washbag and towel, throwing clothes out of her suitcase until she finds the ones she wants for the day, all the while singing tunelessly — that at least she does get from me.

"I'm off for a shower, Mum. See you in five."

"Wait," I say to the empty room. Before I have a chance to feel maudlin, Elspeth appears in the doorway with three mugs of tea. She steps between Izzy's strewn clothes, shoes, and Sebastian, who's rolled off the bed in the night and is lying face down on the carpet.

"Sorry," I say. "I didn't bring her up to be so messy."

"I'm used to it. Aaron's just the same. His room's only tidy now because he's not here. And we were the same at their age, remember?" I nod, thinking of our untidy house share on North Street.

"Lucy was the worst," I say. "Never learned what the kitchen sink was for." We laugh, remembering the piles of dirty dishes, the pots and pans encrusted with grease and burnt food.

"A nightmare," Elspeth says, handing me the tea. "I wonder what she's doing now?"

It's not the first time one or the other of us has asked that question over the years. Lucy left St Andrews not long after Moira's murder. Always a little fragile, she'd seemed to unravel more and more that term, until, at the Easter break, she went home and never returned.

Later, the rest of us felt guilty for not appreciating the extent to which the tragedy had affected Lucy. No one foresaw that she would not return for her final year.

We tried to keep in touch. I wrote to her several times when I was in my final year. She seldom replied. Shona wrote to her too, with the same level of success. We learned that after six months at home, she had gone to Australia, to stay with a cousin of her mother's. There were one or two postcards after that, then nothing.

More recently I've searched for her online, on Facebook, not really expecting to find her. If Lucy is still as paranoid as she used to be, she'd be unlikely to have an online presence.

I hope that wherever she is, whatever she is doing with her life, she is happy.

I sip my tea. Elspeth picks Sebastian up off the floor and places him on Izzy's pillow. She pulls the cover up, then sits down and we chat, just like we did years ago in our house on North Street.

"Duncan's great," I tell her.

"I think I just might marry him." She gives me a thoughtful look. "What about you, Ros? Is there anyone special in your life at the moment?"

"No." I don't even try to pretend. Elspeth wouldn't be fooled. Her brain is logical and incisive, but she's good at reading people too. "I don't know. I meet men and go out with them, but it's just going through the motions. I don't feel anything. It's like I'm dead inside. It's not grief, either. Now I go whole days without thinking of Doug. Do you know, soon he'll have been dead more years than we were together? And I'm getting to be so old."

It's not often that I indulge in self-pity, and I feel a twinge of embarrassment. I'm not expecting sympathy from Elspeth. When I said she's good at reading people, I didn't mean she's the touchy-feely type. She's good at offering practical advice. This morning, though, she surprises me by taking my hand and giving it a squeeze.

"You've concentrated all your love and energy on being Izzy's mother — and father. She's a credit to you. It's your time now." She pokes me in the ribs. "And less of this old woman talk. I'm the same age as you and I've never felt more alive, or been happier. And it's not all down to Duncan."

It's not original advice. My colleagues at work and my friends at home have been saying much the same thing for weeks. Book a holiday. Take up new challenges. Get out there. I know they're right. Maybe I'll heed their advice once Izzy's settled at university and I have more time on my hands than I've had for years. There's nothing like boredom to make you give your life a shake-up. But it's not boredom I'm afraid of. It's loneliness, all that time to dwell on my empty life.

Before I can say anything, Izzy bounds back into the room, wrapped in a white fluffy bath towel, wet hair twisted in a knot atop her head.

"Great shower, Elspeth," she says. "It's time we got a proper shower at home, Mum."

That's what I'll do, I think. Throw myself into some home improvement projects. Izzy won't recognise the house when she comes home at Christmas.

"I'll go fix us some breakfast," Elspeth says. "Full Scottish, everyone?"

I take a quick shower. The aroma of fresh coffee and sizzling bacon wafts up the stairs. Izzy and I follow it to the kitchen. Elspeth is standing over the cooker, dressed in a stripy butcher's apron, looking uncharacteristically domestic.

Duncan pours coffee and orange juice. Despite declaring herself 'too excited to eat,' Izzy devours bacon, eggs, sausages, black pudding, potato scones, and toast and marmalade as though she hasn't eaten for days.

After breakfast, Duncan insists on helping Izzy carry her bags down to the car.

"Who was Moira?" Izzy asks, as we pull away from the kerb.

I'm so taken aback that I almost stall the car.

"Who?" I ask.

"Moira. I wandered into the spare room next to ours by mistake, and I couldn't help looking at some of the books in there. I picked one off the shelf and a photograph slipped out. It was of a girl leaning against some old rocks on the beach. It had the name 'Moira, St Andrews, 1988,' written on the back. Was she someone you knew?"

I feign disinterest. "Probably just someone Elspeth knew at uni."

Izzy seems satisfied with that. It seems curious that Elspeth has kept that picture. I'd assumed she'd have been happy to erase all memory of Moira from her mind. She must have taken it from Moira's room before her parents came to collect her things.

We approach St Andrews from the east, along the coast road. As we descend the long curve of Kinkell Braes, the town begins to unfold before us. St Rules Tower rising from the ruins of the medieval cathedral, the cobbled stone pier jutting out into the North Sea, and the long stretch of the East Sands all tug on my heartstrings. This view of the town, more than any other, always brings a lump to my throat. Nostalgia for long distant family holidays and my time as a student.

The morning passes in a blur of unloading the car and settling Izzy into her room. When the dreaded moment arrives and I must say goodbye to my daughter, I know I shouldn't linger. Izzy is trying not to show it, but I know that she's impatient for me to go. She's keen to start striking up conversations with all these potential new friends in her hall of residence. I know she's going to be fine.

"One last hug," I say. We hold each other tightly for a moment, and although it almost kills me to do so, I force myself to pull away first.

"Love you, sweetheart. Goodbye."

"Love you too, Mum. Bye."

I'd promised myself I wouldn't cry, and I manage to honour the promise until I reach the car, where I snort into my handkerchief.

I don't feel like driving back to Edinburgh straightaway, so instead I park the car and walk into town. I've only been back to St Andrews once or twice since I graduated, and each time I've been struck by how little has changed. Many of the buildings' façades have altered and there seem to be far more shops than in my day, but everything else is instantly recognisable.

I walk along Market Street as far as the Whyte-Melville memorial fountain, where I pause for a moment, remembering the giddy excitement of going to the Lammas Fair as a child. Then I cut through to North Street, inevitably coming upon our old house. At my first sight of it, all I can think of is Moira. Her death overshadows everything good about the time I spent there. Elspeth, Shona and I have repeatedly turned down invitations to reunions and get-togethers. With Izzy studying here for the next four years, I'm going to find it hard to avoid the house, but for now, I hurry on past, eyes focused on the way ahead, not on the past.

Before I know I'm doing it, I am walking down to the harbour and across the footbridge to the sea front, where I pick up the path alongside the beach. The tide is out, leaving behind a wide expanse of rippled damp sand. There are lots of men and women my age, walking with young people Izzy's age. Parents and children spending time together before the inevitable parting later in the day.

When I reach the hill at the end of the beach, I climb the steep slope to the cliff path. It doesn't take long to reach the point where Moira's body was discovered. I stand for five minutes or so, looking down at the rock and spindle, and the other rock formations that make this part of the beach so characterful. But there's a cold wind blowing off the grey North Sea and I don't linger too long.

I can barely remember what Moira looked like. All that remains in my memory is an impression. As you grow older, memories either astonish you with their vividness, or dissolve when you most want to hold onto them.

I make my way back, choosing to walk along the beach. Now my memories are once more of childhood holidays — running down the slope from the caravan site with my bucket and spade, eager to start digging in the sand. Or of playing on the swings in the park overlooking the beach or putting on the green by the harbour.

I am so absorbed in my memories that I don't notice the dog, a giant, wet German Shepherd, until it bowls into me and shakes out its fur, showering me with cold sea water.

"Bronn!" A man's voice booms out. I swing around to see the owner of dog and voice, striding towards me across the damp sand. I have an impression of bulk, hirsuteness, a long raincoat and stout walking boots.

"I'm sorry. I let him off the leash and this is how he repays me."

"It's okay," I reassure the man. And it is. My jacket is waterproof. I'm not one to make a fuss over things that don't matter. "I'm a dog lover."

"That's a blessing. There are some people who'd sue me over an incident like that."

"That's not me." There is an awkward moment as we look at each other. Something seems familiar about this man. I sense he's thinking the same about me.

"I know you," he says at last.

"I know you, too," I say. "But I don't have a clue where from."

"That makes two of us." He smiles. "Another life, perhaps?" We regard each other with a mixture of puzzlement and curiosity.

"Let's try names," I suggest, and before I can introduce myself, he gets in first.

"I'm Innes Nevin."

My own name dies on my lips as I register the shock. I look at him more closely, taking in the thick, greying hair and beard, the lines around his eyes, and the eyes themselves, which are what finally persuade me he's telling the truth.

"Well, clearly my name means something to you." There's amusement in his eyes now, but also bafflement. "I used to be a policeman. I hope this meeting in our past lives wasn't on the wrong side of the law?"

I know my appearance has changed over the years. My hair was mousy brown back then, and permed eighties-style. Now, four times a year my hairdresser wraps it up in different coloured foils, creating strands of blonde and copper amidst the grey-brown. I wore glasses back then, too, huge, as was the style. Oh, and I'm a couple of stones lighter. I work out these days.

"I remember you, but you'd have to be a pretty great detective to recognise me. Roslyn Maitland, née Anderson. I lived in the house on North Street with Moira Mackie. You were one of the police officers who came to tell us that Moira had been murdered."

26

Nevin contemplates me for a moment or two. "How strange. I know you and yet you look . . ."

I help him out. "Completely different. Everyone says so. Everyone who knew me in the eighties, I mean. My own daughter doesn't recognise me in photographs from that time. I've just brought her here. She's starting her first term at St Andrews."

Normally in a situation like this, there's an exchange of pleasantries, and a quick parting of the ways. But neither of us makes a move to go. It's as though there's a mutual understanding that we have a lot more to say to each other before we part.

Bronn, who's been circling around, sits down, clearly convinced that he's going to be here a while. Nevin and I seem to be caught up in the moment, neither of us having a clue what to say next. I'm on the point of giving him a polite smile and continuing my walk when he says, "I'm sorry. About what happened back then."

"About Moira?"

"About all of it. The investigation. The death of that young man."

"He killed Moira. There's nothing for you to be sorry about."

His face is hard to read. Moira's must have been his first murder case.

"I've thought about that case a lot over the years."

I nod. It's been the same for me. From a completely different angle to him, of course. He is looking out to sea. It must be strange for him, still living where it happened, walking along this beach, with the memories all around him.

"Look," he says uncertainly. "Are you in a hurry? Do you have someone waiting? A husband or partner?"

"I'm a widow."

"I'm sorry."

"Nine years, now. Nearly as long as we were married."

He nods, continues to look at a point on the horizon, where a tanker sits, grey and leaden as the sea. A gull screeches overhead and quick as a flash, Bronn is on his feet, poised for action. He jumps into the air comically, as if he believes that flight is possible, even for a dog.

"I, er, wonder if you'd like to have a drink?" Nevin says.

"I'm driving to Edinburgh later, but a coffee would be nice."

Nevin calls Bronn to him and we continue along the beach. As we near the harbour, he puts the dog back on his lead.

"Are you still a police officer?" I have a vague notion that police officers can retire with a good pension after so many years' service. Nevin looks to be in his mid- to late forties. Same as me.

"No," he says. "I left the force last year, after thirty years' service, mostly as a detective. How about you? What did you do after you graduated from here?"

"I moved to London, worked as a civil servant for about a year, jacked it in, went to art school and became an art teacher. I taught for about twenty years, then I went a bit mad and gave up teaching to do freelance work. Mostly, I do portraits of people's pets."

"You're still in London?"

"At the moment. I've been thinking of moving." I don't mention that the house Doug and I bought in the early nineties is now worth a fortune. I could stick a pin in the map and move almost anywhere. Edinburgh would be my first choice, but I'm still not sure. It's not that I'm attached to London, more that I'm afraid of change.

Nevin asks if I mind having coffee in a pub, as there aren't many dog-friendly coffee shops. He chooses a bar on the Scores, which I recognise from my student days, although it's undergone a name change, like most of my old haunts.

"It must be strange," Nevin says, returning from the bar with a pint of beer and a mug of coffee, "your daughter being here, at your old university."

"Yes," I say. "She's only ever heard good stories about my time at St Andrews, so I guess it's my own fault." I don't mean to sound negative, but there's a hint of bitterness in my tone. Nevin doesn't miss it.

"You weren't pleased? Because of what happened?"

"Izzy doesn't know anything about that."

Nevin sips his pint. If he's surprised, he doesn't show it. Then he says, "In nearly thirty years of being a policeman, I never came across a case that haunted me more."

There's something quietly shocking about his declaration. In all those years, he must have worked a lot of cases, seen some terrible things.

"It wasn't just her age," he continues. "I worked on murder investigations in Glasgow where the victims were much younger."

Which makes it even more disquieting. You would expect 'disturbing' cases in a big city. St Andrews is a quiet seaside town, the gem of the 'East Neuk' of Fife, and has been a seat of learning for centuries. I'm being naïve, I know. Evil is at home in any environment.

Bronn is lying on the floor under the table, snout resting on his paws. Every so often he lets out a weary sigh. It's not boredom. He's tired himself out playing on the beach and his eyes are drooping. I have a sudden urge to slip under the table and lie beside him, just to feel something warm and living, but Bronn's fur is still damp and claggy with sand. I haven't touched my coffee.

"It was your first murder investigation, wasn't it? And you were so young. It was bound to leave its mark on you."

He had used the word 'haunted.' I think of him, lying awake over the years, plagued by Moira's ghost, and it makes me warm to him.

Nevin doesn't answer until his glass is half empty. "A lot of aspects of your friend's case were frustrating. For one thing, we never found out where Moira had been all weekend before her body was discovered on the Sunday morning. And Stuart Brogan's suicide robbed us of any explanation for why he killed her."

I wrap my fingers around my mug and try to work out what Nevin wants from me. His tone is regretful, apologetic almost. I'm unsure whether that's on my behalf, or whether it's because he's had to notch this investigation up as one of his failures. My own feelings about the investigation were always ambivalent — relief over Moira's killer being apprehended so swiftly, tinged with disbelief and sadness over her needless death.

All I can do is repeat my earlier comment. "You shouldn't blame yourself. You were a very junior officer at the time." Nevin gulps down the rest of his pint and places his glass on the table with a thump loud enough to draw enquiring looks from other customers. I've touched a nerve.

As a conciliatory gesture, I offer to buy him another pint. When I return from the bar, his mood has changed again, and he smiles as he accepts his beer. For a moment we are silent, Bronn's deep breathing and occasional snorts the only sound in our secluded area of the bar.

Then, "I never believed that Stuart Brogan killed Moira Mackie," Nevin says quietly. As I take in his words, I gaze at the glass of mineral water I've brought back from the bar. Bubbles rise to the surface, dissolve, more rise to take their place. "No one could account for Moira for the best part of two days before her body was discovered."

I nod. This is not new information. "Yes. Her body wasn't found until the Sunday morning, but none of us had seen her since the Friday." I struggled with the hard part. "It was said that Brogan strangled her and dumped her body on the cliff path sometime late on Saturday afternoon or evening. But he took his life before the police could obtain details from him, such as how he managed to abduct Moira, and where he took her."

Nevin listens, poker-faced. He takes a long drink from his glass and looks around the bar, as though checking there's no one close enough to hear. I sense he's about to take me into his confidence. I'm right.

"A couple of weeks ago, I received a letter from John Menzies's widow. You remember Menzies?"

"Your boss?"

"Yes. Apparently, in the last months of his life he was very confused. He was suffering from dementia. There was a story that he kept returning to again and again. About a murder investigation he once worked on, in Scotland. His widow was confused too. Her husband had told her he won a lot of money on the lottery and moved to Canada, where they met. She had no idea he'd once been a policeman. She was even more confused when he grabbed her arm one evening and asked her why she kept calling him Bob, when his name was John. John Menzies. Until then, she'd believed the man she'd been married to for twenty odd years was called Bob MacDonald."

Nevin pauses, sips his beer, continues. "Menzies also told his wife that in his former life as Detective John Menzies of the Fife police, he'd helped frame a suspect for a murder he didn't commit. The suspect's name was Stuart Brogan. Menzies also mentioned me by name. That's why Barbara MacDonald tracked me down."

There's a prolonged silence as I absorb what Nevin has told me. An obvious question arises. "You said Menzies was confused. Was he suffering from some form of dementia? If so, what he said could simply be the demented ramblings of a dying man."

Nevin looks at me, frowning. "Do you remember what happened to Menzies?" he asks. It's my turn to frown. He continues. "About a month after Moira's case was closed, Menzies was alleged to have drowned in a boating accident."

A far distant memory stirs in my mind. Of Shona, telling me that something had happened to the detective who'd come to North Street to tell us about Moira. The details are long forgotten. "Alleged?"

"His body was never recovered. It's entirely possible Menzies didn't die in that accident. He could have deliberately faked his own death and gone off to begin a new life in

Canada under a different name. After his death, his wife found his birth certificate along with some other papers, proving his real identity."

I sit back in my chair, feeling light headed. I think of Lucy and her ludicrous conspiracy theories. They don't seem so silly now. "This is all . . ."

"Hard to believe. Tell me about it," Nevin says. "A couple of weeks ago, believe me, I was thinking the same as you're thinking now. It's a lot to get your head around."

"No offence, given that you're a retired policeman, but have you been to the police?"

"No."

"But you intend to?" Nevin's silence is disconcerting. He fiddles with his beer mat, then takes another long drink.

"I don't know yet. There's scant evidence to merit reopening an old murder investigation. A solved one at that. Particularly since, as you say, Menzies wasn't in his right mind when he told that story to his wife. Maybe that's all it was. A story."

"But she found Menzies's ID. If what this woman says is true, then Moira's real killer might still be out there." I give an involuntary shudder.

"Yes," Nevin says quietly. "And there's another concern. Menzies wasn't a wealthy man, and I'm pretty sure it costs to start a new life with a fake identity."

I can see where this is going. "You think he had help? But that would mean . . ." Nevin nods. There are plenty of possibilities, most so unlikely, I'm reluctant to speculate aloud for fear of sounding fanciful. I leave the talking to Nevin.

"Some kind of cover-up is the obvious assumption. Menzies was paid not to ask too many questions, and to keep his mouth shut. He accepted the money out of greed — or fear. Whoever was willing to pay him to frame Brogan must have had a very good reason for wanting the identity of the true killer to go undiscovered. That person may be the killer, or it may be someone connected with the killer, or even someone who wished to protect the killer. Either way, they aren't going to look favourably on anyone who starts asking questions, even after all this time."

Something tells me that Nevin isn't the kind of man to be deterred easily. I'm not sure what to make of his taking me into his confidence. On the one hand, I'm grateful that he's shared the information, but on the other, I wonder at his motive. We barely know each other. We have a connection, of course. Moira is here in this bar, squeezed between us, her restless ghost waiting for the truth to be uncovered. I have a sudden premonition that she will continue to haunt us until we know what really happened to her. Still, I ask Nevin, "Why are you telling me all this?"

Nevin shifts in his seat, as if making more room for Moira. "I'm sorry. It's just, meeting you on the beach so soon after the call from Menzies's wife, when my head was full of thoughts about the original investigation . . . Well, I don't believe in fate, but you must admit it's an extraordinary coincidence."

"Not so much in the grand scheme of things," I say. "You live here, my daughter's going to be studying here for four years. This is a small town. We'd probably have bumped into each other sooner or later. It just so happens that it was sooner."

"Aye. You're right." He gives a sigh. "I shouldn't have burdened you with all this."

I shrug. "What are you going to do?"

"What I should have done twenty-eight years ago." Nevin turns to look me in the eye. "Investigate Moira's murder properly, and bring her killer to justice."

I realise it's what I'd been hoping he was going to say. "I'd like to help."

Nevin is fingering his beer mat again, flipping it between his fingers like a giant cardboard coin. He sets it aside and looks at me. I hold his gaze. The years spool back, and I see the same quiet intelligence in his eyes that I noted years ago when he stood in the living room of our house on North Street — a young, inexperienced officer, embarking on the first big investigation of his career.

There's a silence, during which I fear he is trying to think of reasons to discourage me. So, I'm taken aback when he says only, "Thank you."

"What will you do next?" I ask. Nevin sighs, stretches his long legs out under the table, momentarily forgetting about Bronn, who yelps in protest and stirs. Nevin pets him until he calms down. The dog stands, places his muzzle on Nevin's knee, whines forgivingly.

"Well, this one's getting restless, so another walk, I suppose," he says, seeming to evade my question. But then he adds, "I've asked Mrs MacDonald to make copies of the documents she found relating to John Menzies and send them to me. She's agreed not to talk to anyone about this affair yet. Didn't need much persuading. I think she's still in two minds whether any of it's true. I've also been going over the investigation in my head — and in an old notebook that I dug out. The memories are surprisingly accessible, probably because it was my first experience of investigating a murder. To be perfectly honest, I haven't planned beyond that."

"I'd like to do whatever I can to help. Moira was my friend. I want justice for her too. And there's Stuart Brogan's family. They've had to endure the torment of everyone believing their son was a murderer. He might have been wrongly accused and driven to suicide out of desperation. They deserve to know the truth."

Bronn yawns and places his paws on Nevin's knees. The table rises, toppling our empty glasses. They land on the carpet with a thud, miraculously unbroken. Nevin reaches down and picks them up, while Bronn laps at the spilt dregs. I glance at my watch. "Look, I've got to go back to Edinburgh this evening. I'm staying with my friend Elspeth tonight. I don't know if you remember her and Shona? From North Street?"

"I remember. There was another girl. Lucy, wasn't it?" Either he has a good memory, or he's come across us all in his notes.

"Yes. Lucy Parry. I'm seeing Elspeth and Shona tomorrow. Is it okay if I tell them what you've told me this afternoon?"

"Actually, I'd appreciate it if you could keep all this to yourself for the time being," Nevin replies. "I can't swear you to secrecy, of course. But I am asking you to please consider not saying anything. Then again, perhaps one or two well-placed questions that won't arouse suspicion?" I give a nod to show that I understand, and he thanks me.

Outside, we exchange contact details. I've almost forgotten where I am, and am taken by surprise, momentarily, by the sight of the sea, stretching grey and unsettled into the distance. Bronn gives another whine and gazes longingly at the beach. Neither Nevin nor I make any move to go. It doesn't seem right, parting like this after the conversation that we've just had. We are strangers, yet not strangers.

"I'll call you," Nevin says, hesitantly.

"Yes," I say. I want to add, *I'll look forward to hearing from you*, but in the circumstances, it doesn't seem appropriate.

CHAPTER SIX

Elspeth and I met in my second year at St Andrews. I'd arrived late for a lecture, and she spotted me casting my eyes around the theatre for a seat. From the middle of a row near the back, she called out, "There's one here," and gratefully I scrabbled over the little clique of disgruntled students on the end of the row to join her.

After the lecture, Elspeth asked if I'd like to come to the students' union for a coffee, and I accepted readily. It was a month into the term and already I was feeling overwhelmed. I'd hoped it was going to be different this year. Better. But so far, I hadn't made any real friends yet. Just like in my first year, when I'd seemed to drift around the outside of various friendship circles, never quite able to move beyond the circumference.

I almost hadn't returned after that first, unhappy year. My parents had no idea just how bad things had been. I'd made up stories to convince them that I was having a good time and making lots of friends. I knew they worried about me, and I wanted to put their minds at rest. They'd had enough worry in their lives, after losing my older sister when I was sixteen. If ever I contemplated harming myself in those dark, early days, I only had to remind myself that

I'd be leaving them childless, and somehow I would rally the inner resources to enable me to carry on.

Elspeth's offer of coffee was a lifeline. As we queued up and ordered milky coffees and bacon butties, she told me that she was in her second year, and that she came from Edinburgh. Since Edinburgh was the nearest city to my village, I knew it well, and we spent a pleasant hour talking about our favourite shops and haunts.

"We probably saw each other walking around town loads of times," Elspeth declared. "I could have sat next to you at a concert, maybe even have spoken to you, never realising that one day we'd be friends."

Friends. I savoured the word. It was like primary school all over again, finding that special person across a scary, hostile playground, with a mixture of relief and pity for the ones still searching.

It was flattering to hear that Elspeth already counted me as a friend. She had a strong personality, something that I admired. I had been shy and unconfident since losing my Leah. She'd been my best friend as well as my sister, and I missed her terribly.

As the weeks passed and I spent more and more time in Elspeth's company, I realised that she wasn't perfect. She could be a bit possessive, critical of other people, unfeeling even. I put it down to her strong character. Elspeth seemed like just the sort of person I needed in my life at that time. Someone to shore me up, relieve me of the burden of being sociable. I'd had a difficult few years since Leah's death. After meeting Elspeth, my mood began to improve. My whole attitude to life at university — and hence life in general — began to change for the better.

Elspeth and I met Shona towards the end of our second year. Shona overheard us talking about moving into a house in town for our third year, and introduced herself. All three of us met Lucy at the information board in the students' union. She was poring over some postcards advertising accommodation.

"Are you looking for somewhere too?" she asked us somewhat unnecessarily. She was dressed in workman's dungarees dyed a shade of mauve, over which she wore a black donkey jacket a couple of sizes too big. The lapels of her jacket and the strap of the canvas army bag slung crosswise across her body were covered in badges declaring her political and musical affiliations. Her hair was long on one side and cropped on the other, revealing ears with multiple studs. She had an English accent.

"Er . . ." Elspeth said, uncertainly.

"Yes," Shona said. I don't remember saying anything.

"Great. What about this one?" The girl stuck a finger on a card advertising a house on North Street that was available from the beginning of October.

"It's for five people," Elspeth pointed out.

"No problem," Shona said at once. "There's a girl in my yoga class I could ask."

"Great. By the way, I'm Lucy," the strange girl said. "Hope none of you mind sharing with a Sassenach." Lucy, it turned out, was from Yorkshire.

"Is it just me, or is there something a bit odd about Lucy?" I said to Elspeth later.

"It's just you," Elspeth replied. She was joking. "It's not just you. She's a bit weird, but not in a bad way."

"You didn't think it odd that she just sort of assumed we wouldn't mind sharing with her?"

"A bit," Elspeth mused. "Did you see all those badges? The way she was dressed? Complete dog's dinner. Doesn't have a clue who she is, or what she stands for."

Despite her forthrightness, I got the impression Lucy wasn't a particularly confident person. It made me warm to her. She was, of course, just the sort of person Elspeth would approve of as a housemate. Slightly vulnerable. A bit lost. Easy to dominate. Though Shona didn't seem to be any of those things, Elspeth seemed to take it for granted that she would be another housemate. That left only the fifth member of our household to consider.

"I could ask the girl in my yoga class to meet us all for a drink, and give you all a chance to vet her," Shona said.

"Yes, we need to make sure she's suitable," Elspeth remarked.

"I expect she'll be fine," Lucy said.

"What's her name?" I asked.

"Moira," Shona said when she could get a word in. "Her name's Moira Mackie."

* * *

Moira Mackie was already seated and drinking coffee when the three of us turned up at the appointed meeting place, a café in the centre of town. It gave her a tactical advantage. I'd been expecting to watch her as she walked in the door, but instead, Moira was the one appraising us.

Shona did some brief introductions. Moira's eyes fixed on each of us in turn as our names were mentioned. It made me feel slightly nervous. Even Elspeth seemed uncomfortable under that scrutinising gaze.

Shona had been anxious that we all take to Moira as a prospective housemate. On the way to the café, she'd fed us morsels about Moira's appearance and personality, such as, "Moira's really beautiful," and, "Moira's very clever. Bound to get a First." I think it grated on Elspeth a bit, though she didn't say anything.

Shona also dropped a snippet of gossip. Moira Mackie was having an affair with a lecturer in the history department called Andrew Kelso. Doubtless, this piece of information was intended to impress us. She was unaware that Elspeth had had a crush on Dr Andrew Kelso since taking his modern history module the previous year. Knowing Elspeth as I did by then, I couldn't help feeling this didn't bode well for Moira's chances.

By the time we turned up at the café, Elspeth and Lucy had formed quite different opinions of Moira.

"She sounds perfect." Lucy.

"I'm not so sure. Sounds like a bit of a stuck-up bitch, if you ask me." Elspeth. She looked to me for support. I told her I'd make my mind up after meeting Moira, which I could tell irritated her. Elspeth always expected me to take her side, which, more often than not, I did.

After half an hour in Moira's company, I was completely won over. Lucy, too, seemed utterly charmed by her seemingly easy-going and open personality. Only Elspeth remained unimpressed.

When Moira excused herself to go to the toilet, she immediately voiced her opposition. "So, what does everyone think?" she asked in a hushed tone. "I for one am not in favour. I don't think she'd fit in with the rest of us at all."

"What's wrong with her?" Shona asked.

"I thought she seemed quite nice," I ventured.

"Me too," agreed Lucy.

Elspeth crossed her arms. "She's completely false. I can't believe you lot can't see it. So full of herself, blowing her own trumpet . . ."

Shona leapt to Moira's defence. "When? All she said was that she'd make a good housemate because she's considerate and tidy." Lucy nodded. To me, Elspeth's accusations seemed unjustified. At the risk of sounding disloyal, I said, "I thought she came across as pretty genuine." Elspeth's withering look made me feel like a traitor.

"Show of hands," Shona said. "Before she gets back. All in favour." Her own hand shot up in the air. Lucy's quickly followed. With an apologetic glance at Elspeth, I stuck mine up too. There was a pause, and after clattering her coffee cup down on its saucer, Elspeth raised a reluctant hand. "Fine," she said, sourly. "But don't blame me if she turns out to be the housemate from hell."

"Great. That's agreed then. Moira is our fifth housemate," Shona said.

Right on cue, Moira returned from the toilets. Was it my imagination, or did a look pass between her and Shona?

I couldn't help suspecting that Moira's withdrawal had been premeditated.

"It's unanimous. You're our new housemate." Shona's announcement was met with beams of pleasure from Moira and welcoming smiles from Lucy and me. Elspeth sat, arms still folded across her chest, jaw hard set, a forced smile on her unforgiving face.

"So, what's everyone doing over the summer?" I asked. "Elspeth and I are working in Jenners in Edinburgh until September, then we're going travelling for a few weeks before term starts."

"Butlins for me," Shona said, with a distinct lack of enthusiasm.

"I was thinking of going to a kibbutz," Lucy said. We all made polite noises. Nobody really believed that Lucy was serious. She seemed the sort of person who was full of grand ideas only to bottle out when it came to the crunch. She'd probably stay at home all summer and work in her local supermarket.

Everyone looked at Moira. "Actually, I'm thinking of staying here."

"Are you going to be working?" Lucy asked.

"I've got a job at one of the caravan parks. They've offered me accommodation in a little caravan on site. Should be fun."

She was staying in St Andrews to be near Andrew Kelso, I imagined. I glanced at Elspeth and guessed from her look of annoyance that she was thinking the same.

"Why don't you and I go somewhere in September?" Shona said to Moira. "I have a couple of weeks after my job ends. We could go travelling together."

"Thanks. Maybe I'll do that."

I noticed no one thought to invite Lucy along on their trip. She sat there staring at her lukewarm tea, probably wishing she hadn't mentioned going to a kibbutz.

Moira accompanied us back to North Street to view the house. It had three bedrooms on the first floor and two on the second. Downstairs there was a small kitchen at the back and a living room at the front. Elspeth nudged me and whispered. "Let's make sure we get here first in October, so that we can have the top floor. I don't want to be anywhere near Moira."

"I hope you're going to make an effort to get along with her, Elspeth," I said. Elspeth pulled a face. "It's going to be really crap if you cause an atmosphere just because you're jealous of her shagging Andrew Kelso."

Elspeth never liked her faults being pointed out to her. "I'm not jealous." Her face softened a bit. "I'll try. For you. But don't expect me to worship at her feet like the rest of you."

"What are you two whispering about?" Shona asked.

"Nothing," Elspeth assured her. "Just saying how much we're looking forward to sharing with Moira come October." She smiled sweetly.

"To new friends," Moira said, pretending to hold up a glass.

"New friends," we all echoed, though I suspect Elspeth's words were uttered through gritted teeth.

CHAPTER SEVEN

It is almost dark by the time I cross the bridge spanning the Firth of Forth and leave Fife behind. Ahead of me, the lights of South Queensferry twinkle in the gathering dusk. Overhead, the clouds form a shifting montage of dark and light. I think of Izzy and a lump comes to my throat. It feels like I am leaving her far behind on another continent, and not just a bridge's span away in Fife.

Back in Edinburgh, Elspeth greets me with a hug. Her son really is on another continent, I remind myself. *Pull yourself together, Ros.*

"You're later than I thought you'd be. Couldn't tear yourself away?"

I wish I could tell her about the strange coincidence of my meeting with Innes Nevin. He hasn't sworn me to secrecy, but I know I must honour my promise to keep it to myself, at least for now.

"You've got time for a shower if you want one," Elspeth says. "Table's booked for half past seven."

The spare bedroom seems vast and empty now that I don't have Izzy to share its space. It is also cold. Someone — Elspeth? — has opened a window and the evening air sneaks in, carrying with it the distinctive smell of hops and a chilly draught. I pull down the sash, pausing a moment to take in the view of rooftops and hills.

The brooding Pentlands put me in mind of Innes Nevin. He is a big man, tall and bulky but it's muscle, not fat. There is nothing left of the slender, chiselled boy he had been back when he was investigating Moira's murder with Inspector Menzies.

It had taken some time for me to recognise him on the beach, but when we were close and I caught sight of his eyes, something clicked immediately. I remembered how astute he had been on his first visit to our house on North Street. He had picked up on the slightest nuance of silent communication between Elspeth and me.

I shower quickly and change into a black shift dress and heels. I add a few pieces of silver jewellery, and I'm ready to go.

"Are you nearly ready?" Elspeth calls up the stairs.

"What's Duncan doing this evening?" I ask, noticing his absence.

"He's playing tennis with a friend from work. He'll be home in an hour or so. He's going to pick us up later."

"That's kind of him."

Elspeth has ordered a taxi. "We could walk there in twenty minutes in our flats," she laughs, "but not in these heels." Elspeth is only five foot two, so she wears scarily high heels to compensate. I remember her practising how to walk in them years ago. She was determined to gain the extra height as a way of asserting herself in what was still a male dominated profession back in the eighties.

The taxi driver deposits us at the top end of the Royal Mile, near the Castle.

"The Witchery by the Castle?" I say, unable to suppress my delight.

Elspeth grins. "My treat." She knows I love this famous old eatery. It's where Doug proposed to me, and where we celebrated when I discovered that I was pregnant with Izzy. It's a faintly gothic establishment with oak-panelled walls hung with tapestries, and leather seating, deeply romantic and atmospheric.

"Thank you," I whisper, knowing this wouldn't be Elspeth's choice of venue at all.

"Well, you aren't in Edinburgh that often. I can eat at the Tower any time."

An excited voice calls out our names. It's Shona. The first thing I notice about her is that she looks tanned and healthy. She's spent the last five years in Australia. Her short, spiky hair is white, without a hint of grey. It suits her.

"You look stunning," Elspeth says, kissing the air around Shona's cheeks.

"You don't look so bad yourself," Shona says, hugging Elspeth but not too closely. She winks at me over Elspeth's shoulder. Elspeth picks up on Shona's Australian twang.

"'Struth, Shona. You've turned into a right Aussie. We're going to have to call you Sheila from now on." Her accent is execrable.

Shona ignores her and holds her arms out to me. "How long has it been?" she asks. I've done the calculation in advance, and I suspect Shona has too.

"Far too long," I say, smiling.

I imagine I can taste the salt sea air of St Andrews in Shona's hair. When it comes to making associations with people, my senses seem to go into overload. With Elspeth, it's the scent of musk from the cheap perfume she wore before she began her professional life and could afford the more expensive brands. With Lucy, it would be the sticky sweet aroma of patchouli from the joss sticks she burnt to mask the smell when she was smoking dope.

With Moira, it would probably be the taste of malt whisky, which she introduced me to one evening at a pub on the Scores. And Doug? The velvety feel of his shorn hair after an unforgiving haircut.

"This where we're eating?" Shona asks, nodding at the entrance to the Witchery. She turns to me with a twinkle. "I take it this is your choice?"

"Actually, Elspeth booked it," I say.

"Oh well, nothing like eating within a hair's breadth of where they used to routinely burn women for being different."

It was an unsavoury fact that the Witchery overlooked the place on Castle Hill where hundreds of women had been burned at the stake during the witch hunts of the sixteenth and seventeenth centuries.

"Come on, or they'll be thinking we're not coming and cancelling my reservation," Elspeth says, ushering us along the pavement and through a gap between buildings, into a close, where the restaurant's entrance is concealed, off the Royal Mile.

I give a deep sigh as I sink into one of the red leather seats at the table our waiter has shown us to. Of course, this place reminds me of Doug, but the memories are happy ones, and I feel my gloomy mood — a mixture of sadness at saying goodbye to Izzy and unease over my grim conversation with Nevin — begin to lighten.

There's a lot of catching up to do. Working in Australia has been good for Shona, it appears.

"So, I'm thinking of moving back here on a more permanent basis," she says. "I miss the seasons here. It might sound crazy to you, but I can't wait to wear woolly jumpers and boots again. And a cardigan in the middle of summer. It's so relentlessly *hot* out there."

"Any hot men?" Elspeth jokes.

"No." There's a pause before Shona adds. "But there is a hot woman."

This is news to Elspeth and me. I suppress an 'Oh,' but Elspeth isn't quick enough. She squeals. "What?" A few heads turn in our direction, then look away.

Shona shrugs. "What can I say? I'm a dark horse."

"But you were married. For five years," Elspeth points out.

"Yeah, well. Everyone makes mistakes."

"Well, good for you," Elspeth says. "This woman — are you and her serious?" Her eyes flit around the restaurant, as though expecting Shona's lover to jump out from behind a chair and join us.

"Her name's Henrietta. And yes, we're serious. Serious enough for her to be happy to move here to be with me. Though," she smiles a little self-consciously, "as far as I'm concerned, we could live anywhere, just as long as we're together."

"I'm really happy for you, Shone," I say.

"Me too," Elspeth adds. She signals to the waiter and asks for a bottle of champagne. "My treat," she says for my benefit.

I feel a twinge of embarrassment. Both Elspeth and Shona have more successful careers than me. I have the house that Doug and I bought together, and a modest, if not always frequent, income from my art work, but I can't afford to splurge on champagne.

Shona asks how I feel about dropping my daughter off in St Andrews. "Does it feel weird when you go back? Maybe I should go sometime, just to see if the place still haunts me." She has never been back.

It is sad that our memories of our time at university are tainted by tragedy. Usually when we have a reunion like this, there's a tacit understanding that we don't dwell on that part of our past. Which has often meant that no one mentions Moira.

The waiter arrives with the champagne and fills our glasses. We've already had a bottle of red and I'm feeling slightly drunk. Maybe it's the fact that the three of us haven't been together for a long time, or maybe it's because it's a conversation that is long overdue, but all of a sudden, we are talking about what happened that penultimate year at St Andrews.

It's Shona who sets the ball rolling. "So," she says, pausing between mouthfuls of smoked salmon, "I was thinking about Moira the other day."

She drops it into the conversation casually enough, but I notice her fork quivers slightly as she conveys it to her mouth. Elspeth chews her steak slowly, as if by doing so she can put off acknowledging that Shona has said anything at all. I swig some champagne.

"Oh, come on," Shona says. "You guys! Stop acting like you haven't heard me. We've pussyfooted around this topic for years. Don't you think it's time we talked about it? I for one am sick of having this giant woolly mammoth in the room whenever we're together." She pauses. "I think about her a lot. I suppose I was in love with her. Wouldn't have acted on it in a million years in those days though."

Hearing her say that, right after her revelation about her sexuality, made sense. She'd been closer to Moira than the rest of us. How sad that she'd never felt she could tell any of us about her preferences back then. That she'd felt pressured into a conventional marriage to conform to a social norm.

She's right though. By not talking about Moira, we've made the subject one that cries out to be discussed. Maybe we should have cleared the air years ago.

If there is a moment when it would be appropriate to bring up my encounter with Nevin on the beach, it is now. I say nothing, even when Elspeth, to my surprise, agrees with Shona.

"We were so young and sheltered there, weren't we? Moira's murder was our first real taste of the big bad world."

Elspeth's feelings about Moira are complex, because she hated her. It's hard for her to pretend otherwise just because Moira was murdered. It's no surprise to hear her generalise our experience.

I think of what Innes Nevin said about Moira's case still haunting him and say, "It was like the end of innocence."

I've had my share of tragedy in my life, I think. First losing Leah, then Doug. At least Leah had had a peaceful death, surrounded by the people she loved, and who loved her. Moira's death by violence had seemed to pave the way for Doug's. Opened my eyes to the latent evil in the world.

Shona presses my arm.

"We tried for closure once, didn't we?" she says. When Elspeth and I look puzzled, she prompts us. "That ceremony? On the cliff path near the rock and spindle?"

I remember. The four of us — Lucy, Elspeth, Shona and I — making a sad pilgrimage along the cliff path to the place where Moira's body had been discovered. It had been Lucy's suggestion. Of course, the word 'closure' hadn't been fashionable back then.

"Isn't that what the funeral is for?" Elspeth had asked.

"Funerals are for families," Lucy had insisted. "We need something that's just for us. Something . . . personal." Despite her avowed atheism and her alleged anarchism, Lucy was a deeply spiritual person. Not that she'd ever have admitted it, but after Moira's death, she seemed less inclined to suppress that aspect of herself.

And so, for Lucy's sake mostly, we had huddled together on the clifftop in the freezing cold of an unforgiving February day, the wind almost knocking us sideways and the roar of the North Sea drowning out our voices as we read out our eulogies. After a while it started to rain, a persistent, chilling drizzle that dampened our spirits and extinguished the candles that Lucy had brought along for us to hold.

Afterwards, we traipsed back down the hill and along the East Sands, to dry out in the house on North Street.

How did we all cope in the aftermath of Moira's murder? Elspeth threw herself into working hard and striving for her goal of getting a good degree. She'd spent the following academic year in Germany as part of her languages course, obtained a First the year after that, and gone on to train as an accountant. Even now, she still works far too hard. But then, after the initial shock, she was the one least likely to be left grieving Moira.

Shona went off the rails for a bit, drinking and having a crazy social life, but she got her degree and then discovered her passion for travelling. She landed herself a job where she could combine the two. You could say that she coped by never standing still for long enough to reflect on the past.

And me? Well, I've managed by just getting on with my life, marrying Doug, being a parent. Being ordinary. But there's something I don't often admit, and that's the all-pervasive feeling of dread I've carried with me since Moira's death. A sense that life is cheap and fragile, which Doug's violent death only seemed to confirm.

I'm making it sound like all our lives have been blighted, even defined by Moira's murder, when it's really not like that. Affected, yes, but defined? Who knows? I'm not a psychologist. Elspeth is the daughter of a Presbyterian minister, and grew up imbued with a solid work ethic. It would be more of a wonder if she hadn't become a driven individual.

Shona's Great-Great-Aunt Agatha had been one of those doughty Victorian spinsters who defied convention and travelled the world unaccompanied. Is it so surprising that Shona's racked up enough air miles to go to the moon and back several times over?

Admittedly, my life achievement report would probably read 'should have taken more risks.' But maybe it's just in my nature to lack ambition. Moira was the sort to take risks, and look where it got her.

Inevitably, Lucy's name comes up.

"I think about Lucy, too, every so often," Shona says.

"Who knows what became of her?" Elspeth answers with a shrug. She might as well have said, "Who cares?"

"Funny how a person can just disappear like that," Shona goes on.

I think immediately of Nevin. Of what he'd said about Inspector Menzies, drowning alone at sea, after allegedly falling out of his fishing boat, and I wonder suddenly at the coincidence of two people connected with Moira disappearing.

But Lucy didn't disappear. She just stopped keeping in touch.

"I've looked for her online a couple of times," Shona says. She makes a circle with her thumb and forefinger. "Big. Fat. Nothing."

"I've looked too," I say. We look at Elspeth, who shakes her head. She seems bored with the conversation. She gives the empty bottle of champagne a shake as the waiter walks past, and he stops to take her order.

"We'll have another one of these," she says, winking at Shona and me. I would like to continue talking about Moira and that final term at St Andrews, but Elspeth deftly steers the conversation in a different direction.

"So," she says. "Who's having dessert? The raspberry Pavlova here is to die for. And, Shona, I want to hear more about Henrietta after we've ordered."

And just like that, the past is buried again.

CHAPTER EIGHT

After the long summer break, we moved into the house on North Street, keen to begin our third year at St Andrews. Elspeth and I were not, after all, the first to arrive, and we ended up on the first floor, with Moira sandwiched between us. Lucy and Shona occupied the two rooms on the top floor.

Inevitably, alliances formed. Shona grew close to Moira. Elspeth and I remained best friends. I suppose Lucy was always the odd one out. But she seemed content to tag along with any combination of the rest of us. From the start, I was nervous about how Elspeth would behave towards Moira. More nervous still when Moira made overtures of friendship towards me.

Soon after we moved in, Elspeth insisted on drawing up a list of 'house rules,' which everyone had to sign. There were even financial penalties for infringing them. Fifty pence for leaving the bathroom in a mess, thirty pence for leaving dirty dishes in the kitchen sink, that kind of thing. The amounts were intended to reflect the severity of the offence. Elspeth wrote 'Fines' on the lid of an empty biscuit tin and left it on a shelf in the kitchen. Every so often, she'd empty the tin and we'd all go for a drink on the proceeds. Elspeth liked order and central planning that worked for the common good.

Moira opposed the setting up of rules but went along with it for the sake of keeping the peace. Poor Lucy proved to be a persistent offender. She was untidy and forgetful, though she tried hard to conform.

I suspected that Lucy spent a lot of time trying too hard to be the person she thought other people wanted her to be. I always felt slightly protective of her because it was so easy for people to take advantage of her. As Moira — and Elspeth — found out quickly enough.

Elspeth's behaviour towards others could be calculating and manipulative, traits it turned out that she shared with Moira. Both treated Lucy shabbily at times, exploiting her eagerness to please for their own benefit. They'd send her out on errands, persuade her to cook the odd meal for them. Each of them berated the other for treating Lucy this way, seemingly blind to their own guilt.

"Sometimes I think they're too alike to get on," Shona once confided. "But Moira lacks Elspeth's mean streak." Her gaze had lingered on me challengingly when she said this. Out of loyalty to the friend who had rescued me from loneliness or something worse, I made no comment.

Elspeth was insanely jealous of Moira. Everything jarred, from her popularity with men to her natural academic ability. Elspeth was clever, but she had to work hard to obtain good results. It maddened her to see Moira achieve top marks for essays without seeming to put the hours in. Above all else, she was jealous of Moira's relationship with Andrew Kelso.

One night, not long after we moved into the house on North Street, I woke at around two in the morning with a headache. I crept downstairs to fetch a glass of water and an aspirin. As I passed the living room, I overheard a series of low moans, and looking inside, I saw Moira astride a bearded older man, whom I recognised instantly as Andrew Kelso.

I was twenty years old at the time, but I'd only had sex a couple of times. The first was with a boy I met at the students' union disco. We'd both been drunk, and I couldn't swear that we'd actually done it, but the next morning I heard him boasting about it to one of his flatmates and made up my mind that I was no longer a virgin. I'd been desperate to lose that label for ages. My other sexual experiences had been similarly disappointing.

Seeing Moira with Andrew was a revelation. I knew I should look away but I stood, transfixed, unable to take my eyes off them. I had to admit there was something magnificent about Moira at that moment. I thought of the clumsy fumbling around with the boy from the disco, me crushed under his weight, eager for it to be over. I had no idea sex could be as exciting as this.

I crept back upstairs, minus the water and the aspirin, and straight into Elspeth's room where I shook her awake. "I've just seen Moira and Andrew Kelso shagging on the sofa," I whispered. Elspeth squinted at me, disbelieving.

"What?" she said, groggily. I grinned at her, savouring the moment. "Who gives a shit," she said, sourly.

"You're jealous." I bounced on the edge of Elspeth's bed, irritated with her for pretending she didn't care.

"Crap. I wouldn't shag him if . . ." Elspeth's voice trailed off. She was looking across at her bedroom door, which was standing open. I followed her gaze. Moira was standing in the doorway, her hair dishevelled, Andrew Kelso's shirt wrapped loosely about her.

"Enjoy the show?" she asked, looking straight at me with faint amusement. She swivelled on one foot and walked away in the direction of the bathroom.

My hand covered my mouth. "She saw me watching," I said, appalled.

Elspeth gave an unkind laugh. "Teach you not to be a peeping Tom."

"How could I avoid it when they were doing it in plain sight?" I protested. "I went down for a glass of water." But I had lingered longer than was necessary. There was no denying it. Elspeth knew it too.

"So, is he just as fit without his clothes on?" she said, rubbing sleep from her eyes.

I gave a nervous giggle. "Couldn't really tell. Moira was on top."

"Oh!" Elspeth's exclamation of surprise told me she was not as sexually experienced as she would have the rest of us believe. I had long suspected that the boyfriend in Edinburgh, whom she claimed to have been 'copulating like crazy with' on visits home, was a myth. The only time she mentioned him was when the topic of sex came up. Then it was 'Gav this' and 'Gav that.' You'd have thought there wasn't a single position in the *Kama Sutra* that Elspeth and Gav hadn't mastered.

But the legendary Gav hadn't visited Elspeth once since her return to St Andrews, and Elspeth hadn't been home more than a handful of times. The last time I'd asked about him, she'd shrugged and said that she thought they didn't have much in common any more.

"So, does everyone know about their affair now?" I asked. Moira had sworn us all to secrecy.

"Not that I'm aware of."

"Well, they weren't being exactly discreet just now," I said with a giggle. I went to bed, obsessing slightly over what I'd seen.

There was an awkward moment in the morning when I met Moira coming out of the bathroom. I wasn't sure who should be apologising to whom. Moira spoke first. "Sorry about last night. I wasn't expecting anyone to come downstairs. I'll make sure it doesn't happen again." She seemed a bit edgy, and I realised that she was probably afraid that I might gossip, and that word of her affair with Andrew would get back to his wife. I mumbled something about their secret being safe with me.

"It's not you I'm worried about," Moira said. "Elspeth doesn't like me. I wouldn't put it past her to shop us to Andrew's wife. I told Shona it was a bad idea to tell you lot about Andrew and me. She thought it would help me get the room. But Elspeth can't stand me being with Andrew, can she?"

"I'll have a word in her ear," I said. I felt confident that Elspeth wouldn't tell Andrew's wife about Moira. She'd told me she enjoyed the sense of power over Moira that came from keeping her secret. "Maybe one day I'll call in a favour for my continued silence. Should the need ever arise."

After that night, Andrew was often present in our house.

Shona wasn't keen on him. She was unfailingly polite to him, but never more than that. I was a bit in awe of him. Elspeth became even more obsessed with him, if that were possible, though she flatly denied it whenever I confronted her. As for Lucy, she admired Andrew from a distance. He wasn't really her type. Lucy was attracted to male versions of herself.

"You know she's two-timing him, don't you?" Elspeth whispered to me one evening when Moira and Andrew were upstairs engaging in a particularly noisy sex session. I looked at her in astonishment. "It's true. She's been seeing a local boy since the summer holidays." Elspeth must have picked up on my annoyance, for she added quickly, "I only found out yesterday. Shona told me. I was going to tell you, but you've been living at the library."

It was true. I had an essay due in a couple of days and I'd been pulling some late nights.

Elspeth's tone was slightly disapproving when she talked about Moira's behaviour. She was the daughter of a Presbyterian minister, after all. Though she'd grown up to be an atheist, like me, she was still sloughing off the encumbrances of her upbringing.

Over the coming months, we grew accustomed to Moira's complicated love life. Some of us even helped her juggle the two, so that neither Andrew Kelso nor the local boy, whose name was Stuart Brogan, ever met. At least, not in Moira's bedroom.

I remember one occasion when I kept Andrew talking in the kitchen while Lucy saw Stuart to the door. Moira appeared, unruffled, wrapped in a towel, purportedly straight from the shower, to show Andrew up to her room. She winked at me to show her thanks.

Once, I asked Moira how she coped with her duplicitous lifestyle.

"I never intended for it to happen," she said. "I was single at the beginning of the holidays. Andrew had told me it was over between us. His wife was due to give birth in July and he'd decided he should try to be faithful. I didn't take him seriously, of course. I knew he'd be back. But I thought, why shouldn't I have a bit of fun with Stuart in the meantime?"

I listened, enthralled, as Moira told me of her first meeting with Stuart Brogan.

"It was one afternoon, after I'd finished early at the caravan site. I decided to walk into town to do some shopping. I arrived at the harbour just as the fishing boats were returning with their catches. A young fisherman winked and smiled at me from the deck of one of the boats, and I waited until his boat drew up alongside the harbour wall. I was captivated by a vision of sinewy, sunburned arms, and the roguish twinkle in his blue eyes, and by the strands of gold that burnished in his gingery fair hair," Moira said with a flourish. "I sat down on a lobster pot while he helped unload the morning's catch, and waited for him to finish."

"Go on," I said, enjoying the tale.

"It was love at first sight," Moira said, then hastily corrected herself. "Well, I suppose lust would be more accurate, but who cares? Honestly, Ros, the air on that harbour-side was fairly fizzling with sexual tension. Everyone could sense it."

I laughed, but only lightly. To tell the truth, I was a little in awe.

This boy, Moira claimed, made her realise that men, too, could be beautiful. When Stuart — she'd learned his name from the shouts of his father and the other men — stepped off the boat at last and stood, hesitant, in front of her, she'd kissed him, a long passionate kiss that drew calls and wolf whistles from the other fishermen.

"Stuart's dad said, 'You didn't tell me you had a lassie,'" Moira said. "He automatically assumed we were together, not that we'd only just met. Stuart went along with the pretence. He walked into town with me, reeking of fish. I told him to go home and have a wash and a change of clothes, then come and meet me. I waited for him in the grounds of the cathedral. I was lying on the grass, my face turned to the side, when a cloud passed over, or so I thought. I squinted up and there was Stuart's beautiful face blotting out the sun. It was just like a scene from one of my mum's Mills and Boon books."

By now, I was hanging onto Moira's every word.

"We kissed, and," Moira lowered her voice, "would have gone all the way if we hadn't been in a public place. Stuart was rock hard."

"Okay, that's enough," I said, contriving a laugh.

"Stuart came back to the caravan that night and every other night he could manage for the rest of the summer. He was heartbroken when I told him I was going off travelling with Shona."

"So how come you started seeing Andrew again?"

"It was the day before I was due to join Shona," Moira said. "I saw Andrew and his wife, Annie, in St Andrews. She was pushing a pram. I caught Andrew's eye as they drew near, and he looked so panicked I nearly laughed out loud. Surely it couldn't do any harm for a student of his to stop him in the street and coo over his newborn? Anyway, later I was browsing upstairs in one of the bookshops, when I felt someone touch my arm. It was Andrew. As soon as our eyes met, I knew he was still crazy for me. He told me he'd made a terrible mistake splitting up with me, said how much he missed me. I knew it was probably partly because he wasn't getting it from his wife, but I was still flattered. I think it was his voice more than anything, Ros. He has such a sexy, husky voice. It's the thing about him that turns me on the most, apart from, well, you know, just about everything else about him. It was all the encouragement I needed. He'd told Annie he needed to go upstairs to look for a book. We didn't have much time. You should have seen his face when I told him

I was going off on holiday the next day. I told him I'd get in touch when I got back, but he said he couldn't wait that long. He begged me to see him that day. Trouble was, I had Stuart coming to the caravan that evening for a last night of passion before I left."

"Moira!"

"I took pity on Andrew — well on myself too, to be honest, and asked if he was free later in the afternoon. Fortuitously, Annie was going to her sister's in Crail. I told him we'd have to go to his place as I couldn't have him at the caravan in case my boss found out. Honestly, Andrew was so relieved, he even forgot to remind me to be careful not to be seen when I arrived at his house."

Moira paused for a moment. I couldn't help thinking that she'd taken on a lot and that at some point, it would all start to unravel. If it hadn't already. I thought of the morning when Andrew and Stuart had almost come face to face in our hallway, and feared the worst.

"I must admit, I resented Annie Kelso at that moment," Moira continued. "I looked out the window and saw her pushing the pram along in front of her. I could just make out a little pink head poking out from one of those lace-trimmed quilts. That was when I realised I'd forgotten to congratulate Andrew on the birth of his child. I didn't even know if it was a boy or a girl." She paused again. "Not that I really cared, but I thought I'd better try to remember to ask when I saw him later. It was a boy, by the way. They called him Karl. After Karl Marx, I suppose. Andrew's a tad left wing, as you know. Oh, and for Andrew's grandfather. He was German."

"Okay," I said, when she'd finished, "I see how it all came about, but I still don't get why you want to juggle two men. Which of them do you like more? Can't you just choose between them, and make your life a bit less complicated?"

Moira shrugged. "I was on the rebound from Andrew when I met Stuart. I'm fond of him, but there's no chance at all that I'm going to fall in love with him. I'll have to tell him soon, I suppose. I just want to enjoy sex without the complications of commitment for a little longer."

"And Andrew? Are you in love with him?"

"Maybe a little. But I know Andrew's not the faithful type. If he wasn't cheating on his wife with me, he'd be cheating on her with someone else." A mischievous glint flashed in her eye. "Maybe even Elspeth Blair."

My laugh was slightly uneasy. Laughing behind Elspeth's back always felt like a betrayal.

"Does my promiscuity shock you?" Moira asked.

"No," I said, meaning it. "Of course not." I didn't add that I felt a bit sorry for Stuart Brogan, whom I suspected was under the impression that Moira had real feelings for him.

"Elspeth doesn't approve, does she?" she said.

"Er . . ."

Moira helped me out. "It's partly because of her religious background, though she'd deny that. And partly because she'd love to shag Andrew herself. That's why she hates my guts."

There was a brief silence. If Moira was waiting for me to agree, she'd be waiting a while, though she'd only said what I was thinking.

"You just can't say a word against her, can you?" Moira said. Her tone was slightly pitying, which irritated me.

"Elspeth's alright," I said. "You just have to understand her."

"Well, there's one thing I do understand about Elspeth Blair."

"What's that?" I asked, curious.

"She'd cut my throat soon as look at me."

CHAPTER NINE

I drive back to London the morning after my night out at the Witchery with Elspeth and Shona, my head still full of my conversation with Innes Nevin. I stop at the service station I stopped at with Izzy, and drink coffee, half-wishing that she was with me now. My phone vibrates. A text. From Innes Nevin.

My heart beats a little faster as I tap on the message to read it in full. It's nothing to get excited about, just something along the lines of how he hopes he hasn't upset me with his story about Menzies. I think he must have been slightly panicked that I would blab to all and sundry, for he's reiterated his request that I keep what he told me to myself for the time being. I'm glad that I managed not to mention our meeting to Elspeth and Shona, even after the second bottle of champagne.

My gaze lingers on the last words in his message. 'If you were serious about your offer to help, I would be happy to meet with you again.'

Happy to meet with you again.

With a sigh, I put my phone back in my bag, trying not to read too much into the word 'happy.'

I don't answer Nevin's text for a couple of days. For one thing, I'm busy finishing off a job for a client. For another,

I'm kept occupied with a barrage of messages and pictures from Izzy, who seems to be taking to student life with enthusiasm. I'm relieved and happy for her, and touched that she is remembering to include me. I think back to my own first weeks away from home, glad that Izzy's experience of university is proving more positive. There was a telephone in my hall, but there was always a queue to use it in the evenings when I felt at my lowest ebb, and the nearest public telephone was a walk away in the dark and cold.

When I do reply to Nevin, I tell him I was serious about wanting to help. I ask him what I can do. Then, just as I am about to hit 'send,' I add another few lines telling him what Shona said about looking for Lucy online. I also tell him that Lucy failed to return to St Andrews for her final year, after Moira was murdered and Brogan took his own life. I don't know why I mention it, except that I am thinking of Menzies disappearing, and it occurs to me that, in a way, Lucy too disappeared.

Nevin's response arrives immediately. He asks if I know where Lucy's parents lived, and I remember that she was from Yorkshire. The following day he calls with the news that both of Lucy's parents are dead. He hasn't been able to track Lucy herself down yet.

"You think she went to Australia after quitting her course?" he asks. "Maybe she decided to stay there. There's a chance she got married and changed her surname, which'll make her more difficult to trace." After a pause, he adds. "But not impossible." I get the impression that he doesn't attach much significance to Lucy's 'disappearance,' so I don't press him to keep trying to trace her.

"I'm coming back to St Andrews in three weeks to see Izzy," I tell him. "Perhaps we could meet and discuss how I can help you find out what happened to Moira?"

"Thank you. I'll be in touch." The call ends abruptly, leaving me doubting whether he really does want me to become involved. It's a little over a fortnight since our meeting on the beach. I wonder what he has managed to uncover in that time. I don't know whether I can assume that he would keep me updated of any new discoveries, but I check my texts frequently, just in case.

After the call, I don't feel much like working. I've been finishing off a portrait in oils of a Pyrenean Mountain Dog, with silky white fur and wonderfully expressive eyes. He's a lovely creature and reminds me of the dog in my favourite childhood TV programme, *Belle and Sebastian*, about a little boy and his dog living in the French Alps.

With a sigh, I set my brushes aside. I don't feel I can do justice to Polo the Pyrenean Mountain Dog this morning. There are other commissions waiting — dogs, cats, even a cockatoo with the unlikely name of Spartacus. I don't lack for work, but none of my subjects are inspiring me today.

Feeling restless, I decide to give the house a good clean, but it doesn't take long. Now that I'm alone here, there isn't a lot to do. Even Izzy's bedroom is spotlessly tidy. I linger a while in her space, looking at her books and knick-knacks, indulging in nostalgia. I miss Sebastian resting on her pillow, miss the clothes strewn across the floor and the film of make-up on her glass-topped dressing table. I knew it was going to be hard to let her go, but this is almost like grieving.

I know that if I continue in this vein I'll start thinking about Doug, so I grab my coat and go for a walk. I'm privileged to live in a leafy part of Chiswick, only a few minutes' walk from the Thames Path. Doug and I bought the house, a three-bedroom Victorian end-of-terrace, in the early nineties. His parents gifted us a lump sum to help with a deposit, and the mortgage is now paid up. I don't know exactly how much my house is worth, but like most people, I look on Zoopla whenever a nearby property is sold, and marvel at the price. Sometimes I wonder why I'm still here.

Part of the answer to that is provided when I reach the lovely stretch of footpath at the Strand on the Green and look across to Oliver's Island, a tiny forest afloat in the middle of the river. On the wide bank of sand by the water's edge, a heron picks its way through the silt to the river in search of fish. There's the sound of gulls cawing and a taste of brine in the air that reminds me of the seaside and, inevitably, of Innes Nevin.

It's not just the view, which is lovely and surprisingly peaceful on this late October morning. It's all the memories of my life here that would be so hard to leave behind.

"Tosh," Izzy would say.

"Maybe when Izzy finishes primary school," I'd say. Then it was, "When she's finished her A levels." But here I am still, and Izzy's gone. Even if she gets a job in London when she finishes her degree, she won't necessarily want to move back home. Besides, how likely is that? She's told me countless times that she'd like to live and work in Edinburgh after she graduates. Visits to her grandparents in Edinburgh as a child have imbued her with an incurable love of the city.

The walk clears my head and gives me an appetite. I warm up last night's leftovers — an unimaginative pasta dish — for lunch, and eat at the kitchen island, watching a squirrel steal some nuts from the bird table before disappearing into next door's garden. I wash up, resolving to spend the afternoon working on Polo's portrait, but when I sit down my enthusiasm wanes and I can't seem to concentrate on the task at hand.

I wonder if I'm coming down with something. My head aches slightly and I feel shivery, but the latter could be because the central heating isn't timed to come on for a couple of hours and there's no heat in the house.

It's an endless, wasted day. No, not entirely wasted.

By the end of it, I have come to a decision.

The following morning, I call an estate agent and tell them I'd like to put my house on the market.

CHAPTER TEN

My introduction to Stuart Brogan took place in the New Year after we all moved into North Street. He arrived at our house on a cold January evening to take Moira to the pictures. There was an adventure film showing at one of the local cinemas, but Moira wanted to go to a French language film that the film society was showing in the students' union.

Stuart looked like someone who worked outdoors a lot. Young as he was, his face already had a weathered look, and there were patches of dry skin on his cheeks. It gave him a rugged attractiveness. He looked strong and lean. I could sort of see why Moira thought him beautiful.

While Moira was getting ready, we chatted for a bit. He was quite shy, but I managed to find out that he had left school at sixteen to go to work on the boat owned by his father and his uncle, that he had an older sister, and that he liked playing golf. Well, he was in the right town for that.

"Stuart?" Moira's reappearance put paid to further conversation.

"Has Ros been bombarding you with questions?" She kissed him on the cheek, but Stuart wanted something less chaste. He pulled Moira to him and kissed her hard on the lips, while his right hand strayed to her breasts. I looked away, embarrassed. I was about to go upstairs when Moira called to me, "Come with us, Ros."

"No thanks," I said, but curiosity got the better of me. That, and the fact that everyone else was out and I didn't relish the thought of spending the evening with only my textbooks for company. Also, despite her entreaties, I had a hunch that Moira was teasing me. She didn't really expect me to say yes. I changed my mind.

"Actually, alright. I'll just nip upstairs and get my hat and gloves." I was rewarded with a look of hastily disguised surprise from Moira, and one of outright annoyance from Stuart.

Moira linked arms with me as we walked along Market Street, which clearly irritated Stuart. He scowled, lit a cigarette, and walked in front of us all the way to the students' union.

As soon as the film started, Stuart put his arm around Moira and pulled her close to him. I tried to ignore them, but when Moira uttered a series of quiet moans, I sneaked a glance. Stuart's hand was between her legs, moving rhythmically. I swallowed and looked away, embarrassed again. I couldn't help thinking of the night I'd caught her and Andrew Kelso on our living room sofa.

When the lights came up, I excused myself and went to the toilet. I told Moira and Stuart not to wait for me but when I left the building, they were standing a short distance from the entrance, both blowing smoke rings into the frosty evening air.

As we walked back to North Street, an argument broke out between them. Moira had just asked if Stuart had enjoyed the film and he remarked that he thought it was 'shite.' Moira accused him of thinking that everything that wasn't a Hollywood blockbuster was 'shite,' and he accused her of being a 'stuck-up snob.'

"And you're a philistine," Moira retorted, irritating him further. He pushed her away — a little roughly, I thought. He strode along in front of us, fuming inarticulately, until Moira caught up, took his arm and leaned in to whisper something in his ear. Whatever she said, it broke the ice between them. Stuart's anger was replaced by a lustful smile.

"Let's get a drink," Moira suggested. "You coming, Ros?"

"I think I'll just get back," I said, tired of being the odd one out. Moira nodded. She took Stuart's arm and steered him away. I walked home, thinking that Moira would be breaking up with Stuart very soon.

Shona was home when I got back. When I told her about my evening, she scowled. "I don't know what she sees in either of those men she's involved with."

"Well, they're both good-looking."

"Are they? Not that I'd noticed," Shona said. At the time she was seeing a second-year theology student called Alan. He was madly in love with her, but he was a devout Christian who didn't believe in sex before marriage. None of us thought the relationship would last. Not because Shona didn't have a religious bone in her body, which she didn't, but because we all thought the ban on sex slightly ridiculous.

"I suppose Andrew's more her match intellectually."

"Maybe so, but their politics aren't in tune. Moira doesn't even make a pretence of being left wing," Shona said. Andrew Kelso was a committed socialist. He'd spent a year studying in Leipzig in the early eighties, on an exchange programme with Edinburgh University. He claimed that the experience had modified but not altered his views. "In fact, I think she's apolitical."

"Unlike Elspeth," I commented. Elspeth's views were more in tune with Andrew's. Sometimes when Andrew was round, he and Elspeth would discuss politics. Their exchanges were often fiery, with Andrew playing Devil's advocate, but never confrontational. Unlike Moira's discussions, political or otherwise, with Elspeth, which frequently ended up with them squaring up to each other on the rug in the middle of our sitting room, like two feral dogs ready to tear each other to shreds.

It wasn't just politics that led to these arguments. If Moira said black, Elspeth would say white and off they'd go again.

Moira returned somewhere around midnight, minus Stuart Brogan, and sporting a bruise on her cheek that would probably be a black eye by the morning.

"It wasn't Stuart," Moira assured us, seeing our questioning looks. We were all gathered in the sitting room, playing cards. Shona was incensed.

"Stuart Brogan hit you?"

"I walked into a lamp post." None of us believed her.

"Crap. You have to stop seeing him, Moira."

"Well, I'm intending to, just not quite yet. He's so good in bed. And I can handle him." Shona shook her head in apparent disbelief. Lucy stared in shocked silence, as did I.

Elspeth, shuffling the deck of cards, commented sourly, "Then you deserve whatever he gives you."

"Elspeth!" For once, even I couldn't support Elspeth. Moira ignored the comment. She turned to Lucy.

"Luce, is there any of that gorgeous chocolate cake you made left? I'd love a piece with a cup of tea." Eager to please, Lucy trotted off to the kitchen to put the kettle on.

"What's everyone doing at the weekend?" Moira asked.

Elspeth, Shona and I gave a collective shrug. "The usual," Shona said, and Elspeth and I nodded. The usual consisted of the pub followed by a film at one of the local flea pits on Friday evening, the students' union bar followed by the disco on Saturday evening, and most of Sunday recovering from a hangover.

"Thought so. You're all so boringly predictable." She yawned widely. "I'm going to Aviemore with Andrew. His wife and kid are going away to her mother's, so Andrew and I have a whole weekend together for once."

"What will Stuart think about that?" Shona asked. She'd been lying stretched out on the sofa, and now pulled her knees to her chest to let Moira sidle up next to her. Moira gave a throaty laugh.

"He can think what he pleases. I've told him I'm not available, and besides, he's going to Glasgow for the football."

There had been other occasions when Andrew and Moira had gone away together. Andrew attended a lot of conferences and talks at other universities. He was specialising in something to do with Eastern European politics and economics. When Moira went with him to these events, she would sneak into his hotel room, or meet him in whatever town or city they happened to be visiting, always being careful not to be seen with him in public areas.

"Why Aviemore? I mean, what are you going to do there at this time of year? It'll be freezing," I said.

"Well, I don't expect we'll be out that much," Moira said with a wink. "Andrew's booked us a room at a five-star hotel. He's going to meet his German cousin for a few hours on Saturday afternoon. Apparently, he's over for a walking holiday and it's a convenient place for them to meet." Moira pulled a face. "Apart from that we'll have the whole weekend together. Ooh thanks, Luce." Lucy handed her a mug of tea and a slice of cake. "I'll think of you all, downing your pints at the union bar and queueing up at the chippy after the disco while Andrew and I are drinking champagne, and making love in front of a roaring fire."

Elspeth was unimpressed. "I hope the pair of you get your bare arses burnt."

CHAPTER ELEVEN

The morning after my momentous decision to put my house on the market, I receive an early morning call from Innes Nevin.

"I've located a relative of your friend Lucy Parry. She lives in Norfolk, in a place called Aylsham. Do you know it?"

"As a matter of fact, I do. We had some family holidays in Norfolk when Izzy was little, so I know it quite well."

"Well, the person I've tracked down is a cousin of Lucy's. Her name's Cathy Sharp. I have an address and phone number. Have you got a pen and paper handy?"

"Just a minute." I grab what I need, then ask Nevin to fire away.

"I've been thinking," he says after reading me the details. "Maybe it would be worthwhile you paying her a visit." Does this mean that he's changed his mind about the significance of Lucy's failure to return to St Andrews, and her subsequent disappearance?

"Sure. I'm not doing anything this weekend. I'll give her a call and see if she's willing to talk to me." As soon as he ends the call, I phone Cathy Sharp. She's somewhat surprised to hear the reason I'm contacting her, but agrees to a visit readily enough.

My restlessness does not abate. Over the next couple of days, I force myself to complete the portrait of Polo and deliver the finished work to his proud owners, who are overjoyed with the result. They are hanging his likeness above the fireplace before I've even left their house.

On Saturday morning, I leave Chiswick at half past eight. The satnav tells me I'll arrive at my destination around noon, but it doesn't factor in any breaks (I take two), so it's almost one by the time I park outside Cathy Sharp's house in Aylsham.

A woman roughly my age answers my knock and invites me inside. I follow her into a pleasant kitchen at the back of the house. One wall is made entirely of glass and offers a view of an expansive garden, with mature trees that are almost bare at this time of year, though the lawn is unraked and ablaze with colour in the late autumn sunlight.

"This is a beautiful location," I comment. "Blickling Hall is just a mile or so from here, isn't it? We took our daughter there once when she was little. There was a National Trust treasure hunt with a pirate theme. She loved it."

Cathy smiles. "My kids used to love those family days at Blickling too. Would you like some tea or coffee?"

"Thanks. Tea would be good."

"You said that you knew Lucy when she was at St Andrews?" Cathy asks as she puts the kettle on.

"Yes. We shared a house with some other girls — Elspeth, Shona and . . . and Moira."

"The girl who was murdered. And now you're trying to get in touch with Lucy?"

"Yes."

"Any reason in particular? It must be what? Nearly twenty-five years or more since you all left university?"

"Yes. My daughter's just started her first year at St Andrews. I was up there recently, and like you do, I got to thinking about the past. I've always wondered about Lucy."

"It's taken you rather a long time to get around to wondering what became of her, if you don't mind my saying so." Cathy's tone isn't hostile. She places a mug of tea in front of me.

"We did keep in touch for a bit after she dropped out. We were all concerned about her. I suspect now that she was heading for some sort of breakdown. I wouldn't have thought that at the time, though. That sort of thing wasn't really talked about much back then, so the signs wouldn't have been apparent to us." Cathy nods. "I know about Lucy's parents. They died in a car accident, didn't they?"

"Yes. Such a tragedy," Cathy says.

"How awful. Lucy must have been devastated."

"She was. She flew back for the funeral. She was a wreck. My mother tried to persuade her to stay, but Lucy was determined to return to Australia. Maybe she thought there was nothing left for her here."

"Poor Lucy," I say, genuinely sad to learn of this tragedy in her life. "Were you and Lucy close?"

"As children, yes, but we grew apart. Lucy became quite opinionated as a teenager. She tended to see everything in black and white. No shades of grey. I don't think she always believed the things she said. She just liked to shock. She was so . . . what's the word? Mercurial. She'd flit from one cause to another, randomly. One minute it was animal welfare, then it was the Palestinians or CND. She was forever looking for a cause to devote her life to. I think she was really just trying to find a way to fit in somewhere."

"Yes, that sounds like Lucy," I say, recognising the troubled young woman I knew. "I never really understood why Lucy never returned to St Andrews for her final year. She was very upset over Moira, but to throw away three years of study . . . She would have been allowed to defer sitting her exams for a year, I'm sure. It seemed like such a waste."

"Yes. It upset my aunt and uncle that she dropped out like that. But Lucy was ill, you know. Depression. I think what happened to her friend was a sort of trigger."

I nod, sad that I failed to reach out to Lucy more. Especially as I had had some experience of being depressed in my first year at St Andrews.

We are both silent for a few moments. Cathy sips her tea and gazes out at the garden. "I really must get out there one day and rake up those leaves. But they look so pretty, don't they? I can't bear to do it until the damp weather comes." I get the feeling that she is being evasive. With a sigh, she gets up and goes over to a Welsh dresser and pulls out a drawer. After a bit of digging, she seems to find what she's looking for, and sits down again, holding an envelope, which she passes to me.

There are five or six postcards inside, all with pictures of Australian scenes: the opera house at Sydney Harbour, Ayres Rock, Alice Springs. At some point, the cards must have been pinned to a board, for there's a tiny hole in each, and the circular indentation left by a drawing pin. I turn the cards over and can't help smiling when I see Lucy's familiar handwriting and her name squeezed in at the bottom under the address.

"She sent me these just after she went back to Australia after the accident. She spent some time travelling before settling in Adelaide. Lucy's fine," Cathy assures me. "You'll be somewhat surprised to hear that she's back in the country and has been living in St Andrews for the past four years."

Cathy's right. I am surprised. I ask why she didn't just tell me this on the phone. She apologises. "I'm afraid I'm a bit protective of Lucy. She went through a lot back then, and she's been so well for so many years now that I'm just a bit hesitant about people who might stir up old memories."

I feel as though I've passed some sort of test. "I won't do that," I say, though I'm a little afraid that even seeing me might set Lucy off again. It will be necessary to tread carefully.

Cathy studies me for a moment or two. Finally, she agrees to contact Lucy and pass on my details. "If she's happy for me to give her details to you, I'll do so."

Innes Nevin could probably locate Lucy easily enough. I could probably locate her myself without too much trouble, but I agree to wait.

On my drive back to Chiswick, I imagine how it will be seeing Lucy again after all these years, and realise that I am looking forward to our reunion.

CHAPTER TWELVE

Much to Elspeth's annoyance, Moira was full of herself after her weekend in Aviemore with Andrew Kelso. She returned around eight on Sunday evening and straightaway began telling us all about it. I expected Elspeth to make a show of leaving the room as soon as Moira began to hold forth about her trip but she sat, stony-faced, on the sofa throughout, punctuating Moira's story with a series of disapproving or disbelieving noises.

"Start from the beginning," Lucy insisted. "What happened after he picked you up on Friday evening?"

"Well, not a lot to begin with. It was a pretty boring journey, and it rained all the way. After we'd booked into our hotel room and," Moira lowered her voice conspiratorially, "indulged in a little lovemaking . . ."

"Oh, for fuck's sake," Elspeth said, while the rest of us smiled.

"Which, for the record, was orgasmic." Grins from Shona, Lucy and I, rolling eyes from Elspeth. "We had the most gorgeous meal in the hotel restaurant. Andrew ordered champagne, which was exquisite."

I'd never tasted champagne. I was pretty sure Shona and Lucy hadn't either. Elspeth, who eschewed alcohol on most occasions, remarked that champagne was very overrated.

"After dinner we went upstairs and, well, the rest of the evening is too X-rated to describe. And most of Saturday morning. Sunday afternoon was a real anti-climax. Andrew met up with his cousin, Hans, so I had to amuse myself."

"What was Hans like?" Lucy asked.

"Middle-aged. Intense. Stern. Very serious. I don't know . . . German?" Hans, it seemed, had failed to leave a positive lasting impression on Moira. "I didn't really talk to him much. Andrew sort of hinted he'd prefer to talk with him alone. They don't get together very often and there was a lot of catching up to do. I think Andrew was trying to save me the boredom of spending more than a few minutes in Hans's company." Moira paused, examined her fingernails. "Actually, I got the impression that Hans rather disapproved of me."

"He'd rather Andrew had brought his wife instead?" Shona said.

"Maybe. But it didn't seem like disapproval on moral grounds. Maybe it was just his manner. Whenever I came within earshot, he'd stop talking abruptly. Bloody rude, if you ask me." She shrugged dismissively. "As if I'd be interested in anything a boring old fart like Hans had to say anyway. God, he must have been about forty."

"You're just miffed that he didn't fancy you," Shona teased. "You're so used to men worshipping you."

Elspeth grunted, and Moira turned to her with a flash of mischief in her eyes. "You'd have got on well with him, Elspeth. Ooh, by the way, Andrew told me a little bit of gossip about you while we were away."

I looked at Elspeth. I couldn't think of anything she'd told me recently that would evoke the sudden fury in her expression. "What gossip?"

"About you and a certain Piers Thornton?"

"That's none of your business."

"There's no need to be embarrassed," Moira said. "Andrew said Piers is seriously sexy. Or hadn't you noticed?"

"Who's this Piers then, Elspeth? Spill the beans," Shona said. I shot Elspeth a look that I hoped conveyed my disappointment that she hadn't told me about her lover. And maybe a smidgeon of sympathy for her being put on the spot like this by Moira.

"He's a PhD student at Edinburgh University. Andrew Kelso was one of his tutors when he was doing his degree at St Andrews." Elspeth spoke in a monotone, but with a dangerous edge. Her eyes were fixed on Moira.

Moira's tone was contrastingly jaunty. "Andrew is good friends with Piers. They have a lot in common. They both specialise in boring stuff about Eastern Europe, particularly the GDR." She turned her sweetest smile on Elspeth. "Next time Piers is over we should double up. I'll talk to Andrew about it." Moira yawned and, with a playful wink, announced she was exhausted.

After she'd left the room, Shona said, "Well, you're a bit of a dark horse, aren't you, Elspeth Blair?" She looked at me. "You didn't know, Ros?" I glanced at Elspeth, feeling nervous.

Moira's remark about a double date had left her ablaze with anger. "I hate that spiteful bitch," she spat. "I don't believe Andrew blabbed to her about Piers and me. Moira must have found out about him and decided to wind me up by saying Andrew told her." No one commented. It was blindingly obvious that Andrew Kelso must have told Moira about his former student.

It was obvious no more information on Elspeth's relationship with the mysterious Piers would be forthcoming that evening. Her ill humour drove Shona and Lucy from the room. I sat for a while longer, not really hoping for an apology for being left out of her confidence, but still harbouring some hope that she'd throw a titbit of information my way. After all, I'd told her about all my pathetic — and infrequent — sexual encounters. Eventually, I understood that Elspeth couldn't have spoken even if she'd wanted to. She was literally speechless with rage.

The following morning, I was surprised to find that Elspeth had already left the house by the time I got up. My morning lecture had been cancelled, so I stayed at home and attempted to do some revision. Around noon, I heard the door slam, and after ten minutes or so, I went downstairs where I found her in the kitchen, warming a tin of soup on the cooker. A loaf of wholemeal bread lay, uncut, on the table, atop a white paper bag bearing the name of the baker's shop in town whose doughnuts were popular with students. "Want some?" Elspeth asked, without turning from the cooker.

"Yes, please. I'll slice the loaf." I extracted a bread knife from a drawer and began cutting the loaf into doorsteps. Elspeth poured the soup into bowls and we sat, dunking and eating companionably, our lunch unspoilt by any hint of lingering acrimony from the evening before.

"That's warmed me up," I said. The bedrooms in the house on North Street all had electric bar fires which demanded to be fed twenty pence pieces on an alarmingly regular basis. Downstairs, the only heat source was another electric fire in the sitting room. I'd been studying all morning in a chilly room, with a duvet wrapped around my shoulders and a hot water bottle stuffed up my jumper to save money on the electricity. Even after the warming soup, my feet were still freezing. "Let's put the fire on in the sitting room. There's plenty of money in the kitty."

Elspeth looked on in disapproval as I dropped coin after coin from the kitty — an old tea caddy — into the meter. "We're only meant to use this fire when we're all in the room," she reminded me. Everyone contributed to the kitty, so everyone should benefit.

It was one of her house rules which was frequently flouted.

"I've got some twenties in my room. I'll put them in the kitty later."

For ten minutes or so, we talked about how our academic work was going, then Elspeth said, "I suppose you're bursting to ask me about Piers?"

There was no point in denying it. I was still feeling aggrieved. I wanted to know why it was such a big deal if people knew she had a boyfriend. "We're supposed to be best mates. I don't have any secrets from you," I whined.

"Fine. I'm sorry I didn't tell you about him. Satisfied?"

I gave a grudging nod. "I suppose."

"I met him at a lecture I attended back in December. Andrew Kelso introduced us."

"And Moira wasn't there that time?"

"No. Andrew's wife was with him."

Poor Elspeth, I thought. She'd fancied Andrew from the first moment she heard him open his mouth at a lecture. Before Moira, there had been only the obstacle of a wife standing between her and happiness with the man she adored. A married man was off limits, but she could dare to dream.

"Maybe Annie Kelso will get pregnant and die in childbirth, and Andrew will turn to me in his grief and discover that I'm the one he was meant to love," Elspeth had said to me once, sounding like a character in a nineteenth-century novel.

Finding out about Moira's relationship with Andrew had taught Elspeth a crude life lesson. "I should have seduced him first and bugger the consequences," she lamented when she heard.

"So you've been seeing this Piers since December?" I asked.

"Yes. We had a drink with Andrew and his wife, then they went home. Piers and I had another couple of drinks before he caught a taxi to Leuchars to get the Edinburgh train. He gave me his number and made me promise to call him the next day."

"Wow. He must have been pretty smitten."

"I think he was." Elspeth blushed, reminding me of one of her more endearing qualities. She was mostly without vanity.

"I'm so pleased for you, Elspeth. But why all the secrecy?"

"No real reason. It's just . . . I didn't want to jinx it." She looked at me shyly. "Are we still friends?"

"Of course. But promise me one thing." Elspeth raised an eyebrow. "Make a bit more effort to get on with Moira. It's the Easter holidays soon, and then we'll be into our last term of the year. You're going to Germany next year, aren't you? So you only have to put up with her for one more term after this one."

Elspeth seemed to consider this for a moment or two. Then she shook her head. "Sorry, Ros. I can't promise to get on with her. There's no way that bitch and I are ever going to see eye to eye."

Exasperated, I got up and stuck another couple of twenties in the coin box. "Well, at least try not to kill her," I said.

"Can't guarantee that either."

I turned around. Elspeth's eyes sparkled with mischief. "Kidding," she said. I smiled. I recalled her fantasising about Annie Kelso dying in childbirth, and wondered what horrible fate Elspeth's imagination was conjuring up for Moira.

CHAPTER THIRTEEN

"So, Lucy's actually living in St Andrews now. Small world, isn't it?" Innes Nevin says. I'm speaking on the phone with him a couple of days after my visit to Cathy Sharp's house.

"Could Lucy have known something about Moira's death? Maybe that's why she disappeared?" I ask.

Nevin is polite. "Hmm. I doubt that had anything to do with it."

I wish I could see his face. I want to know if he's rolling his eyes, or pondering, or merely bored with my chatter.

I tell him about my plans to return to St Andrews. "It's half term next week. Izzy doesn't have time to come home. It's a reading week for her, but she's happy to spare me some time if I come up for a visit. I just have a few things to sort out down here first."

Like getting a set of keys cut for the estate agent, who can't wait to start showing people around my house. There's a silence, so I add, "If you think that I could do anything to help, that is."

The silence stretches. Finally, he clears his throat, speaks gruffly. "Cost you a fortune to book accommodation here. You could stay at my place. I have extra bedrooms. That's if you wouldn't consider it awkward."

"Oh!" The suggestion takes me completely off guard. "Er . . . That would be . . . nice . . . I mean, convenient." I feel like an idiot. What gets into me when I talk to this man? I sound like a tongue-tied schoolgirl.

"Good. Let me know when to expect you." He gives me his address, and asks me to call him when I'm on my way.

"Of course. Speak to you soon. Goodbye, er, Innes."

"Goodbye, Roslyn."

After the call, I start to have doubts about what I have just agreed to. I remind myself that we're both adults. Innes is sort of a friend, isn't he? And friends often invite their friends to their homes.

A little voice inside my head bleats, *You've only just met him*. Another says, *You've known him for years*. Finally, I reconcile the two by deciding it's a sort of business arrangement. If I'm going to help him solve the mystery surrounding Moira's murder, it makes sense for me to be close to him. *Oh? How close?* the first voice mocks.

I'll have to think of something to tell Izzy. She's going to think it weird when I say I'm going to stay with a man I hardly know. Perhaps I'll tell her we are old acquaintances. That I'm going to do a portrait of Innes Nevin's dog, and that instead of just sending me photographs, he's invited me to stay and meet my subject. I might even throw in a wife. Might as well complicate things properly.

Innes and I haven't discussed how long I will be staying at his house, so I decide to take things as they come. If I'm away for longer than a week, there's a possibility that someone might view my house in my absence and put an offer in before my return. Do things move that quickly with the housing market? The estate agent assured me there would be plenty of interest, and that I can expect a quick sale at or near my asking price. It's a little scary to think that I might be homeless in a few short weeks.

I haven't told anyone of my plans. I don't have many friends in London nowadays. The people I've connected with over the years have mostly moved on. The reason I lingered here so long after Doug's death — the belief I clung to for years, that he was coming back and if Izzy and I just stayed put, he would be able to find us — is long buried. I know Doug is never going to stand on the doorstep of this or any other house to fulfil the promise he made on parting: "I'll be back in time for Izzy's birthday."

Doug's body was never recovered. For years, I told myself that this meant he wasn't dead. A lot of people tried to convince me that there was incontrovertible evidence to the contrary, but I clung to my belief. Even after a visit from Mike Anning, a friend and fellow journalist who brought me Doug's broken spectacles and the photograph of Izzy and me that he carried with him always, now dog-eared, torn at the edges and smudged where Mike had tried to wipe off the traces of Doug's blood. He'd been in a jeep with Doug when they were attacked. Doug was the one made to kneel by the roadside and take a shot to the head while Mike was spared. One life or another. It's all arbitrary.

After seven years, coincidentally the length of time that needs to elapse before a marriage can be annulled when one spouse goes missing, I began to let go of Doug. The thing that bothered me most, after I accepted the fact of his death, was that the people responsible for the atrocity were never brought to justice.

My thoughts turn back to Moira and the possibility that her killer might similarly have evaded justice. Who really killed her? It is legitimate to ask this question again now, given what Menzies told his Canadian wife about Brogan's potential innocence. But how does a person begin to investigate such a thing after so many years?

Was Moira abducted by her killer? Or did she go with him — or her — willingly? Andrew Kelso had only his wife's word as an alibi. Surely that must mean he could now be regarded as a major suspect? I wish I possessed the brain of a trained detective. I can't see Andrew as a murderer, but who else had the motive — or the opportunity — to kill Moira?

There is an obvious candidate. Her name pops into my head, and I can't dismiss it immediately, although Elspeth was with me most of the weekend that Moira was killed. Still, I can't stop myself calling to mind a deeply unpleasant incident that occurred just two weeks prior to Moira's murder. Elspeth had come disturbingly close to causing Moira actual harm.

That incident had shocked Elspeth, scared her half to death. Which was enough to convince me that she wouldn't really have hurt Moira. It had even prompted her to seek help for her issues. She'd broken down in tears when she told me how, after several sessions of therapy, she'd uncovered the true source of her hatred of Moira.

Who then? If I'm to be of any help to Innes, I will need to reimagine the past, look closely at people and events, and try to interpret them differently.

But first, there is the present to consider. The following day, I hand in a set of keys to the estate agent and learn that three viewings have already been arranged.

Back at home, I go over what I've packed. The usual mix of jeans and tops, but I've also thrown in a couple of nice dresses and some heels. I don't know whether it's a sign of being prepared for all eventualities, or if I'm hoping to impress Innes. I add some books and some art materials. Now my suitcase stands, zipped up, in the hallway. I pull my winter coat out of the cupboard and root around for some warmer gloves and a hat. It's a long time since I've experienced a Scottish winter, and I'm taking no chances.

The journey seems to take longer than last time, when I had Izzy for company. This time I don't stop in Edinburgh. I've hit the evening rush hour and am obliged to join a tediously long queue of traffic waiting to filter on to the bridge.

I have Innes's postcode on my satnav, but it still takes me some time to locate his house, which is not in the village itself but near the cliffs and reached by a single-lane track.

It's almost dark by the time I arrive, but I can just make out Innes's house, a white-washed stone cottage. A dog barks when I knock on the door. Bronn. I realise that I am excited at the prospect of seeing him and Innes again.

Innes appears at the door, one hand on Bronn's collar, restraining the dog from jumping up on me. "It's okay," I assure Innes. "Dogs will be dogs. Let's just get it over with."

"Are you sure?" Innes laughs, and I nod. I prepare myself for Bronn's unrestrained welcome. His tail thumps against my legs. Slobbery kisses wet my face and hands. Eventually he calms down.

"Where are your bags?" Innes asks.

He accompanies me to the car and retrieves my suitcase from the boot. I hope he doesn't think from the weight that I'm intending to move in for good.

He lugs my case upstairs to a pretty bedroom. It has a feminine feel.

"I hope I'm not pinching your daughter's room."

Innes looks wistful. "This was Greta's room. She's married now. She and her husband live in Glasgow. I've put you in here because of the view, although it's a bit bleak this late in the year."

I cross to the window. At this time of the evening, in the encroaching darkness, the sea is merely hinted at by a swell of liquid blackness at the end of Innes's garden but it looks close enough to touch. I imagine I can taste salt in the air of the bedroom.

"Actually looks quite beautiful on a sparkling summer's day," Innes assures me.

"It looks beautiful now," I say, smiling.

"Right." Innes sounds doubtful. "Well, come summer you're going to be really impressed."

There's an awkward silence. Innes clears his throat. "I'll leave you to unpack. When you're ready, there's a nice pub in the village. I thought we could eat there. As long as you don't mind a brisk ten-minute walk in the cold?"

I'm still wearing my winter coat, and I hold up my arms to show how I can barely move for padding. Bronn gives me an apologetic look and follows Innes from the room.

Innes's cottage is a bit remote, lonely even. It must contrast sharply with his years of city living in Glasgow. His description of the view as 'bleak' could equally apply to the location. He seems to have no neighbours. It makes me wonder if the pub really is just ten minutes' walk away.

Innes looks surprised when I come back downstairs after only ten minutes. I shrug. "There wasn't much to unpack. It was mostly books." I think of the dresses and wonder if I should have changed. A walk to Innes's local in the cold doesn't seem to warrant it.

We strike off along the cliff path, Bronn bounding on ahead, a darting silhouette in the moonlight. Innes has brought a torch and he shines it on the path to light our way. The pounding of the sea makes conversation challenging. I have to shout to be heard, and strain to catch Innes's words before they are snatched away by the howling wind.

As I suspected, the ten-minute walk is more like twenty. I imagine Innes striding alone along this path, his long legs devouring the distance at twice the pace. At last, he veers off the path and we turn a corner. Ahead I make out lights, rooftops, and the sound of a wind chime tinkling somewhere not too far away.

"The village," Innes says. "You can't see it from the road you came on. There's a pub, a wee shop, and a scattering of houses." His voice booms. He's forgotten to stop shouting now that the noise from the sea has abated.

The pub is brightly lit and welcoming. I'm not sure what I imagined it would be like, but it exceeds my expectations. Innes nods at a couple of people at the bar and selects a table in a secluded corner. There's not a great deal of choice on the menu. Innes recommends the fish and chips, and I'm happy to go with that. We're in a fishing community, after all.

Bronn stretches out under the table. Innes goes to the bar with our order and I sit quietly, thinking of Izzy, who is only a few miles along the coast. I wonder what she is doing.

Innes places a glass of white wine in front of me. "It'll be about ten minutes." He sits down. "Has your friend Lucy been in touch yet?"

I shake my head. "I'll send Cathy Sharp a text tomorrow to let her know I'm in St Andrews. Maybe she'll prompt Lucy to contact me. I hope Lucy doesn't still think of me as part of the problem she ran away from all those years ago."

"You'd be surprised how often people run away from their problems," Innes comments.

I can't help thinking of my attitude to Doug's death. Of my irrational belief, even after I'd been shown evidence to the contrary, that he'd somehow survived and was coming back to Izzy and me. I invented all sorts of excuses for his failure to return, even the awful possibility that he just wanted to leave his old life behind. There's more than one way of running away from your problems, I think.

I must have let my thoughts show, for Innes seems to be studying me.

"Are you okay?" he asks.

"I'm fine. Lucy was the last person to see Moira alive, you know." I correct myself. "The last of us, I mean, her housemates. She saw Moira talking to a man she didn't recognise. He didn't look like a student as he was a bit older. Might have been staff."

Innes frowns. "I've been going over the case in my head. I don't remember seeing anything about that. Are you sure?"

"Yes, she told us after your first visit. I think she was too shocked to remember when you were there, but after you'd gone, we all tried to think when we'd last seen Moira, and we worked out that Lucy saw her last. She was going to contact Menzies and let him know, just in case it might be useful in, you know, working out her movements that day."

"That's news to me." Innes's face is set, stony.

"Maybe she forgot?" There is another possibility. I voice it with caution. "Or, she told Menzies and he didn't act on the information."

Innes turns stiffly away from me and is silent for a few moments. I sense he doesn't want me to see his reaction, but it's not hard to guess what it is. I follow my theory to its logical conclusion, knowing it will incense him more. "Because he was already involved in framing Stuart Brogan."

Our fish and chips arrive. Bronn looks up, alert with expectation for a few moments, and then resignedly places his head back between his paws. To my surprise, the waiter returns to our table with a bone, and, having sought permission from Innes, gives it to a delighted Bronn.

Innes is on first name terms with the young waiter, whose name is Josh. He asks after his parents, enquires how he's getting on with his Highers and his application to study languages at Edinburgh University. All without the slightest suggestion of the anger that I sense is roiling away inside of him.

When the waiter moves away from our table, I reach for the vinegar and splash it over my chips. Innes passes the salt and I sprinkle it more liberally.

"I can only guess how that must make you feel, knowing that your colleague was corrupt. But you shouldn't blame yourself. You were young and inexperienced . . . and . . . and . . . he took advantage of that. You couldn't possibly have known what he was up to . . ." I stop, remembering how irritated he'd been the last time I tried to convince him it wasn't his fault. Nothing less than making amends by finding out what really happened to Moira will assuage his feelings of guilt and shame.

He seems to nod, but maybe he's just relaxing the tension in his neck. Or flinching. Then he says, "Andrew Kelso still works at the university. He's Professor Kelso now."

"His wife provided his alibi, didn't she?"

"His first wife. Yes," he says.

"So, she divorced him then?"

"Apparently she left him about a year after Moira's death."

"Surprised she lasted so long." Andrew had been well and truly outed as an adulterer in the weeks following the discovery of Moira's body.

"He remarried. Twice. His present wife is half his age. Kelso's son is older than her."

"Celebrities do that sort of thing all the time," I say, and ask Innes what he thinks about Andrew Kelso as a suspect, considering the new information about Menzies. "Would his first wife stick by the alibi she gave him, I wonder? He could have persuaded her to lie for him, and after Brogan was accused, she'd have had no reason to feel guilty about it."

Innes dots tartare sauce over his fish. "Hmm. As I recall, her story was that their baby was unwell with croup the weekend Moira was killed. She alleged that Kelso came home early Friday afternoon and never left the house all weekend. They took it in turns to walk the floor with their sick child."

"What about her?"

Innes's attention shifts from his sauce to me. "What? The jealous wife?"

"Is that so outlandish? Was she ever considered as a suspect?"

"There was a sexual element to the crime, which pointed to a male perpetrator."

"Oh, yes. Of course." I sprinkle more vinegar over my chips and dust them lightly with more salt. "I know Moira was killed before DNA testing became routine, but isn't it the case that you can go back and test old clothes — for example, if you have a new suspect?"

"That can be done, but it isn't an option in this case." I frown and Innes explains, his voice a low growl. "There was a fire. All the evidence from the investigation into Moira's death was destroyed."

I lower my fork, fish still on the prongs. Our eyes lock. "Back to Lucy and her conspiracy theories, aren't we?" I say. "You've got to admit, that's quite a coincidence, given the rest of what we know."

Innes sighs, takes a gulp of beer, stares at a man walking unsteadily towards the gents. I'm sure he's not going to respond to my remark. He can't make it up as he goes along. He needs evidence. So, I'm surprised by his next words. "Conspiracy theory isn't a term I'd favour, but I am intrigued by the coincidences."

"How can I help?" I ask. Innes points at my empty glass and asks if I'd like another. I'm already feeling a little light-headed. "My round," I insist.

While I queue at the bar, I consider how ill-equipped I am to be a detective. I've spent my life in the classroom. What do I know of criminal investigation techniques, except what I've seen on television and read in detective novels? There is one element in my favour. I am driven to know the truth about what happened to Moira, and I'm not the sort of person who gives up easily.

Innes has a question for me when I return from the bar. "How do you feel about accompanying me to interview Stuart Brogan's sister, Isla Farrell? His parents are both dead. She's the closest living relative, apart from some cousins who live in Aberdeen."

"I can do that. You may need to give me some pointers as to what sort of information we're looking for."

"Good," Innes says. "I don't think she'd react well to being approached by me alone. I was part of the original team that investigated the murder her brother was accused of committing."

The story had not been picked up by the wider press. I remember a picture of Stuart's mother and father, Eddie and Maureen, on the front page of the local paper. It was a couple of days after their son's suicide. The picture wasn't even a recent one. It showed the Brogans standing in front of their fishing boat, the *Merry Mermaid*, looking fresh-faced and happy. It had clearly been taken years before and didn't exactly fit the occasion.

"Eddie Brogan gave Menzies a hard time." There was no judgement in Innes's tone. "He turned up at the police station protesting his son's innocence. The day after Stuart took his own life, he threw a punch at Menzies. I remember it took two of us to haul him off. Menzies was on the floor."

"Eddie Brogan may have had right on his side after all. His son might well have been innocent."

Innes's eyes crinkle up at the corners, but not with laughter. The memory still stings, I can see.

"Menzies wanted to press charges." Innes is thin-lipped.

"You persuaded him not to?"

Innes snorts. "John Menzies wouldn't have listened to anything I had to say on the matter. It was the chief who dissuaded him — Callum Gibb." Innes frowns. "Gibb should have conducted a more vigorous investigation."

"Have you spoken with him recently?"

"Gibb? He'd be an old man now, if he's alive at all. I doubt he'd even remember Moira Mackie. Still, wouldn't do any harm to talk to him, I suppose."

Something about the way Innes mentions Moira's name brings a lump to my throat. He cares. It's not just his sense of pride that's taken a blow. He cares deeply that an injustice has been done to so many people.

Innes is a father. Becoming a parent changes the way you see other people's children. It's for the families that he wants justice. Even if they'll never know it's finally been done.

This realisation causes me to reassess my own reasons for finding out the truth about Moira's murder. It's true I feel a sense of outrage at a killer never having been brought to trial for his crime, at the terrible tragedy of Stuart Brogan's suicide, the unimaginable sorrow of his and Moira's families. But uppermost in my mind has been my own curiosity, my desire to know what really happened. I feel humbled by Innes's compassion.

"What should we say to Isla Farrell? I'm new to this game."

"What game?"

"Playing detective."

Innes smiles. "I'm new to it too." I shoot him a puzzled look. "Being a private detective. I never had to think up excuses to interview people before. All I had to do was show my police ID."

"I can't think of a single reason why we'd be asking questions about a murder that took place more than a quarter of a century ago. Unless we were reporters, of course. Somehow, I don't think a member of Stuart's immediate family would want the muck on him raked over again. Especially if she still believes in her brother's innocence."

We ponder the problem for a few moments. Finally, Innes says, "I think we'll have to go along with telling her a version of the truth."

"About Menzies?"

"Perhaps leaving that bit out."

"But how . . .?" I'm interrupted by Josh the waiter, who asks us if we'd like to try the spotted dick and custard for pudding. We both decline.

As soon as he's out of earshot, Innes says, "Here's what I propose. I'll introduce myself as Innes Nevin, one of the police officers who worked on the Moira Mackie investigation. I'll be honest, tell her I've retired and that I'm writing a memoir of my time on the force. So far, so true — memoirs apart. I'll explain that I've been haunted for years by her brother's suicide because I witnessed a lack of rigour in the way that John Menzies conducted the investigation. Hopefully, she'll draw her own conclusions from that, and think I'm suggesting I can help prove her brother's innocence. Or at least cast some doubt on the findings of the original investigation."

I'm quiet for a moment. "We'd be giving her false hope . . ."

"Does that make you uncomfortable?" Innes spears me with his intense, blue gaze. Everything about this makes me feel uncomfortable, but if I'm going to let that bother me, I might as well quit now. Go back to London, take my house off the market, carry on as though what Innes told me about Menzies that day on the beach is simply an apocryphal tale that he made up as an excuse to get my phone number.

So, I say, "No. I'm okay with it."

"Good."

"So, what's my role? With Stuart's sister? How are you going to explain my presence?"

Innes thinks for a moment. "Would you be offended if I introduce you as my PA?"

"Hmm." I let him stew for a couple of seconds before assuring him, "No, that's okay. As long as you don't call me your secretary."

Innes widens his eyes in mock astonishment. "What do you take me for?"

"Seriously, I meant it when I said I wanted to help. I only wish I'd known Moira better. I think she thought of me as a friend, a confidante even. But . . ."

But Elspeth wouldn't have stood for that. I'd deliberately not grown any closer to Moira than the bounds of my friendship with Elspeth had permitted. I regret it now.

"Kelso and Brogan. Was she serious about either of them?" Innes asks.

"She was attracted to each of them for different reasons. Both were physically attractive, though their looks weren't similar. Nor were their personalities. Andrew was suave and seductive, Stuart brooding and testosterone-fuelled. Moira referred to him as her 'bit of rough,' the brawn to Andrew's brain. As for serious, maybe she believed herself a little in love with Andrew, but not in the purest sense of the word. Moira liked sex. She liked men. She was simply making the most of being young and free to have a good time."

I say this now without any hint of disapproval, though at the time I'd felt a slight sense of moral opprobrium at her behaviour, a vestige of my Catholic upbringing, which I renounced as a teenager.

I think of Izzy and wonder at the romantic adventures that lie ahead of her. I'm pretty sure she had sex with a boy from school whom she dated for about six months. She never discussed it with me, which hurt me a little, as I'd always made it clear that she could talk to me about anything. But I understood her reasons.

Innes shows that he is perceptive. He's caught on that my thoughts have strayed. "How is your daughter settling in?"

"Well, as far as I can tell, she's making friends, enjoying her lectures, keeping up with the workload. So far, so good. She's also been looking for a job, just a few hours a week to help keep her debts from soaring."

It wasn't something I'd had to worry about. I'd had my tuition fees paid, and because my parents were on a low income, I'd been entitled to a full maintenance grant.

Innes nods. "That's good. Regarding Moira, let me know if anything else comes to mind."

"I will. Perhaps being here, focusing on the past, will awaken sluggish memories. I do so want to help." It seems to have become my mantra.

"I know." Innes's tone softens. "Are you finished? We should get back before the weather worsens." He turns his face to the window, and I see that it has begun to rain.

Outside, a worse wind has whipped up, and the roar of the sea puts a stop to any conversation. We retrace our steps out of the village and back to the cliff path and I brace myself against the wind and the rain, heavy now, battering against my coat and stinging my face. My hood won't stay up and it's too difficult to hold it in place and battle against the elements, so by the time we reach the cottage, I'm wet and bedraggled.

Innes hands me a towel and lights the wood-burning stove. In a short while the whole cottage seems to glow with warmth. We sit until well after midnight, sipping brandy and going over what we will say to Stuart Brogan's sister. Eventually, Bronn reminds us that he has needs, and Innes reaches for his coat.

After we say goodnight, I climb the stairs to Greta's bedroom and slip into bed, snuggling under the duvet, even though the warmth from the stove downstairs has permeated the whole house. I fall asleep to the unaccustomed sound of the North Sea pounding in the background.

CHAPTER FOURTEEN

Relations between Elspeth and Moira continued to be tense after the Christmas break. Typically one of them would goad the other, resulting in a toxic atmosphere for a while, until it all blew over and we'd enjoy some short-lived harmony in the house.

It continued to infuriate Elspeth that Moira, who rarely seemed to do any work, invariably did well academically.

"What can I say? It's a gift!" Moira would trill whenever any of us asked her how she did it. "Natural ability" was another of her offhand responses.

"I just don't get it. She doesn't come across as all that clever. Makes you wonder how she's doing it," Elspeth complained, the implication being that Moira was sleeping her way to a good degree.

After yet another of Elspeth's rants about how Moira didn't deserve her academic success, Lucy's only comment was, "So what? At least she doesn't go around boasting about her marks." This was a thinly veiled criticism of Elspeth's tendency to crow for days when she got an essay back with a good grade. As for Shona, she never had a harsh word to say about Moira.

"I can't stand her," Elspeth confessed to me one afternoon in the library. I followed her gaze to where Moira was sitting at one of the wide tables on the ground floor, holding court to three or four young men. Her flirtatious laughter pealed out across the floor, attracting tuts and disapproving looks from students at nearby tables. Libraries were still quiet places in those days.

"Who does she think she is, treating the library like a bloody social club? People are trying to work." Elspeth banged her book shut and began gathering her things. She didn't have a lecture until the afternoon, so I wondered where she was going. "Upstairs, for some peace and quiet," she said in a vehement whisper when I enquired. As she passed Moira's table, she gave her a glare. Moira responded with a self-satisfied smirk.

It wasn't long before things between the pair began to escalate. Elspeth would make snide comments about Moira's habits and appearance. Sometimes she'd walk out of the room whenever Moira entered, or deliberately exclude her from conversations. Things came to a head in an unpleasant incident one memorable day in early January.

Shona and Lucy had hit on the idea of planning a surprise party at our house for Moira's twentieth birthday. Elspeth was against the idea, of course. She refused to help plan the event and was adamant that she wouldn't attend.

"I mean, it's not as if Moira was ever anything other than pleasant to you before you started being funny with her. I can't understand why you took such an irrational and illogical dislike to her."

Shona's words weren't random. She'd chosen them carefully to appeal to the way Elspeth liked to see herself. Cool and level-headed, rational, and above all, logical in her approach to every aspect of her life. I still shiver when I think of Elspeth's response.

We were in a pub on Market Street — Shona, Lucy, Elspeth and I. Elspeth didn't know it, but we'd lured her there for the sole purpose of confronting her over her dislike of Moira. It had led to an unpleasant atmosphere in the house, and we were all a bit sick of it. Shona had even gone so far as to suggest that we ask Elspeth to leave if she couldn't get along better with Moira. I disagreed, but Lucy sided with Shona.

Elspeth's eyes narrowed at Shona's remark. She sat, fiddling with her pack of Old Camel cigarettes, eventually taking one out and lighting up, but instead of putting it to her lips, she rolled up her sleeve and calmly pressed the red-hot tip against her arm.

"Elspeth!"

Shocked, I jumped up, shoved her hand away. An angry burn mark stood out on her arm, surrounded by a trail of grey ash. There was a faint odour of burnt flesh. Shona and Lucy gazed on in stunned silence. "What the fuck do you think you're doing?" I demanded.

Elspeth hadn't so much as flinched. It must have hurt but she seemed oblivious to any pain. "That," she said, her calm gaze on Shona, "was an irrational and illogical act."

"Bloody hell, Elspeth. What were you trying to prove?" Shona shook her head. She leaned back in her seat, pint glass in hand. Elspeth offered her a cigarette. "Anyone got a light?" she said. "I've run out of matches."

"Thank fuck for that," Lucy said. Everyone laughed, but nervously. Looking closely at Elspeth, I saw a glint of something in her eye. It wasn't exactly satisfaction but I couldn't help thinking of that old saying about the cat that got the cream.

With a shrug, she said, "Moira rubs me up the wrong way. I suppose I could make a bit more effort to get on with her. Sod it, I'll come to her bloody party." Shona, Lucy and I sat nodding. We had got what we wanted.

But it felt as though Elspeth had called all the shots. She'd been the one in control. I couldn't help but think of my earlier conversation with her, when she'd said she and Moira would never see eye to eye. It didn't fit with her saying that she'd make an effort to get on with Moira.

Her relations with Moira seemed to improve for a bit after that.

Until the party.

We held Moira's birthday the following weekend. Her parents had come over from Glasgow for the day. They were an unassuming, middle-aged couple, who spoke with broad Glaswegian accents. Both seemed too old to be the parents of a twenty-year-old. I thought I remembered Moira saying that they'd been in their forties when she was born. Moira looked nothing like either of them and, watching her interact with them, I got the impression that she felt she was in their way.

Mr and Mrs Mackie had lived through the Second World War and had already brought up two children before Moira came along. Moira's late arrival must have seemed less a blessing than a disruption of their plans for middle-aged peace and quiet. I could see why she'd found getting away from them and coming to university a liberating experience.

We planned the party for the Saturday. It was supposed to be a surprise, but Moira probably caught on, for it was the third such 'surprise' party in as many months. Lucy, Shona and Elspeth had all had birthdays recently.

Still, Moira managed to look convincingly astonished when she walked into our house to find around twenty-five people crammed into our small sitting room. Shona had kept her out of the way for a couple of hours while Lucy and I decorated the place with homemade bunting and balloons. One of Shona's friends had brought along his ghetto blaster and a shoebox full of mix tapes to ensure a steady stream of music. Everyone had brought some booze.

As we all sang 'Happy Birthday,' followed by 'For she's a jolly good fellow,' I watched Elspeth watching Moira. She wasn't singing, but merely mouthing the words as though it hurt to move her lips. When she looked at me, I narrowed my eyes. Elspeth rolled her eyes to the ceiling, but she joined in with the cheering at the end of the singing.

It was a party much like every other party I'd attended as a student. Everyone drank too much, couples snogged and groped in darkened corners, the music went up a notch every so often until it was booming, and the neighbours called the police, who duly arrived and warned us to turn it down. Later, when the pubs closed, there were the inevitable gate-crashers, but by then no one cared if they'd been invited or not.

Around one in the morning, I found myself squeezed into a corner of the first-floor hallway with a boy from my history class. He had one hand up my T-shirt fondling my breasts, and the other was making its way up my inner thigh. My head was spinning, and I felt slightly nauseous. I pushed him away. Despite his best efforts, I was completely unaroused.

Staggering away from him, I caught sight of Elspeth standing outside Moira's open bedroom door. Seeing me, she gave a start. I asked her what she was doing, my words sounding slurred and far away. "Nothing," she snapped. But there was a guilty look on her face.

"That's Moira's room." A brilliant feat of observation on my part.

"I know." Her voice was chilly. I stood on tiptoes to try to see into the room, but Elspeth had positioned herself in the doorway, blocking my view.

"Is she in there?"

"No."

"Were you in her room just now?"

"No." I must have looked disbelieving, for Elspeth repeated her denial, and claimed that she'd been on her way to the bathroom.

"Can I go first? I'm desperate," I asked, no longer interested in what Elspeth had been up to.

"Good party," I called out to her from behind the bathroom door, which I'd left ajar. There was no answer, and when I emerged once more onto the landing, I saw that the door to Moira's bedroom had been closed.

Around three in the morning, people started to leave, at least those who were able. The ones who'd drunk too much were passed out on chairs or floor cushions, where they'd lie until morning.

I'd been slumped on the sofa for a good hour, conscious only of the music, and the dwindling number of bodies in the room. I stood up and the room tilted. "I'm so pissed," I said to an unresponsive body at the other end of the sofa.

There was a sudden, piercing shriek from upstairs.

The zombies around me that weren't actually comatose covered their ears. It was a shriek of anger rather than pain, which was just as well, as I doubt anyone would have been able to respond to an emergency. I fought my dizziness and mounted the stairs, slowly.

Moira was standing on the landing, a look of dismay on her face. I staggered towards her and followed her gaze to her bedroom. Lucy and Shona were right behind me.

Moira's clothes had been pulled out of her cupboards and drawers, and lay strewn across her bedroom floor in tatters. It was Shona who stated the obvious. "Shit, Moira. Someone's ripped your clothes to shreds."

Moira didn't answer. I'd never seen her look truly angry before that moment. Her top lip curled over her teeth, giving her a feral look. Red blotches stood out against the pale skin of her face and neck. Her whole body shook with rage.

"Not someone," Moira snarled. "Fucking Elspeth Blair." She turned on her heel and marched up to Elspeth's room, with the rest of us right behind her. Without knocking, she burst inside, and light spilled into the room as she flicked the switch. In seconds, she was at Elspeth's bedside, shaking her awake, dangling a pair of ripped jeans accusingly in Elspeth's face.

"Moira! What the hell?" Elspeth blinked in the harsh light. She rubbed her eyes and twisted herself into an upright position. To tell the truth, I found it hard to believe that she could have been asleep with all the commotion that had been going on.

"Oh, spare me the 'I don't know what this is all about' bullshit! You've been in my room cutting up my clothes!"

"I have not."

They stared at each other for a full ten seconds, before Moira took a decisive step forward and slapped Elspeth across the face.

There was a collective gasp from Shona, Lucy and me. We watched as Elspeth, cheek reddening from Moira's slap, leapt out of bed and threw herself at Moira.

What followed was impressive. I'd seen 'girl fights' in the school playground, and they were usually of the hair-pulling, scratching and biting sort, punctuated by a lot of high-pitched squealing. Not so this one.

In response to Elspeth's leap, Moira instantly stepped backwards and adopted the kind of fighting stance I'd only ever seen on TV. She spun around, right leg raised, and delivered a sickening kick to Elspeth's stomach.

We all gasped. Elspeth howled in pain. Shona and I exchanged glances. *Where the hell had Moira learned how to do that?*

"You fucking cow!" Elspeth screamed, clutching her gut, unable to rise. I went to her aid, skirting nervously past Moira, who seemed slightly shocked at what she'd done. Shona and Lucy stared after her as she stomped from the room.

I was suddenly sober. "She's broken my bloody ribs, I'm sure of it," Elspeth groaned. I recalled the nauseating thud of Moira's foot impacting with Elspeth's middle, and didn't doubt it.

Shona offered some reassurance. "I've had broken ribs. I don't think you've got them. You're just winded, I think."

Lucy hovered at the bedside, looking stoned, shaking her head in disbelief. "She must have done karate at school or something," she commented.

"It wasn't me," Elspeth intoned sullenly, rubbing her ribs. "I never touched her bloody clothes."

No one commented. It was on my lips to ask her what she'd been doing standing outside the door to Moira's bedroom earlier on, but I held back. I could see that Shona and Lucy were conflicted over Elspeth's guilt. Elspeth's eyes sought out mine. I kept quiet. After all, I hadn't seen her do anything more than stand in the hallway.

We left Elspeth's room. When we passed Moira's door, it was closed. Shona hesitated for a moment as if she might knock, but in the end, she walked away.

I woke the next morning hideously hungover. The memory of the 'fight' returned slowly.

I crawled out of bed around midday and went downstairs to find Elspeth in the living room, clearing up the detritus from the party.

"Bloody hell, Elspeth, it's freezing in here," I said, but despite the very fresh air blowing in through the open windows, an unpleasant odour still hung in the air — of stale cigarette smoke and empty lager cans — and I understood the necessity for the cold.

The furniture was still arranged around the walls where we'd cleared it the day before to maximise the floor space for dancing, but otherwise the place looked remarkably clean and tidy. "You must have been up for hours to have cleared all that mess up."

"I was in too much pain to sleep much." To prove her point, Elspeth winced as she straightened.

"Do you think you should go to casualty?"

"No. I think I'm just bruised."

"Is anyone else up?"

"You mean, have I seen Moira shit-face Mackie this morning?"

Obviously I wanted to know if they'd faced each other yet. "Lucy and Shona are still in bed, as far as I know. They haven't been downstairs. I heard Moira go out before I got up this morning."

"That's surprising, though you and Moira were probably the only ones not stoned or pissed as newts last night." It was the one thing Elspeth and Moira had in common. Neither of them was a big drinker.

"I don't expect to see Lucy before tea-time. She'll sleep the sleep of the dead for hours." Elspeth looked at me with faint disapproval. "How are you feeling? You look like shit warmed up."

"I've felt better. Nothing a cup of coffee and some fried bread won't take care of." I moved to get up, groaned, collapsed back on the sofa.

"Oh, for goodness' sake. I don't know why you drink so much, Ros. You know you can't handle it. Sit there. I'll bring you some breakfast." But before Elspeth left the room, she asked, "You did believe me last night when I told you I had nothing to do with ripping up Moira's clothes, didn't you?"

I nodded uncertainly. The truth was, I wasn't sure. "If not you, then who?" I said, risking her ire.

"Who knows?" Elspeth said with a shrug. "I'm sure I'm not the only one who can't stand her."

When she returned with a mug of coffee and said fried bread, dipped in egg allegedly to make it healthier, I asked, "Have you still got the list of people we invited to the party?" As if I needed to ask.

"Of course. Why wouldn't I?"

"Let's take a look. See if we can narrow down a list of suspects."

"Okay, but you're forgetting something. About twenty gate-crashers walked in the door after the pubs shut. There were loads of people here I didn't recognise. Including that guy who was all over you on the upstairs landing. Who was he, by the way?"

I felt myself redden. "Er . . . I don't know. He had evil breath, though."

The sound of the door opening and closing caused us both to start. It was Moira. She looked startled to see Elspeth. She cleared her throat and said, "I'm sorry for accusing you falsely last night. It was a natural sort of assumption to make, given that—"

"I can't stand you?" Elspeth said, sourly.

"Yes. Well. There's no accounting for taste," Moira said, "Most people seem to take to me. I guess you're the exception that proves the rule."

"Have you any idea who might have done it?" I asked.

There was the slightest hesitation. "No. Probably just someone who'd had too much to drink and thought it would be a good practical joke."

"Not a very funny one."

"How are your ribs?" Moira asked Elspeth.

"Painful."

"Well then, no real harm done."

"I'm glad you think so." They glared at each other.

Anxious to break the deadlock, I asked, "Where did you learn to fight like that, anyway?"

"My brother," Moira said. "He loved that TV series, *Kung Fu*. The one with David Carradine? Took lessons and taught me. He said it's good for girls to learn a bit of self-defence." She looked at her watch. "I'm off out again in a minute. When I told Andrew what happened to my clothes, he offered to buy me a new wardrobe. Never look a gift horse in the mouth."

Elspeth turned on me the moment Moira left the room. "You could have been more supportive, Ros. We are best friends."

I stared at her but didn't say, *I didn't tell her I practically caught you coming out of her room.*

Shona and Lucy came downstairs soon afterwards, giving the lie to Elspeth's prediction that Lucy wouldn't surface until tea-time. We told them what Moira had said. Somehow or other the whole question of who had perpetrated the malicious act of destroying Moira's clothes blew over, and we never did look at that guest list. I couldn't help wondering, though, whether Elspeth's early rise, her efforts to set the house in order before the rest of us came downstairs, even her stilted conversation with Moira, arose from the depths of a guilty conscience.

* * *

As if the episode with the ripped clothes hadn't provided enough drama, only a couple of days later our household was shaken by another crisis.

This time Elspeth, Shona and I heard the news second hand.

It was a Saturday morning. We were enjoying a leisurely breakfast in the kitchen. Elspeth and I were still in our dressing gowns. Shona had been out for an early morning run and was sitting at the kitchen table, showered and dressed, her hair wrapped in a towel. An acrid smell of burning pervaded the air, a sign that Elspeth had decided to have toast for breakfast instead of her usual cornflakes. At weekends, she bought an uncut loaf from the baker's and sliced it into doorsteps too big to fit in the toaster without burning. She was scraping the worst of the charring off her latest burnt offering when Lucy shuffled into the kitchen.

"Good morning," she said in a subdued tone.

"What's up?" Shona asked immediately.

Before Lucy could answer, Moira entered the kitchen, a dark look on her face. She crossed to the sink to rinse a mug under the tap, elbowing past Lucy, who was pouring milk over her bowl of muesli, and causing her to spill milk over the table. Moira didn't apologise. After making her tea, she stomped out of the kitchen, ignoring everyone except Lucy, to whom she gave a glowering look in passing.

"What the hell is up with her this morning?" Elspeth said as soon as Moira was out of earshot. Her eyes fixed on Lucy. "Have you done something to upset madam?"

"Something terrible," Lucy said, sounding miserable.

Elspeth pushed aside her blackened toast, a wicked gleam in her eye. Shona raised an enquiring eyebrow. *Here we go again*, I thought. More drama.

Lucy pushed her muesli around in the bowl. "I told her I wouldn't say anything." The kitchen was instantly eerily silent. You could have heard a pin drop. "And I can't."

"No way we're letting you off with that, Lucy!" Elspeth said. "Come on! You can't leave us in the dark. We won't tell her you told us." Elspeth, round-eyed, was sincerity itself.

Lucy should have known better, but she looked to be weighing up Moira's wrath against the admiration she would earn from the rest of us for being the bearer of tasty gossip. In the end, she couldn't help herself. She spilled. Breathlessly.

"Stuart Brogan came here last night when you were all down the pub." Lucy had had a cold and stayed at home. "He caught Moira and Andrew Kelso in bed together. They fought. Moira had to pull them apart."

"Shit!" It took a lot to impress Elspeth. She stared open-mouthed at Lucy, shock rapidly turning to delight. This was obviously the juiciest piece of gossip she'd heard for a long time.

"Huh! Bound to happen sooner or later," Shona commented. She turned to Lucy. "But why is Moira pissed off at you?"

"Yesterday afternoon she gave me a note to take to Stuart Brogan. He was supposed to be coming around in the evening, but Moira had seen Andrew earlier in the day and he'd told her his wife was going to her mother's until Sunday. The note was to tell Stuart she'd got her period early and had really bad cramps, and that he shouldn't come here."

"Let me guess," Elspeth said. "You forgot to deliver the note."

"It just completely slipped my mind."

"Typical Moira," Elspeth said. "Gets you to do her dirty work and then blames you when it goes tits up."

"She's right, Lucy. This isn't your fault," I said. "You aren't responsible for Stuart and Andrew finding out about each other. Like Shona said, it was bound to happen sooner or later." Poor Lucy. I knew she must hate Moira being angry at her.

"Can't expect to have your cake and eat it forever," Elspeth hooted, rubbing her hands in glee. "God, what I wouldn't have given to be a fly on the wall."

Lucy looked stricken. "You . . . you can't tell her I told you, Elspeth. Please." Elspeth let out a long, exasperated sigh. Lucy gave her a pleading look. Finally, Elspeth promised that she wouldn't breathe a word.

"And don't behave all smug around her so that she guesses, either," I cautioned Elspeth, knowing her only too well. Not for a nanosecond did I believe that she intended to keep her promise to Lucy.

"I'll be inwardly smug," Elspeth promised, zipping her lip with her finger. She passed Lucy a slice of burnt, buttered toast. "Here you go, Lucy. I reckon you deserve some of my Tiptree marmalade on that for making my day. Now, let's have all the juicy details."

"It was awful," Lucy said. "Moira called me a moron. Said I was a useless waste of space who couldn't even be trusted to run a simple errand. And she was right. I am useless."

Shona and I offered words of reassurance, while Elspeth waited impatiently for Lucy to continue.

"Stuart turned up at nine. I was in the sitting room. I saw him pass the window and I was going to run to the door and tell him not to come in, but he was already in the hall when I went to answer his knock. I . . . I'd come in earlier and forgotten to lock up after myself. He . . . he ignored me when I said he shouldn't go upstairs."

We waited, mouths agape, while Lucy, in a hushed voice and with a nervous glance at the door, got to the climax of her story.

"There was a lot of angry shouting. Stuart was doing most of it. I ran upstairs and was just in time to see him drag Andrew out of Moira's bed, stark naked. He was making fists of his hands, just like a . . . a boxer."

"What was Andrew doing?" Elspeth asked.

"He was, you know, covering his . . . bits," Lucy said. "He probably thought Stuart would kick him where it hurts. Which meant he couldn't really defend himself when Stuart threw a punch at him. Andrew's got to have a black eye today. He's going to have some explaining to do to his wife."

"Serves him right for cheating on her," Shona said.

"Poor Andrew. That Stuart Brogan looks like a real brute." Leave it to Elspeth to take Andrew's side.

"What happened next?" I asked.

"Well, Andrew managed to punch Stuart before Moira got between them. I thought Stuart was going to punch her too but he suddenly got himself under control. He made this sort of howling sound, like a wild animal, and ran right past me out of the room. Nearly knocked me down the stairs."

"What did Andrew have to say when he realised Moira'd been cheating on him?" Shona asked.

"As soon as Stuart was gone, he started questioning her. Funny, I don't think he quite grasped what Stuart's presence meant at first."

"It wouldn't possibly occur to him that he might not be enough for any woman," Shona commented dryly. I was inclined to agree. Andrew Kelso was a vain man.

"Then, suddenly it must have clicked," Lucy said. "He was furious."

"Was he still naked?" Elspeth asked. I rolled my eyes.

"Yes. But then Moira caught sight of me watching from the hall and she came over and shut the door, so I didn't see anything after that."

"Did you listen? What did you hear?" Elspeth again.

"They had a shocking row. Moira called him a hypocrite and a coward, and he called her a whore." There was a collective gasp. Even Elspeth seemed outraged at the insult. Shona was incensed.

"Fucking hypocrite," she railed. "So like a bloody man to use a word like that to describe a woman who isn't a fucking virgin. I bet he doesn't think of himself as a whore despite all his shagging around."

"This went on for about twenty minutes," Lucy continued. "Then I realised Andrew was coming towards the door, so I scurried off to my room. I heard him bang the outside door downstairs, and then Moira came to my room and started shouting at me." Lucy dissolved in tears.

"Poor Lucy," Shona said, giving her a hug. I made her a cup of tea.

"Have some more marmalade," Elspeth said, offering Lucy the jar.

If Moira had wanted to keep the news of the bust-up from the rest of us, she should have forgiven Lucy — or at least pretended that all was well between them. Unfortunately, she ignored poor Lucy and even treated her shabbily over the next couple of days, leaving her out of conversations and criticising everything from her accent to her choice of clothes. I longed to take her to task over her unkindness to Lucy, but feared making things worse by giving away that I knew about the fight. Elspeth had no such qualms.

"Leave her alone," she cautioned Moira, after overhearing her lay into Lucy for forgetting to turn off one of the bathroom taps. "It's not her fault you've had a bust-up with your boyfriends."

"What?" Moira's eyes flashed dangerously.

"Don't play the innocent. We know all about it," Elspeth said. "Seems to me like you should take responsibility for your own mistakes and leave Lucy out of it. And don't look at Lucy like that. You would have told us all about it soon enough. You were just choosing your moment. I bet you just love the thought of having two men fighting over you."

"Elspeth Blair. I swear . . ." But just what Moira was about to swear was left unsaid, for, with serendipitous timing, Andrew Kelso walked into the room, half-hidden behind an enormous bouquet of red roses.

"Am I interrupting something?" he asked.

"Oooh! Are those for me?" Moira squealed.

"Roses for love . . . and . . . forgiveness?"

Elspeth rolled her eyes. After Moira had ushered Andrew out of the room, she hissed, "Everything always turns up roses for that bitch. Stuart Brogan had a lucky escape if you ask me."

The following morning it was back to business as usual. Moira floated about the kitchen on cloud nine. Elspeth scowled into her bowl of cornflakes while Moira recounted in all too colourful detail the amazing make-up sex she and Andrew had indulged in for half the night.

"Yes, we heard," Shona commented, yawning.

A few days later, Moira informed us that she'd seen Stuart Brogan. "He was still furious, of course, but I can't do anything about that. I told him from the start I wasn't ready for an exclusive relationship. Pity it's over in some ways, though. He was great in bed, but on balance, Andrew's more experienced . . . and more use to me."

After a dismissive shrug, she added, "Stuart will get over it in time. Though for now, I'll be giving him a wide berth. Honestly, if looks could kill, I'd be dead already."

CHAPTER FIFTEEN

Stuart Brogan's sister, Isla Farrell, greets us at the door. Her house is on a small estate in Cupar, a town roughly nine and a half miles from St Andrews. She peers closely at Innes.

"Aye, I remember you," she says, apparently satisfied that he is indeed the PC who investigated Moira's murder years before. "You're wearing well, I must say. Come on in out of the cold." She shows us into a bright, airy sitting room. "Aye, it was a terrible business right enough. I remember it like it was yesterday. My mum and dad never got over it."

A girl of around six is sitting on a comfortable sofa with a tablet balanced on her knee. "My granddaughter, Belle. Off you go upstairs for a bit, Belle. I need to talk to this lady and gentleman. If you're a good girl, we'll go to the park when I'm finished."

Without a word of protest, Belle pads out of the room. As soon as she's out of earshot, Isla says, "The police were wrong about Stuart. He didn't kill that girl. We grew up together and I know he didn't have it in him to do a thing like that."

The reality of what it must have been like for Stuart Brogan's family hits me again. Mr and Mrs Brogan's anguished protestations of their son's innocence had washed over me at the time, arousing only the faintest stirrings of sympathy amidst stronger feelings that they were somehow to blame for turning their son into a cold-blooded killer.

Today, I see things differently. I look at Isla and wish I could confide in her what we know about John Menzies. But I still don't know if it's the truth or just another version of it. I'm reduced to telling her I'm sorry for what she and the family have suffered.

"Ach, well, my mum and dad are at rest from it all now. Reunited with their innocent son in heaven."

I think of the time I accompanied Moira and Stuart to the cinema, how they'd fought. Of Moira returning later with a black eye. Stuart might not have been a killer, but he'd been no angel either.

"Did you ever meet Moira Mackie?" Innes asks.

"Aye," Isla says. We wait, hoping she'll elaborate, but her lips are clamped shut. There's a glimmer of suspicion in her eyes. She looks at me. "You sure you're not reporters from one of those trashy papers?"

Innes reassures her that we are who we claim to be. The suspicion doesn't fade completely, but she gives us the benefit of the doubt.

"Stu brought her back to the house a few times. Never overnight, though. We didn't have a spare bedroom and my parents wouldn't have let them sleep together under their roof. Stu brought her along to Mum and Dad's silver wedding anniversary do at the social club. I could see straight away that she was out of our Stuart's league.

"Stuart was besotted with the girl. He just couldna see past her. Aye, she was bonnie and no doubt that had something to do with it. But he was stupit to think she'd stick with him for long."

There's a faraway look in her eye now. I can tell she's remembering. I feel a twinge of guilt for raising past ghosts. After Leah's death, and again after Doug's, people kept telling me that eventually I'd remember all the good times we'd enjoyed together. I lost count of how many times I heard the words, 'Remember him the way he was before.'

Before he was dragged from his jeep, forced to his knees and shot through the head on a lonely, dusty roadside, far from home and the people he loved and who loved him. For the longest time, all I could think about was the fear he must have felt, and the thoughts that must have raced through his mind in those last, anguished moments.

"I'm sorry if our coming here is dredging up bad memories for you," I say.

Isla studies my face for a moment, then says perceptively, "I'm not the only one who's haunted by the past, by the looks of it."

I tell her that I lost my sister and my husband. As I speak, I am aware of Innes looking at me with concern. My confiding in her this way creates a bond between Isla and me. "What sort of things did Stuart tell you about Moira?" I ask.

"Well, he went on and on about her looks, as you'd expect. I'm not saying she didn't have a good figure but she was on the skinny side. I used to kid Stuart about her no' havin' any curves." Isla is a curvy woman and I suspect she always has been. "He thought she was perfect. He was blind when it came to that girl, she had him twisted round her pinkie." Her expression hardened. "Little did he know she was cheatin' on him wi' that professor."

Andrew Kelso wasn't a professor back then, but neither Innes nor I point this out.

"Mrs Farrell," Innes says, "what do you remember about the weekend Moira Mackie was murdered?"

"Och, it was terrible. I still remember Stuart coming home in the middle of the night, out of his head on drink. Wailin' and bawlin' like a big bairn. He woke the whole house up. That was on the Monday, after he found out about her murder. Another couple of days and Stuart was dead too." Isla gives a sniff.

Innes gives her a moment or two to recover. "I'm sorry. I know it's probably painful for you to go through it all again, but I don't have access to the notes from the original investigation. They were lost in a fire."

"Well, there's no' that much to tell. Stu was in a state about it. Then next thing we know, that Inspector Menzies is telling us he's been found hanged in my uncle's garage, with a note in his pocket sayin' that he was the one who killed Moira."

The silence after Isla's words lengthens into minutes. Isla's gaze travels to the hall again. Her granddaughter is very quiet. As if reading my mind, she says, "Belle's a contented little thing. She'll be up there drawing, no doubt. I've never known a bairn who likes to draw so much as that one."

Gently, Innes draws her attention back to his question about the weekend Moira died, and where her brother might have spent it.

"He was away drinking somewhere."

"In a local pub?"

Isla shakes her head. "Stu took to drinkin' too much after he split up with that lassie. He'd take himself off on his own, sometimes to our dad's boat wi' some cans, and just drink himself into a stupor. On the Sunday morning, the morning after the lass was killed, our dad found him on the boat, still drunk. That wasn't the first time either."

"So, no one in the family had seen Stuart that weekend? Until your dad discovered him on the boat? On the Sunday morning?"

"No."

I look at Innes. There doesn't seem much point in prolonging Isla Farrell's misery. We've established that Stuart Brogan had no alibi for the weekend Moira was murdered. Not the best of news. To my surprise, Innes now brings up something that I told him earlier.

"Mrs Farrell, were you aware that your brother hit Moira?"

"Who told you that?" Her eyes flash with anger.

"I did," I say. "Moira came home one night after a date with Stuart. He'd punched her in the face."

"That's a lie."

"I'm sorry, but it's the truth."

114

"You saw him hit her, then, did you?"

I glance at Innes, not knowing how to respond. "Er . . . no. But I'd been with them earlier in the evening and witnessed Stuart being a bit aggressive towards her. He did have a temper."

"I'm no sayin' he didn't. But Stuart would never hit a woman. Anyway, you've got it all wrong. It wasn't our Stuart who gave her that black eye. It was me."

"I don't understand," I say.

"I knew about her and that Andrew Kelso. I'd found out just that afternoon. I saw them together, standing under the fire escape of one of those big buildings on the Scores, out of view of the windows. They were kissin'. It made my blood boil."

"You didn't say anything to Stuart?"

"I hadn't seen him all day. He'd been out on the boat and when he got back I was out with my friends. I remember it was a birthday do. I got drunk and I was on my way to the chippie with one of my friends when we bumped into Stu and Moira. I punched her one in the face. Stu was furious."

I'm confused. Is Isla saying that she told Stuart that Moira was seeing Andrew Kelso *before* he caught them in Moira's bedroom?

Apparently not. "I didn't tell Stuart why I did it. I just told him I didn't like his girlfriend. He probably thought I was jealous of her."

"Why didn't you tell him, Mrs Farrell?" Innes asks.

Isla gives a shrug. "Wasn't up to me, was it? I didna want to interfere. Wish I had though. He'd have left her a sight sooner. And maybe . . ." There's no need for her to finish her sentence.

"I have some photographs of them. Would you like to see?" she says, unexpectedly.

I glance at Innes. Isla clearly wants to share her memories of her brother. And it might make her remember something.

Isla crosses to an old-fashioned oak sideboard and opens a levered door. Inside I can see albums and cardboard wallets bursting with photographs. I hope there's some sort of order to them or we could be here a while. Isla selects a red leather-bound album and brings it back to the sofa. It's one of those where you slot several photos into pockets. She flicks over some pages, stops about halfway through and moves the album closer so that I can see.

"That's Stuart when he was a boy," she says wistfully, pointing to a tousle-haired toddler on a red and yellow tricycle. I smile, hoping that she's not going to show me every single picture of Stuart in the family collection. To my relief she skips several more pages, then stops. I lean closer. Moira's face stares out at me across the years and I give an involuntary shudder.

She looks exactly as I remember her. Even her clothes are familiar: faded jeans pulled in with a belt to emphasise her tiny waist, a pretty white blouse with tiny pink rosebuds embroidered on the front, the navy blazer with the striped lining that I remember coveting. She'd bought it in the Oxfam shop one day when I was with her and I wished I'd found it first. Stuart is in the picture, too, his arm around her.

"I took that picture," Isla tells me. "It was down by the harbour. You can see the pier in the background." She turns the page. "Looks a bit like Princess Di there, doesn't she? Who could have predicted their lives would be so short?"

The next photograph is of Moira standing alone at the end of the pier, gazing poignantly out to sea. Looking like she knows what's coming.

"You know that professor she was seeing was a bit of a commie, don't you?" Isla says suddenly. "Moira could be a bit opinionated herself. I was always worried she'd fill our Stuart's head wi' all that socialist rubbish. He had no interest in politics until he met her."

As I remember, Stuart had no interest in politics after he met her either.

"Don't get me wrong. I was no lover of Maggie Thatcher, but that other lot were worse." It is unclear whether Isla is referring to the Labour opposition at the time or to some wider communist threat.

I recall my parents' paranoia about the Soviet Union, their fear that another war was coming. The Cold War wasn't a distant memory then. In 1988, despite glasnost and perestroika, it was still an ever-present threat. But none of this had anything to do with Moira's death, so I don't comment.

A small voice calls from upstairs. "Granny!"

"We'd better go." I can see that Isla wants to get back to her granddaughter. "We've taken up too much of your time already."

She sees us to the door.

"That wasn't very helpful, was it?" I say to Innes when we are back in the car. "Though I didn't know it was Isla who punched Moira that time."

I assume she would have come forward if the case against her brother had gone to trial, to prevent the incident being cited as an example of Stuart's violent behaviour towards Moira. "I must admit, believing that he hit her made it easier for me to accept his guilt. Moira said it wasn't him, but we all thought she was lying. I suppose she was too embarrassed to come right out and say it was Isla."

What else might have been uncovered, had Menzies not concocted evidence to damn Stuart Brogan? *The truth*, a small voice whispers inside my head. Whatever that was. "Isla was wrong about something though," I say.

"What?" Innes asks.

"Moira didn't give two hoots about politics. She pretended she did because Kelso was into all that. Sometimes she used to talk the talk, but she didn't believe a word of it. It used to annoy Elspeth. Back then she was really into politics. I imagine Moira liked to wind up Stuart's family by exaggerating her left-wing leanings." I pause to buckle my seatbelt. "Anyway, none of this has any bearing on her murder."

Innes looks thoughtful. I remember him telling me that in a murder investigation nothing can be considered insignificant.

As soon as we return to his house, Innes takes Bronn for a much-needed walk. I stay behind to catch up on my emails. First, though, I make some coffee and settle into an armchair for a ten-minute read. The room is cosy and I feel my eyelids begin to droop. The words on the page start to blur. Rousing myself, I stand up and stretch.

I go through the kitchen into the small lean-to conservatory at the back of the cottage. It is chilly in here, but the view is spectacular. Several gulls are perched on the wooden fence at the end of the garden. One cocks its head and eyes the house sideways on. I have a sudden memory of a predatory gull I'd seen down by the harbour side, pecking at the eyes of a dead fish in the sludge when the tide was out. The image makes me shudder. I think of Moira, lying exposed on the cliff path, her face turned upwards to the bright moonlight, her killer's face mirrored in her unseeing eyes.

I hear my phone ringing in the kitchen. I don't manage to reach it before it stops, and it switches to voicemail. It's Izzy, her voice sounding thin and strained. "Mum. Something's happened. Can you come?"

CHAPTER SIXTEEN

Izzy.

In my haste to call her back, my fingers turn into thumbs. I fumble through my contacts, thoughts racing through my mind. Something's happened. Is she ill? Hurt? Please don't let anything bad have happened to my baby.

The sound of her voice makes me gasp.

"Mum!"

"Darling? What's happened? Are you alright?"

"Don't freak out when I say this, okay?" I assure Izzy I won't, knowing I can guarantee no such thing.

"I'm in hospital."

"But why? Are you hurt?"

"I had an accident. It's okay, nothing serious. Mainly bruises. They're worried I might have concussion, so they're keeping me in for observation."

"An accident? What sort of accident?" There's the slightest pause before she answers.

"I . . . I'd rather not say over the phone. Look, how soon can you get here? It's better if I tell you about it in person. And don't go worrying yourself silly. I'm alright."

You don't sound alright, I want to say. Despite her assurances to the contrary, Izzy really doesn't sound at all like herself.

There's an edge to her voice. Is it fear? Tiredness? Maybe she's in shock.

Calm down, I tell myself. She's been in an accident. She's shaken. Anyone would be. She's away from home for the first time and she's had an accident. She needs reassurance. It's not going to help if I freak out.

I take a deep breath, regain control. Or, let me put that another way, I *sound* more in control. I tell her I'll be with her in about twenty minutes.

"Okay. That's great. Thanks, Mum. See you soon." Her voice sounds brittle and I wonder if she's trying not to cry.

"You bet, sweetheart. I'm leaving right now." It's a wrench to end the call, but somehow I manage it.

I scramble around, gathering up keys, handbag, coat and scarf. Now I'm outside in the porch. In my haste to leave, I fumble with the lock. There is the sound of friendly barking, footsteps on gravel. I turn around and am instantly blinded by the glare of a torch. Innes and Bronn are back.

Innes squints at me, keeping the torchlight off my face. "Ros? Are you okay? Has something happened?"

"It's Izzy. She's been in some kind of accident. She's in hospital." My words are punctuated by breathless gasps. I realise I'm shaking. Tears blur my vision.

"Right," Innes says, pointing his remote at his car. The lights flash on and the lock clicks. "You're in no state to drive. I'll take you."

I'm about to protest, but he's right. It's not my panicked breathing, or even my trembling hands, but the thought of having to concentrate on anything other than Izzy that convinces me. I hurry to the passenger side. "Thank you." Bronn is already in the back seat.

"Do you know what happened?" Innes asks as he turns the car round.

"She didn't want to say over the phone. That's worrying, isn't it? Do you think that's worrying?"

"Not necessarily. She probably didn't want to upset you."

"You could be right. I hope it's that and not something . . ." My voice trails off. Something what? Something so bad she can't tell me until she sees me? My chest feels tight. I've never had a panic attack, but it feels like I'm about to have one now.

"Ros." Innes stops the car. His voice is calm, steady. I look at him, embarrassed at my lack of control. "Breathe," he says. Easier said than done.

"S . . . sorry. I promised Izzy I wouldn't freak out, and just look at me." Slowly, my breathing eases.

"She's your daughter," Innes states simply, putting the car back in gear.

We don't speak during the journey to the hospital. Innes focuses on the road ahead and I concentrate on remaining calm. Again, I remind myself that I'll be no help to Izzy if I'm a basket case when I arrive at her bedside.

"You go on inside," Innes says when we pull into the hospital car park. "I'll find a parking space, then I'll wait for you in reception."

Panic seizes me again as I approach the woman at the desk. I take a deep breath, determined to be the strong woman Izzy needs me to be.

"Your daughter's in a side ward, Mrs Maitland. There's a police officer with her."

"Where? I'd like to see her now. Please take me to her." Her eyes look over my shoulder, and I turn to see a young woman standing behind me, stethoscope slung around her neck. She offers me her hand.

"Mrs Maitland, I'm Dr Patel. I've been taking care of your daughter."

"Where is she? Can I see her, please?"

"Isabella—" Dr Patel says.

"Izzy. She prefers to be called Izzy."

"Izzy is doing very well. We've treated her for some minor injuries and she'll be staying overnight purely as a precaution, because she had a rather nasty bump on her head."

"What happened to her? Did she fall off her bike?"

"I am very sorry to say that your daughter was attacked." Dr Patel couldn't have sounded more apologetic if she'd beaten up Izzy herself.

"Was she . . .?"

"No. Your daughter was not raped." Relief floods through me. Followed swiftly by anger.

"Who did it?"

Dr Patel looks apologetic again. "I'm sorry, I don't know all the details. The police have taken a statement from her. I'm sure they'll answer all your questions. Now, shall I take you to Izzy?"

I give a grateful nod and follow her, leadenly, down the corridor. She stops at the door to a side ward, a single room. The curtains are drawn so I can't see inside. Hand on the door knob, Dr Patel pauses, turns to me and says, "Please be assured that your daughter's injuries are superficial. They look much worse than they actually are."

I swallow, take a deep breath and nod. Dr Patel opens the door.

On seeing Izzy's face my first instinct is to recoil.

"Mum," she says, tears welling over the baggy slits of her eyes and onto the swollen mounds of her cheeks.

"Oh, Izzy."

"It looks worse than it is," she assures me, echoing Dr Patel's words. And then, "Ouch!" I've embraced her too tightly.

"I'm so sorry, darling." There are bruises that I cannot see then. "Who did this to you?" I ask.

"Mrs Maitland?" I turn around and see a young woman rising from a chair by the window. I hadn't noticed her when I came in, all my focus was on Izzy. "My name is Nadia Fraser. I'm a police constable."

"Police?"

"Yes. My DS took a statement from your daughter about the assault."

"Do you have any idea who did this to her?"

"The short answer? We don't know. Yet. But Izzy has been very helpful in providing us with information that might help identify her attacker."

"Who would do such a thing?" I turn to Izzy. "Was it someone you know? A boyfriend?" She hasn't told me she's been seeing anyone at St Andrews.

Izzy shakes her head. "No . . . at least, I don't think so. I didn't see his face. He was wearing a . . . a mask." It's upsetting to imagine my daughter's ordeal, and to know that I wasn't there to protect her.

PC Fraser notices my distress. "It seems to have been a random attack. Izzy was out running in the park when a man grabbed her from behind and pulled her into some bushes. She was lucky—"

"Excuse me?" In what world does PC Fraser think a young woman lucky who has been so severely beaten that her own mother can barely recognise her? But I haven't even allowed PC Fraser to finish her sentence.

"Lucky someone else was in the park and heard her screaming."

"My hero," Izzy says, for once not mocking. All I can think of is Izzy screaming, me not being the one to rush to her rescue. It makes me feel like I've failed her. *I'm* her hero. I shake my head. There are so many things I want to ask, but I realise that now is not the time.

Izzy has already given PC Fraser a statement. She doesn't need me making her relive her ordeal all over again. I must put her first. There will be time for questions later. Izzy's eyelids are drooping. She must be on pain medication.

"The main thing is that you're alright. You're safe now." It's the right thing to say. Izzy gives me a weak smile. PC Fraser and Dr Patel exchange approving nods.

Dr Patel excuses herself, saying that I can find her on the main ward if I need to speak with her again. PC Fraser straightens her uniform and heads for the door. "I'm just outside in the corridor. I know you have more questions."

"Thank you." She seems so young. The sight of her brings to my mind Innes as a young, inexperienced officer. The thought that his older self is waiting for me somewhere in the hospital is a source of comfort.

Left alone with my daughter, I resist the urge to ask any more questions. It's enough to sit by her bedside, holding her hand and stroking her hair until she drifts off to sleep. I watch her for a while, worried that she might suddenly wake from a nightmare of her recent experience, but her face — her lovely face, beautiful to me despite being battered and bruised — is a vision of peacefulness. Slowly, and with great reluctance, I untwist my fingers from hers, rub the stiffness from them, and step outside to join PC Fraser.

"You look exhausted," she says.

I have a vague idea that I should contact Innes and tell him he should go home — I'm planning to spend the night here at Izzy's bedside. But first I want to ask PC Fraser more questions. Suddenly, a thought occurs to me: Innes will know the right questions to ask. I need to find him.

"I have a friend waiting for me. Do you mind if he joins us?"

"Of course not." PC Fraser looks relieved. She thinks I mean a partner. She must be glad I'm not having to deal with this alone.

We find Innes sitting in the waiting area. There's no one else there. He looks uncomfortably big and awkward in the orange plastic chair. He stands up as we approach, concern on his face. I love him for that. I introduce them. "My friend, Innes Nevin. Innes, this is PC Nadia Fraser." Innes nods, asks after Izzy.

"She's okay," I tell him shakily. "She was attacked. Beaten up." His mouth opens to ask a question. I know what it is. It's the same thing I feared.

"No," I say, "it wasn't a sexual assault." Innes frowns, looks at PC Fraser.

"We can't rule out a sexual motive. A young man came to Izzy's aid within minutes, so it's possible . . ." There's no need for her to complete her sentence.

"Who's your DI?" Innes asks.

"George Farquhar."

Innes nods curtly. "I take it he's been informed."

"Of course. There's been a forensics team out at the park where Izzy was attacked all afternoon. Izzy was interviewed by a detective sergeant earlier."

"Has forensic evidence been collected from Izzy?"

"Yes, sir." Innes hasn't lost his air of authority and PC Fraser automatically addresses him as she would a superior officer.

"Have there been any other incidents like this one recently?"

"No."

"Do you have any reason to believe Izzy might have been targeted?"

Despite my weariness, Innes's question has me instantly alert. Where is he going with this? It was a random attack, wasn't it? A sick individual waiting for an opportunity. Izzy was simply in the wrong place at the wrong time. Or is he suggesting she's been stalked? Tracked down and hunted like an animal? I tuck my hands deep inside my pockets to hide the fact that they're shaking.

"No. At least, we don't think so. I did ask Izzy if anyone had been pestering her."

I can see PC Fraser is starting to doubt herself, her lack of experience. She is so young. Has she even come across a crime like this before? Innes runs a hand through his hair, making it stand on end.

"This young man, the one who helped Izzy. Has he been questioned?"

"I believe so."

"You believe so?" Innes's tone is dry as dust.

"Are you police?" PC Fraser asks.

"I was." Innes gives a cough. "I'm retired."

PC Fraser's eyes widen. "I've heard of you. You're Innes Nevin. My dad knows you."

Innes stares at her, his expression slowly changing to one of astonishment. "You're Pat Fraser's lass?"

"Aye, that's right."

"Pat and I were at school together," Innes explains, turning to me. To PC Fraser, he says, "You're a sight bonnier than your old man ever was, that's for sure."

PC Fraser smiles politely. She tells me she'll be outside Izzy's room when I return. After she's gone, Innes says, "Look, do you fancy a drink? I think you could do with one. There's a place less than five minutes from here. Bronn can come with us. I should let him out of the car for a bit."

I glance at my watch. I'm reluctant to leave the hospital — it feels like I'd be abandoning Izzy. But the doctor said she'd be asleep for hours.

"Just a quick one, then. I don't want to leave Izzy for long."

"You're staying the night." It isn't a question. Innes is a father. He takes it for granted. "Make a list of what you need me to bring from the cottage."

We leave the hospital and go outside to the car park. Bronn greets us ecstatically. The pub is neither cosy nor welcoming. It's sparse and functional, the hangout of hard-drinking locals who eye us with suspicion as we walk in the door. The barmaid is slow to serve us, even though she's only drying a shot glass and watching a pool game taking place in the bar.

We sit down at a table some distance from the bar. I reach for my drink. The coaster is stuck to the bottom of the glass. Bronn settles beneath the table with a sigh. There will be no bones on offer here.

"I'm so sorry this has happened to your daughter," Innes says. "I'm sure the police will catch the perpetrator. The young man who helped her might be able to give a description."

"Yes. I'm sure you're right." Something's playing on my mind. "Seeing Izzy like that, I couldn't help but think of Moira, what she must have suffered. And of what might have happened to Izzy if that young man hadn't come to her assistance."

"I understand where you're coming from, Ros, but going forward you need to focus on Izzy and the fact that she's okay."

"I know . . . I know. It's just . . . I've been through it before. I know what it's like to lose someone you love to an act of violence."

Suddenly, I am telling Innes about Doug. I end by saying, "When my husband was killed, I refused to believe it. For seven years, I convinced myself that he'd been taken prisoner and was alive somewhere, that he'd come back to us one day. It didn't seem like pure fantasy. Journalists were forever being abducted by hostile parties. There were stories in the news all the time. Or so it seemed to me then." Innes listens without comment. "Even after a visit from a colleague of Doug's who'd witnessed my husband's execution — he was shot in the head at point-blank range — I refused to acknowledge the truth. How stupid was that?"

"You were in shock."

"For seven years? I was deep in denial."

"You must have loved him very much."

"Yes." The lump in my throat prevents me from saying more. We sit in silence, the past cloaking me in a shroud of melancholy.

"I lost someone too," Innes says, so softly I think I've misheard him.

"Your wife? How did she die?"

"One day I came home from work to find her unconscious on our bed. She'd taken some pills. Left a note saying how sorry she was for leaving me in the lurch." His voice is bitter. "I was the one who left her in the lurch. Always at work, never enough time for her and the kids. If I'd been a better husband and father, maybe . . ."

127

Instinctively, I cover his hand with mine. I don't tell him it wasn't his fault because I sense that, despite the self-reproach, Innes has acknowledged this already. He nods.

"I should get back to Izzy."

"Of course." Innes accompanies me back to his car where he finds some paper and a pen for me to write a list of items that I need him to bring from the cottage. As I hand it to him, my hand grazes his. Our eyes meet. We lean closer together, but at that moment, Bronn gives a sudden tug on his lead and a small bark. He's heard something, a rabbit or some small rodent in the bushes.

"Try not to worry too much," Innes says, turning back to his car.

I walk back to Izzy's ward through dimly-lit corridors. PC Fraser is still there, but she bids me goodnight soon afterwards, telling me to call if I need her.

After she's gone, I settle down in the chair next to Izzy's bed, covering myself with the blanket that some thoughtful person has provided. I gaze at my daughter. A stranger walking into the room would be horrified by the sight of her face, but again, I think what a beautiful sight she is to behold.

Still, I hope she doesn't ask for a mirror any time soon.

CHAPTER SEVENTEEN

In the morning, Innes arrives at the hospital with the things I asked him to bring — some toiletries, a toothbrush, a change of clothes. He leaves before Izzy is awake, telling me he'll hang around in reception until I join him.

When Izzy stirs, I move swiftly to her side. She's a little disoriented. "I'm here," I say reassuringly, hoping my words will dispel the panic I see in her eyes as she wakes.

"Mum." Her eyes fill with tears and I hold her delicately, remembering how she flinched when I hugged her the day before. All of yesterday's bravado has gone, and I feel a sudden rush of anger at the man who has reduced my daughter to this watered-down version of herself. I've brought Izzy up to be strong, independent. I won't let her think of herself as a victim.

A nurse comes in, pushing one of those trollies that look 'busy' with medical equipment. She takes Izzy's blood pressure, gives her some medication and then asks if she would like some help to take a shower. She suggests I take a break, so I kiss Izzy and go in search of Innes, who is waiting patiently in reception, reading a book.

"I've got a flask of coffee in the car, and some breakfast. Let's go outside," he suggests.

"Where's Bronn?" I ask when we reach the car and there's no excited animal to greet us.

"I've left him at home. He'll be alright for a couple of hours."

Innes pours coffee into mugs and takes the lid off a large plastic container. Inside are croissants, some fruit and yoghurt. "Thanks. I didn't realise I was hungry, and the coffee is a treat."

As we eat, I stare out the side window, at the brick wall next to the car. It seems like an appropriate metaphor for where we are with things. A feeling of unease prickles through me. I look out the back window at the other cars in the car park, as if expecting to see a face at one of the windows, watching us. Next to me, Innes takes a bite of his croissant, catching the flaky crumbs in a napkin. I know he's watching me out of the corner of his eye.

We eat in silence for a few moments. Innes finishes his croissant, lowers the window and shakes out the napkin he's been using. A couple of gulls appear from nowhere, but they're quickly disillusioned by the measly offerings and fly off. They land on a nearby wall and sit, watchful, in case something meatier follows.

"I should get back to Izzy," I say. Innes packs away our picnic breakfast.

"I'm sorry," I say. "About your wife."

There's an awkward silence. Then, Innes says, "I'm sorry about your husband."

"It's hard, isn't it? Being on your own."

"That's why I got a dog after the kids left. Helps to have another heart beating in the house, or so everyone told me. Can't say I disagree, though Bronn's not much of a conversationalist."

"I could do a portrait of him for you," I offer.

"Thanks, that would be . . . nice." I sense Innes is being polite. He probably thinks what I do for a living is a bit weird.

Before we can carry on our tentative conversation, a car appears out of nowhere. The driver eyes up the parking space next to ours. It's not really wide enough to accommodate his four-wheel drive, so Innes sighs, and signals that he is ready to go.

"Thanks again for breakfast," I say, jumping out. I walk away with a sense of things left unsaid.

Why do I believe in Innes Nevin? I hardly know him, and yet he evokes a sense of loyalty and trust in me that may be unjustified and is certainly untested. I have travelled halfway across the country and into his home with scarcely a moment's thought. Isn't it about time I examined my feelings for this man? Is curiosity about Moira's murder really my sole motivation for being here?

Innes and I are connected by Moira's death but if I'm being honest, I feel another kind of connection to him. It's been a long time since I've let my guard down regarding matters of the heart. Those short-lived relationships in the years after Doug's death were never intended to be anything other than a distraction from my grief, and the loneliness I felt when Izzy was growing up.

Reluctant to cross-examine my feelings, I return to the ward and find that Izzy has an early morning visitor, a young man.

"Mum," she says as I approach, "this is Tom. My hero." Tom blushes scarlet, and I embarrass him further by embracing him on the spot and thanking him effusively.

"It was nothing," he says modestly. "Just what anyone would have done. I'm glad I was in the right place at the right time. I brought flowers." He turns to Izzy apologetically. "The nurse wouldn't let me bring them in. It's not hygienic, apparently."

Izzy smiles, winces. She looks down. I wonder if the pain has reminded her of what she looks like.

"Did you get a look at him? Izzy's attacker?" I ask.

Tom looks crestfallen. "The police asked me that. I couldn't be much help, other than to say it was definitely a man. The police took all my clothes to search for evidence — you know, like hairs and stuff that their forensics people can analyse."

"Thank you. I can't tell you how grateful I— we are, Tom. Are you a student too?"

"Yes. Second-year medic." He says this with a hint of pride. He looks at Izzy. "I hope this won't put you off studying here. It's a terrible thing to happen in your first term." Then he says, "I'd better go. Let you two have a chat." To Izzy, he says, "Would . . . would it be alright if I come again?" He blushes anew as he says this, and my heart goes out to him. I'm already fantasising about him as my future son-in-law.

"Yes," I gush before I can stop myself. "Er . . . Izzy?"

"Sure," Izzy agrees. Her eyes narrow when she turns to me.

"Great. See you soon." Tom backs out the door and is gone. I know I'm in for an ear-bashing.

"Mum! Could you have been any more embarrassing?"

"I see you're feeling better."

"I was until my overbearing mother turned up and shamed me in front of the cutest boy ever, who also just happens to have saved my life." Her mood changes abruptly. "I don't expect him to come back. I mean, why would he? I look hideous."

"Not for long, Iz. Once the swelling goes down, you'll soon be your lovely self again."

Izzy sighs deeply. "I hope so."

We chat for a while. A little later, a young woman pops her head around the door. One of Izzy's friends from her hall of residence. I promise Izzy I'll visit again later and leave them to have a catch up.

I walk a little way down the corridor, looking for a room where I can make a call. There's a day room where patients and visitors can sit when they want to escape the ward. It's furnished with some chairs, a coffee table, a bookcase with a selection of novels — crime and romance titles dominate. Double doors lead to a garden area outside. Unfortunately, the door is locked. I could do with some fresh air. I sit down and call Elspeth.

The call goes straight to voicemail. Elspeth is probably at work. I feel a stab of disappointment. After a moment, my phone rings.

"Ros? Hi. Is everything okay? You don't usually call me at this time on a work day."

"Hi, Elspeth. So glad you're there. I'm in St Andrews. Izzy's had an . . . an accident."

Sharp as ever, Elspeth picks up my hesitation. "What kind of accident?"

"She was assaulted. Last night. She's okay. Looks awful but they're saying it's mostly superficial."

"Jesus! How awful for you both. Look, I'm meeting a client this morning, but I'll drive over this afternoon. You shouldn't be alone at a time like this. Where are you staying?"

"Er . . ." This is awkward. "With someone. A friend."

"Oh, anyone I know?"

"Yes, at least you might remember him. His name's Innes Nevin. He was the young PC who was involved in Moira's murder investigation."

The silence is so profound that I wonder if Elspeth has been called away. Finally, she says, "Well, you're a dark horse, Ros Maitland. How long has this been going on?"

"Nothing's going on." I realise how unlikely this must sound. Elspeth knows nothing of the circumstances that have brought me to Fife and into Innes's home. It's natural for her to assume that we're romantically involved. Not surprisingly, she snorts.

"I met him when I came up with Izzy in October. We got talking. It's, er . . . kind of complicated."

"Sounds it. Look, it's none of my business, Ros. I'm just glad you've got someone to turn to. Would you still like me to come over? I can be there by half three, four o'clock?"

"That would be great. Thanks, Elspeth."

"Give Izzy a hug from me."

"I will." It's going to be hard not to confide in Elspeth.

I wonder what I can do to occupy the time until she arrives. My car is still at Innes's place, so I can't go far. I make my way into town and walk around the shops for a bit. It's weird being here and no longer being a student. I look at the fresh young faces scurrying between lectures and feel a pang of nostalgia. You can go back to a place but after an absence of many years, it's never the same, I know. Too much has happened since my student days for me to recapture more than a shadowy trace of the girl I was back then.

I choose a café and sit down, wrapping my hands around my cup to warm them. My phone pings. Izzy has sent me a picture of her sitting up in bed. There's a teddy bear balloon tied to her bedpost, and a box of chocolates on her bedside cabinet. More pictures follow. Selfies of Izzy surrounded by her friends, all with long hair and unnaturally perfect eyebrows. When did all young women start looking the same?

The thought that Izzy wasn't targeted last night reassures me. She could have been any one of those young women. She'd simply been in the wrong place at the wrong time.

I finish my coffee and potter around a bit more, and then it's time to go back to the hospital. Elspeth arrives soon after me, during a lull in visits from Izzy's friends. "Hi, Aunt Elspeth," Izzy greets her, forgetting to drop the 'Aunt.' Elspeth gives a momentary start when she catches sight of Izzy's face. I'd told her what to expect, but it seems that the warning failed to prepare her for the reality.

"Hi, gorgeous!"

"I'm not gorgeous. I'm hideous." There's no self-pity in Izzy's voice. She's been posing for selfies with her friends all morning and seems to have embraced her temporary face.

"I was being polite," Elspeth jokes back. She hands Izzy a basket of fruit. "I'll send flowers when you get out of this dreadful place."

"It's not so bad," Izzy says, suddenly subdued. Elspeth and I exchange looks. She feels safe here, I realise with a flash of anger.

We chat for a while. A little later, there's a tap on the door and Tom appears. Izzy greets him with the words, "Brilliant timing. Mum and Aunt Elspeth are just leaving."

Elspeth smiles at me. We know when we're not wanted.

"Would you like me to come back later, darling?" I say. Izzy looks positively alarmed at the suggestion.

"Her boyfriend, I assume?" Elspeth's question reminds me that I forgot to introduce her to Tom.

"Actually, no." I explain about Tom rescuing Izzy from a worse ordeal.

"Well, from the look on both their faces, I don't think they'll be just friends for long. By the way, I've booked a table at the Old Course. I hope you don't mind. My treat." Before I can object, Elspeth takes my arm and steers me to her car. On the way, she quizzes me about Izzy's ordeal. "What are the police doing about it?"

I explain that they've screened Izzy and Tom for forensic evidence, and collected whatever they could from the scene. "Unfortunately, the attacker's face was covered, so neither Izzy nor Tom could give a description. And he was wearing gloves and a mask, so there's not likely to be any DNA evidence."

"Let's just hope they get something."

We arrive at the hotel and are shown to our table. As soon as we sit down, Elspeth begins questioning me about Innes.

"So, you and this Innes Nevin? I had to rack my brain to think of him. The name sounded familiar but I couldn't put a face to it. Not that the face I remembered looks anything like his present one."

"Looks? Have you been Googling him? Already?"

Ignoring my disapproving look, Elspeth pours me a glass of wine.

"Seriously, Ros. You mean you haven't looked for him online yourself?"

"No. And you shouldn't have done either."

"It's what everyone does these days, Ros."

I think I've picked up a hint that Elspeth has something to tell me about Innes. She has an air of smugness about her. I don't want to give her the satisfaction of getting one over on me but I'm dying to hear what she's discovered. I take a sip of my wine, say nothing. I'm banking on her being as desperate to tell me as I am to know.

"Oh, come on, Ros. You're bursting there."

"I'm really not."

Elspeth gives one of her annoying snorts. She drops her voice almost to a whisper, leans over the table and says, "I bet he hasn't told you that he was fired from the Glasgow police."

I can't suppress my astonishment. More wine is required — a slug this time.

"So, what did he tell you? That he'd retired?" The look of glee on Elspeth's face is infuriating.

"Yes," I say. "What do you know, Elspeth?"

"Only that your friend is stretching the truth a bit. Well, quite a lot, actually." Her words send a bolt of misery through me. Even before Elspeth delivers her bombshell, I'm feeling like an idiot for trusting Innes.

"Strictly speaking, he did retire but prior to that, he'd been suspended and investigated for corrupt practices." Elspeth sits back, wine glass in hand, her work done. Or almost done. She's eager to provide me with the details. But afternoon tea arrives in the form of an array of dainty cakes and pastries, and crust-free sandwiches. As soon as the waitress moves away, I ask Elspeth to explain.

"He's been accused of planting evidence on a suspect. He was lucky not to be prosecuted himself. Apparently, his wife had just divorced him, and he was judged to be emotionally compromised. Compassionate grounds. You know how it goes. He was allowed to take early retirement in order to save his reputation after what had been a distinguished career." I wonder what it cost Elspeth to add that last sentence.

"As if that wasn't bad enough," she continues, her hand covering her mouth as she bites down on a pastry, "the suspect died in mysterious circumstances before his trial. No one said it was Nevin but . . . Oh God, Ros, you have got to try one of those cream slices. They are so moreish."

In response, I push my plate away and excuse myself. It's too much to take in. Innes has lied to me about so many things. "Ros? Are you okay?" Elspeth's voice calls after me, shrill and grating.

What do you think?

In the privacy of the toilets, I sit in one of the cubicles, thoughts racing, anger mounting. The fact that Innes has failed to mention a case in his past that sounds eerily like Moira's is unsettling, disturbing even. It casts him in an entirely different light and makes me wonder if he's invented this story about Menzies. For all I know, he could be delusional. Then there's his wife. He told me she committed suicide. Even if he had personal reasons for the lie, it made him dishonest at best.

On the other hand, a little voice inside my head cautions me. Elspeth has proven to be untrustworthy in the past over rivals for my attention. Even Doug didn't escape.

Upon my return, she apologises. "I'm sorry, Ros. I shouldn't have dumped that on you the way I did. I don't do subtle. I didn't really appreciate that you might have had deeper feelings for Innes Nevin. You did keep insisting you were just friends."

Elspeth's always had this way of apologising by apportioning a good share of the blame to the victim. I know her of old, and don't hold it against her. I even believe her when she tells me she checked Innes out to protect me.

"Look, I've booked a twin room here. You're welcome to stay with me tonight. I'll drive you to Nevin's cottage so that you can pick up your things. How does that sound?"

I nod, numbly. If we time it right, Innes will be out walking Bronn and I won't have to confront him. Cowardly, I know, but I don't feel I can face him right away. I need time to work out truth from fiction.

We don't time it right.

Innes has been waiting for me to call him. I've forgotten he offered to pick me up from the hospital and drive me back to his cottage.

He seems surprised that I have company. Before I have a chance to say anything, Elspeth butts in. "Ros has come to collect her things. She's decided to stay in St Andrews with me tonight."

"Okaay." Innes's voice is hesitant. He must have picked up that something's amiss. He throws me a questioning look. "Ros?"

"I . . . it's for the best," I say, evasively.

"Is something wrong? Is it Izzy?"

"Izzy's fine. It's . . . it's just . . . so that I can be on hand for her if she needs me."

Innes doesn't seem convinced. He gives me a searching look. Elspeth shifts from foot to foot, no doubt impatient with our dithering. Suddenly, she can contain herself no longer.

"Ros doesn't appreciate being lied to, Mr Nevin."

Innes turns a cold stare on her. "What are you talking about?"

"About your *retirement*?" For a moment, Innes looks confused as he absorbs her words. Confusion becomes anger. His gaze swings back to me. "What has she been saying to you?"

Elspeth pre-empts me again. "Only that you're a crooked cop. Or are you going to deny that you were suspended over an allegation of corruption?"

Innes looks like he will explode. From the kitchen comes the sound of whining, followed by scratching at the closed door. It's Bronn, exhibiting that extra sensory perception dogs have when they know that their owner is upset. Innes's eyes flit to the door, then back to me.

"Ros? You believe this crap?"

Put on the spot, I become defensive. "I . . . how do I know what to believe? You told me your wife took some pills to end her life. Elspeth says your wife divorced you."

"My *first* wife took her own life. I married again in haste, an old friend who'd just lost her husband. A stupid mistake, borne out of mutual grief. We realised immediately that we'd made a big error of judgement and divorced amicably within months. As for that other business, Ros, there are two sides to every story. Let me know when you're ready to hear mine."

With that, he stands aside so that we can reach the stairs. "Post your key through the letterbox when you leave. I'm going out."

As I pack my things into my suitcase upstairs, I hear Bronn's excited barking, followed by the slam of a door.

"Just popping to the loo," Elspeth announces.

As soon as she leaves the bedroom, I cross to the window and see Innes striding out along the cliff path, Bronn bounding along in front of him. Two lonely figures in a grey landscape awash in a mist of uncertainty.

CHAPTER EIGHTEEN

"Ros!"

I swung around in the corridor of the history department to see Andrew Kelso beckoning me into his office. I looked around, as if expecting some other Ros to appear at my side, but there was only me.

"Please, take a seat," he urged. I sat down in one of the spindle chairs arranged around the small room he used for his tutor group. It was so cramped that his students' knees must have touched. The room had a sloping ceiling, leaving little head room. Bookcases lined what wall space was left between floor and sloping ceiling, and of necessity, Andrew's desk was piled up with books and papers. Underneath his desk there were two heaps of books separated by a tunnel of free space, presumably so that Andrew could stretch out his long legs. The tiny room had one saving grace — the glorious sea view, which must have made it difficult for his students to concentrate on their studies.

It was a few days after Stuart Brogan had discovered him in bed with Moira, and Andrew was still sporting a colourful black eye. I tried not to focus on it when I looked at him. Why had he asked me into his office? I suspected it was something to do with his messy love life. I was right.

"Ros, I'm sorry about that scene at your house the other night." I gave a shrug, not sure why he was apologising to me. I hadn't even been there when it happened. Moreover, he'd already been round to the house with that outrageously outsized bouquet and apologised to Moira. Relations between him and Moira were back to what passed for normal with those two.

But after apologising, he just sat, folded into his chair, eyes on the view through his sash window. As the silence lengthened, I started to feel uncomfortable. I cleared my throat loudly. Andrew started, as though he'd forgotten I was even there.

"How well do you know Moira?" he asked suddenly. The question caught me off guard.

"What do you mean? I've been sharing a house with her since October."

"Yes, yes, but how well do you *really* know her?" he persisted.

"I don't understand what you're getting at. We're sort of friends, I suppose. I think we get along okay. Moira's quite easy to talk to." Andrew seemed agitated, as though my response was inadequate. I felt like a student who's unable to back up an answer.

"Who is she close to, then? Who does she confide in? She told me you were a close friend."

"Me?" I stared at Andrew stupidly. "I . . . I didn't think we were all that close." Frankly, I was slightly shocked by this revelation, even a little flattered. "She gets on well with Shona. They often go out together."

His questions came thick and fast. "Does she go out a lot? Ever go away overnight?" I shrugged, feeling uncomfortable again. Suddenly, Andrew blurted out what I thought he'd wanted to ask all along. "Besides this Stuart Brogan, is there anyone else she's been seeing?"

"No! I don't think so. But you should be asking Moira about that, not me." So that was it. He was afraid of further betrayals.

Andrew caught his breath. He ran long fingers through his hair. His agitation was beginning to worry me.

"Does she talk about our relationship much?" he asked. "What sort of things does she say?" I coloured. No way was I going to tell him that I'd been told in pretty graphic detail what the pair of them got up to in bed.

"Er . . . she likes you. A lot. She told me she only went out with Stuart because you told her it was all over between the two of you. Then you changed your mind. She was intending to end her relationship with Stuart, even before . . . before . . ."

"Did she tell you about our trip to Aviemore?"

"Yes."

Andrew leaned forward in his chair. "What exactly did she say?"

I frowned, puzzled. "Only that she'd enjoyed it. Except she didn't like you spending so much time with your cousin. She found him a bit, er, boring."

"Is that all she said about him? That he was boring?" Andrew seemed to relax.

"I don't remember her saying anything more. Surely you don't think Moira and your cousin are seeing each other?"

Andrew shook his head, but I got the impression he wasn't really listening. He was staring out the window again, his gaze on the distant horizon. He seemed deeply troubled. Then again, he was a married man with a baby and a secret lover, and he'd just discovered that this secret lover had been cheating on him. It was enough to trouble anyone.

"I can't understand it," he said. "Why would she cheat on me?" That seemed rich, coming from someone who had cheated on his wife more than once. Andrew Kelso must be an exceptionally vain man, I thought, someone who genuinely believed he was God's gift to women. The possibility of a rival was as unbelievable as it was repellent to him.

I picked up my bag. "Can I go now?" An unnecessary question. I didn't need his permission to leave.

The magnetic sea view had his attention again. Barely looking away from the window, Andrew said, "Yes, yes, yes," each word fainter than the last.

Since he no longer seemed aware of my presence, I muttered a goodbye and headed for the door.

When I saw Elspeth later, she was piqued to hear that Moira regarded me as a close friend. I wasn't going to tell her at first, but the whole encounter with Andrew had seemed so strange that I needed to talk it over, and this fact slipped out along with the rest of it. At first she couldn't contain her jealousy. She was also jealous that I had been alone with the great Andrew Kelso.

"I'd give my left arm to be alone in a room with that man," she said. "It's ridiculous him falling for Moira. She doesn't have a single thing in common with him."

"I think he's really pissed off that any woman would look elsewhere when she's with him. Maybe he doesn't know Moira as well as he thought. Do you think I should tell her about his conversation with me?"

"That's up to you. You're her best mate."

"Her words, not mine." *Great*, I thought. *Now Elspeth's going to sulk.* I wished I'd spoken to Shona instead.

The following day, I asked Moira to meet me for lunch. "That would be nice," she said, before asking warily, "Is Elspeth coming too?" I assured her it would just be the two of us.

I chose a pub on the outskirts of town, a place it was unlikely anyone we knew would pop into by chance. Moira was already there when I arrived, sitting at a table and looking at the menu.

"Hi. Sorry I'm late. Lecture ran over time."

"No problem." She smiled. "Good choice of venue, if a bit off the beaten track." I sensed she'd guessed I'd chosen this pub because I didn't want Elspeth to see us together. Moira must have thought I was a timid mouse.

"You shouldn't let her dominate you, you know," Moira said quietly. I wanted to tell her that was rich, coming from someone who treated Lucy like a serf and who had everyone else (Elspeth excepted) at her beck and call. But of course, I didn't. It wasn't in my nature. And there was another reason. People did things for Moira because they wanted to. I thought of Lucy, fetching and carrying for her, and suddenly I saw that their relationship could have been interpreted in a different light. Lucy was a little lost and Moira gave her a purpose, made her feel needed.

So, instead of saying, 'I don't,' I replied, "I know."

"Why does she have such a hold over you?"

I told her about Leah. How her death had made me want to retreat from the world. Shrink inside myself. "I met Elspeth in my second year here. Besides still grieving for Leah, I was terribly homesick and finding it hard to make friends. To tell the truth, I was thinking of jacking it all in. Elspeth kind of saved me."

"Did it ever occur to you that she might have been feeling just as lonely and desperate as you?"

The idea startled me. "Nooo . . . not really. I suppose I was just grateful that she considered me worthy of her friendship."

Moira threw her arms in the air. "Don't undersell yourself, Ros. You are very worthy of being anyone's friend." Her eyes narrowed. "Elspeth Blair exploits your good nature. Surely you've noticed that she doesn't exactly get along well with a lot of people." She sat back. "She hates me because she knows I see right through her. Well, not just because of that. Because I'm cleverer than her and I have Andrew, and because she thinks I'm trying to take you away from her."

This was news to me. "Are you?" I asked. "Trying to take me away from her?"

"I just want to be friends with you, but Elspeth gets so jealous whenever I try to be. You know it too. That's why we're here, miles from anywhere. In case she spots us together. She's so in control of you."

"She doesn't seem to mind me being friends with Shona or Lucy."

"That's because Shona's got loads of other friends, and Lucy . . . well, she probably doesn't see Lucy as competition." Moira shrugged. "Anyway, what are you having to eat?"

We went to the bar and ordered some food. I had half a pint of cider and Moira had a coke. She didn't often drink. When we returned to our table, I began to tell her about my odd encounter with Andrew Kelso, his strange questions and his apparent agitation.

"Andrew asked you how well you knew me? Who I *confide in*?" Moira said.

"Yes, I think he would have asked me more questions but I told him we weren't that close." Thinking that sounded bad, I added quickly, "That's why I asked you to have lunch with me today. I felt bad that we've been sharing a house for a few months now and I don't really feel I know you all that well."

Moira laughed. "And to tell me about your encounter with Andrew, for which I'm grateful." She looked thoughtful.

"Moira, it's none of my business, but don't you think it would be better if you stopped seeing Andrew Kelso? He gave me the impression of being very possessive."

Moira frowned. "Don't worry, Ros. I can handle Andrew Kelso."

"You've got so much going for you, Moira. You could have your pick of the men around here—"

"So why pick another woman's husband? Is that what you were about to say, Ros? This is the twentieth century, you know. I'd expect an attitude like that from po-faced Elspeth Blair, but not from you."

This wasn't going well. "It's not that at all. I'm just concerned. Look at the men you've been involved with recently. Stuart Brogan hit you and Andrew Kelso is insanely possessive."

Moira gave a weary sigh. "Stuart didn't hit me. Look, Ros. I don't always live by other people's rules or standards. If I want something, I take it. I don't feel sorry for Andrew's wife because she's made a choice. She knows what kind of man Andrew is and she chooses to stay with him. As I've said before, if he wasn't cheating on her with me, he'd be cheating on her with someone else. I know exactly what I'm doing with Andrew, same as I'll know exactly when it's time to call it a day."

Our food arrived. Moira took a bite of her burger and said, "So what else did Andrew say about me?"

"Not much. I think he was fishing, you know, trying to find out if you were seeing anyone else. Finding out about Stuart seems to have him worried that you have legions of other men. He mentioned his cousin Hans at one point."

Moira laughed out loud. "Poor Andrew. He must be feeling insecure if he thinks I'd do it with Horrid Hans."

I laughed too. For the next hour, our conversation was more light-hearted. Moira seemed to genuinely enjoy my company, which surprised and delighted me. I even started wondering if I'd have made other friends eventually, back at the start of my university career, if my grief hadn't driven me to retreat to my room rather than face those overwhelming social situations.

Or if Elspeth hadn't come along and claimed me as her own.

CHAPTER NINETEEN

I wake early with a bitter taste in my mouth and glance across at the twin bed next to mine where Elspeth is still asleep, snoring lightly. My neck is stiff from the unyielding pillow, and I move my head from side to side to relieve the discomfort.

My sleep was restless, flooded with alternating dreams of my daughter in jeopardy, and Innes Nevin's face when Elspeth accused him of lying to me.

I reach for my phone and realise that I'm hoping for a message from Innes, some reassurance that he's been unjustly accused. His words play over and over in my head. *There are two sides to every story, Ros. Let me know when you are ready to hear mine.* I so want to believe he has a story to tell. There are no messages.

I send off a good morning greeting to Izzy and get out of bed. I take a shower, lingering a while, allowing the pounding hot water to ease the tension in my neck and shoulders. Condensation builds on the cubicle door. On impulse, I write Moira's name, my finger squeaking over the glass. The letters elongate in watery streaks, until they are illegible. I erase them with the palm of my hand. It seems a fitting metaphor for Moira's short life, written large on the world only to be expunged by the stroke of another's hand.

There are lots of fluffy white towels on the rail outside the shower. I wrap one around my wet hair and one around my body. Despite the noise from the shower and the extractor fan, Elspeth is still fast asleep. Just as I'm wondering whether to wake her, an alarm sounds, and she stretches out a hand for her phone to turn it off. She sits up, rubbing her eyes, and looks surprised to see me up and about before her.

"I'm used to being the first one out of bed," she says. "How did you sleep?"

How do you think? "Okay."

"Good. No nightmares about Innes Nevin, then."

It's not really a question. As far as Elspeth is concerned, it's time to move on. It's as though my feelings on the matter are irrelevant. She trots off to the shower, leaving me to pack my things. I can't stay here. My budget doesn't run to staying at a place like this. I will need to find a bed and breakfast to stay in until Izzy is back on her feet. It should only be for another day or so. And then? There will be no reason for me to linger in St Andrews any longer.

Breakfast is a quick affair. Neither of us feels like the full Scottish, so we make do with coffee and pastries. Elspeth is mindful of the time. She must be back in Edinburgh to interview a client before eleven. "I won't have time to go back to the hospital again and say hi to Izzy. Give her my love, won't you, Ros?"

I wonder why she came, really. To support me, she claimed, but all she's done is ruin my tentative relationship with Innes. There's a lot of the old Elspeth in her still, I think.

Once I've waved her off, I sit in a lounge overlooking the famous Old Course, drinking more coffee and calling various guest houses to see if they have a vacancy. The third one I call has a room free with parking in a yard at the rear, a bonus when you're on a budget. I collect my bags and go directly there.

The room is small but clean and prettily turned out. After unpacking, I drive to the hospital and am pleasantly surprised to see that Izzy is looking much better this morning, despite the bruising to her face being more colourful. There's an array of 'get well' cards arranged on her bedside cabinet, and a pink teddy bear rests on her pillow next to Sebastian, who seems to have appeared since my last visit. Izzy is dressed and sitting on a chair, fingers flying over the screen of her phone. She greets me without looking up.

"Hi, Mum. Guess what? I'm being discharged today."

"That's great, love." Izzy picks up on my lack of enthusiasm. It springs partly from the events of the previous evening, but there's also anxiety about her safety when she comes out of hospital. She guesses this immediately.

"You don't have to worry about me, Mum. There's good security in my hall and I'll make sure I don't go out unaccompanied until the police tell me it's safe. They've been over it all with me."

This is only slightly reassuring. I remind myself not to allow my fears over her safety to knock her confidence. I nod and smile. Izzy says, "With all that's been going on, I forgot to ask if you were enjoying your stay with your friends here." I don't answer at first. There's a beeping sound from further down the ward that distracts my attention. "Mum?"

"Oh! Sorry, Iz. Yes, everything's fine. They're good people."

"Cool. Will you be staying for long?"

Will I? Is there any point in my staying, now that I don't know if Innes was telling the truth about Menzies?

"Maybe a couple of days," I tell her. "At least until I know you're okay with me not being around."

A nurse arrives and confirms that Izzy will be discharged as soon as her prescription for painkillers arrives, which happens five minutes later. I drive my daughter to her hall of residence, taking care to go slowly, mindful of the pain that any sudden jolt might cause her. It reminds me of that first trip home from the hospital with her when she was barely two days old, Doug driving, me sitting in the back seat, Izzy strapped into her little baby carrier next to me. I'd held my arm across her car seat all the way, not trusting her safety to the thin straps securing her to the seat.

It's a wrench to leave her, but at least she's not alone when I go. Two friends turn up ten minutes after we arrive at her room. One is her new 'bestie,' a slim blonde girl with a Mancunian accent. She assures me that she won't let Izzy out of her sight.

Alone outside Izzy's hall of residence, I feel at a loss for what to do next. The house on North Street exerts a pull on me and, after a short walk, I find myself standing on the street opposite the front door. I doubt that it's let to students now. There's a buggy in the alleyway running alongside the house, a vase of orchids on the living-room windowsill. It's a family home now.

Resisting an urge to knock on the door, I walk on, heading in the direction of the West Sands. It's a cold, blustery day. The North Sea roils, frothing with yellow foam from the churned-up sand. Gulls screech and swoop over the turbulent waves, white streaks in the relentless vista of grey water and sky. The air feels moist and tastes of salt. Before me the West Sands stretch into the distance, two miles of continuous sandy beach backed by dunes planted with spindly marram grass.

I walk along the beach to clear my head, battling against the wind that seems to howl from all directions, sand in my teeth. Afterwards, chilled to the bone and in need of coffee, I head back into town.

Market Street is bustling with afternoon shoppers, and the cafés all seem to be doing a roaring trade. I choose one that seems less busy than the others and select a table by the window where I can distract myself by people-watching.

Snippets of conversation reach my ears. The couple to my right are considering adopting a child after another fruitless round of IVF. At the table behind me, two lecturers from the university are discussing the standard of student essays. It isn't possible to follow the thread of two different conversations, and when the couple get up to leave, I realise

I will never know what decision they reached. They are replaced by a group of students talking loudly about the latest series they have been binge-watching on Netflix.

I close my eyes and massage my temples, and the voices seem to become at once more amplified and less distinct, a cacophony of background noise. I sit like that, eyes closed for several moments, until my phone rings, making me start. It's an unknown number.

"Hello," I say. It's difficult to hear because of the noise and I press the phone against my ear. That's why I think I've heard wrongly when the caller greets me.

"Hi, Ros. It's Lucy."

CHAPTER TWENTY

Inspector Menzies was furious when he discovered that we'd kept Moira's affair with Andrew Kelso from him. He turned up at our door the day after his initial visit, demanding to know what else we'd been hiding. I remember thinking that he must be an excellent detective to have uncovered the details of their secret affair so rapidly.

Even Elspeth was impressed. "Amazing. He doesn't strike you as being exactly Brain of Britain material, does he?"

Lucy agreed. "I bet it was his handsome young constable who figured it out."

"I thought all police officers were just pigs to you," Shona said.

"Some pigs are smarter than others. And better looking."

I'd also noticed that PC Innes Nevin was good-looking. And I agreed that what Lucy said was probably right. Nevin had come across as far more intelligent than the plodding Menzies.

It was PC Nevin who brought us the shocking news of Stuart Brogan's suicide. Elspeth, Shona, Lucy, and I were watching TV when he knocked on our door. Shona let him in. I turned off the TV. I could tell by the solemn look on his face that, once again, he had bad news to deliver. A stunned silence followed his words.

"So, Stuart Brogan killed Moira?" PC Nevin gave no response to Elspeth's question.

"Did he leave a note?" I asked.

"Yes. There was a note."

"What did it say?"

Elspeth answered my question. "I don't suppose PC Nevin is allowed to tell us."

"That's correct," he said. "For the time being."

"But he confessed, didn't he?" Elspeth said. "In the note, I mean. He must have done — otherwise why take his own life? He knew it was only a matter of time before the police worked it out." We took Nevin's silence for assent.

"How do you know Stuart wrote that note himself? You'll continue your investigation, won't you"? I said.

There was a slight pause before he answered. "We found a ring in Brogan's jacket pocket. It matches the description of the one we were told your friend always wore. It was missing from her finger when her body was found."

"Her grandmother's wedding ring," Lucy said in a hushed voice. "It had an inscription on the inside."

"Aye, that's the one," PC Nevin said.

"I can't believe it," Lucy said.

"Why not?" Shona said hotly. "Moira said she was avoiding him after he found out about Andrew because she was afraid of his temper. He'd have beaten Andrew up badly if Moira hadn't got between them that time."

"But surely the fact that he had the ring doesn't prove he killed Moira?" I said. "She might have left it at his house, or . . . or something."

"No," Shona and Lucy said at once. Shona explained, "Moira was wearing the ring when she left the house the day she disappeared. She'd mislaid it. Lucy helped her look for it."

"That's right," Lucy said. "I remember that too. It was on the kitchen windowsill. She'd taken it off to put some hand cream on and couldn't remember where she'd left it."

"Thank you," PC Nevin said, and made a note of it.

We learned quite soon afterwards that the police were convinced of Stuart Brogan's guilt. The discovery of Moira's ring in his pocket, his violent behaviour towards Andrew Kelso, and the fact that he had had no alibi for the time of her death seemed to satisfy the police that he was their man. The case was closed.

Moira's parents wrote to us to say that they were planning on having their daughter buried at a private service when her body was released by the police. It was their wish to have only close family members present, and they hoped we would respect their wishes and not try to attend. That way, they hoped, the reporters would also stay away.

"So that's it then," Shona said, summing up how swiftly the whole event had taken place. Barely a fortnight had passed since Menzies and Nevin had knocked on our door to deliver their shocking news.

We were all deeply affected by Moira's murder, and by Stuart Brogan's suicide. Lucy seemed to unravel more and more in the weeks that followed the two shocking occurrences. Over and over, she would repeat, "It's not fair. It's not right. She should still be here, living her life. Someone like her — clever, beautiful. She should be here, looking forward to a wonderful life. It just makes you realise how . . . how futile it all is."

We did our best to console her but as the weeks passed, our time was again taken up with work and other things. It wasn't that we forgot Moira, just that we carried on with our lives, finding our own ways of coping without unravelling completely. It took us a while to realise that Lucy wasn't coping so well.

"Has anyone else noticed that something's going on with Lucy?" Shona asked one day when she, Elspeth and I were assembled in the kitchen. It was a month or so after Moira's murder and Stuart Brogan's suicide.

"What do you mean?" Elspeth said. She didn't seem particularly interested.

"Well, she's been a bit quiet and withdrawn. I know she's been getting up late and skipping a lot of lectures," I commented.

"Lucy's moods have always been all over the place," Elspeth said, a bit unkindly. "I'll grant she's been on the quiet side lately, but that's almost a relief from the times when she chatters incessantly."

"You're heartless," Shona said.

"I've been concerned about her too, to tell the truth," I admitted. I'd had some experience of grief, what it does to you, and I recognised some of the signs in Lucy. But I was convinced that it wasn't just grief over Moira that was bothering her. "I think she might be a bit depressed."

"That's not what I'd call it." Elspeth, ungracious as ever, put her index finger to the side of her head and twirled it. "She's bonkers."

Shona looked thoughtful. "I know she's got a boyfriend now. Maybe she's just preoccupied with him." This was news to me and, judging by Elspeth's expression, she didn't know anything about a boyfriend either.

"I think his name's Alec, but don't quote me on that," Shona said.

"What's he like?" Elspeth's curiosity had been piqued.

"Shortish. Skinny. A bit punky. I saw them together the week before last and I asked her about him. She asked me not to tell anyone else yet, because it was early days."

"Huh." Elspeth was put out at being left out of the loop. Turning to me, she asked huffily, "Did you know?"

"No! I'm as surprised as you are. Come on, Shona, let's have some details."

"Okay but act surprised when she tells you. Lucy was walking home from the pub one night when she heard a voice behind her asking for a light. She turned around and came face to face with a boy with spiky hair and multiple piercings. Oh, and he was wearing tight-fitting tartan trousers and a pair of Doc Marten boots. And a denim jacket covered in badges, some of which were identical to the ones on Lucy's duffel bag." Shona giggled. "She even told me which ones, but I can't remember."

We all smiled. It sounded like Lucy had met her soulmate.

"Lucy slung said duffel bag off her shoulder to root around for her box of Swan Vestas. In return, the guy offered to make her a rollie. They sat together in the graveyard of the cathedral. He took out a packet of Rizlas and a rusted tobacco tin with an olive-green lid, exactly the same as hers! He was a bit inexpert at rolling the fags, apparently. Lucy said she could have done a better job herself but she didn't comment."

We nodded. Lucy seldom criticised other people.

Shona continued. "After they'd been smoking for a few minutes, he asked Lucy if she was a student. When she told him she was from Yorkshire, he said, 'Dinna ken where that is.'" Shona said this in her best Fife accent. "Then he said, 'You're no wan o' they posh gits, are ye?'"

"He thought she might be a yah? That's hilarious," Elspeth said. "I bet it was her English accent."

'Yah,' was the name given to a certain type of wealthy, public school-educated, usually English student at St Andrews. They were distinguishable by the way they dressed, their clipped, upper-class accents and air of privilege. Lucy couldn't have been less like a yah if she'd tried.

"Probably. Apparently, Lucy found his accent almost unintelligible, but they still managed a tentative conversation." There was a pause. "Not sure I should tell you the next bit," Shona said, to be met with howls of protest. She looked at Elspeth. "Don't tease her about it, alright?"

"Pinkie promise," Elspeth said, crossing her little fingers.

Shona looked doubtful but carried on. "Turns out he's still at school," she said in a hushed tone, and waited for the inevitable squeals of delight to quieten down.

"How much younger than Lucy is he?" Elspeth asked.

"He's seventeen. Nearly eighteen." Lucy was twenty. At that age, the gap seemed enormous. "I wish I hadn't told you. No jokes about cradle-snatching, Elspeth."

"Well, I for one am pleased she's hooked up with a kindred spirit. But surely if that's the case, she should be in a better frame of mind," I said.

Shona shook her head. "No. I think you were right before, Ros. I think Moira's death has sent her over the edge. She must be in a really bad way if even a romance can't buck her up."

Like Elspeth and I, Shona had stopped using the word 'murder.'

"Do you think we should contact her parents?" I said.

"I don't think so. Not yet. Let's wait a bit longer and see if this Alec can cheer her up," Shona said. And so the matter was dropped.

A couple of days after we'd been discussing her state of mind, I spotted Lucy on the second floor of the library. She was sitting at a booth by the window with some books open on the desk in front of her. I could see she wasn't working. She was staring out of the window, looking miserable. I approached her and asked if she had time to join me for a coffee. She jumped, almost out of her seat, and both the books on her desk crashed to the floor.

"I'm sorry. I didn't mean to startle you, Luce. Are you okay?" I bent to pick up the books. They were about Australia and New Zealand.

"Planning on escaping somewhere exotic?"

"No!" Lucy's voice was sharp, defensive. "These aren't mine. They were on the desk when I arrived. Someone else must have left them there."

It seemed like a transparent lie, but maybe they had been left behind, as she said, and she'd opened one and started browsing out of curiosity. Though it seemed a little odd that she had no other books or papers out, especially as I knew she had a couple of essays due in soon. Still, if she wanted to be secretive that was up to her.

"So, is that a yes or a no?" Lucy stared at me blankly. "Coffee?"

"I suppose. It's not as if I'm doing anything constructive here."

Since she only shrugged when I asked where she'd like to go, I chose a café that I knew she liked, and once inside, we ordered pancakes and maple syrup.

"So, how are you feeling these days?" I asked clumsily.

"What do you mean, how am I feeling?" I understood her defensiveness. If anyone had asked me how I was feeling after Leah's death, I'd have been just as angry.

"Well, we're all a bit concerned about you. You don't seem yourself these days. Is it Moira?"

Lucy mumbled something that sounded like, "Of course it's Moira." Then, "What have you all been saying about me? You don't have to say stuff behind my back. If you've got anything to say, say it to my face."

"Calm down, Luce. No one's been saying things behind your back. Shona just said you seemed a bit down. You're our friend. Isn't it natural that we should worry about you? If there's something you'd like to talk about, you know you can talk to me, Elspeth and Shona, don't you?"

"Elspeth?" Lucy said. "I don't think so."

"I know they didn't get on, but Elspeth does feel bad about Moira," I say quietly.

"That's charitable of her. As for Shona, well, she's got lots of friends, hasn't she? I like Shona, but she's so busy she doesn't have time to babysit me. And you, Ros? Elspeth doesn't let you off the reins long enough for you to be a proper friend to anyone else."

"That's not true," I said. I was beginning to get a bit sick of people telling me I was under Elspeth's thumb. Lucy merely shrugged, as though the point wasn't even worth disputing. I felt irritated.

Lucy became apologetic. "I'm sorry. I know you're concerned about me, but there's no need. I think I just need a break, you know? I can't seem to get down to doing any work. My mind's all over the place. The Easter break's coming up. I'll be okay when I get back." Then, in a hesitant voice, she said, "There's something a bit . . . unwholesome about Elspeth, you know. A person who cuts up someone's clothes . . . that's not normal behaviour. It's extreme. It's . . . it's disturbing. Moira was afraid of her, you know."

I was becoming uncomfortable with the conversation. I suspected that Moira and Lucy, perhaps Shona too, had been talking about my relationship with Elspeth behind my back.

"Next you'll be saying Elspeth killed Moira," I said hotly. "She had nothing to do with it."

"I know that," Lucy said. "The thing is, you'd say that even if the police caught her with her hands still round Moira's neck, shouting, 'I've killed her!' Open your eyes, Ros. Everyone can see her for what she is —everyone but you."

The pancakes arrived and we ate in silence for a bit. After Lucy's outburst, I didn't know what to talk about. I'd asked her out to try to help her, but now I was angry. Perhaps realising this, Lucy changed the subject.

"I'm finding it hard to work," she admitted. "What happened to Moira has made me wonder what the point is in anything. You never know what's round the next corner. This town feels claustrophobic to me now. I just need to get away."

"Another year and you need never come back to this town again, Luce. You could go to Australia or New Zealand, anywhere you like. You just have to put what happened to Moira in a box for now and try to concentrate on getting a good degree."

"In a box?" Lucy said.

"I'm sorry, Lucy. I could have put it better. What I meant was—"

"It's okay. Don't feel bad. I know what you meant. It's just that I don't find it easy to block things out. My thoughts won't stop."

"I wish there was something I could do to help," I said. Inviting Lucy out for coffee hadn't been such a great idea after all. I didn't seem to be lifting her mood and she was making me miserable. "Shona's pretty cut up too, you know," I said.

"Yes. Poor Shona. I think she was a little in lo . . ." Lucy's voice trailed off.

159

I wished I could have found some way to broach the subject of Alec, but a promise was a promise. Besides, I could see the state Lucy was in. She was angry, hurting, and her brain was working overtime. Her hostility towards Elspeth, I decided, was simply another symptom of her generally negative frame of mind.

Once we'd finished drinking our coffees, Lucy returned to the library, but I doubted she was going there to work. In her mind, she had already distanced herself from this town, and all of us. I hoped that getting away for the Easter break would give her some respite from her obsessive thoughts over Moira's death, and that she would return, refreshed, for the final term of the year.

I didn't see Lucy much after that. She went home a week before the end of the Easter term and never returned to St Andrews. But just before she left, I was standing on the pavement outside the front door of our house on North Street, waiting to see her off, when she kissed me on the cheek and whispered, in a voice so low I thought I'd misheard, "Take care of yourself, Ros. Elspeth Blair's your friend now, but watch out for her when the wind changes direction."

CHAPTER TWENTY-ONE

For the longest time, I stare at Lucy, unable to believe it's really her.

"I'm for real," she says, smiling. Lucy arrived at the café about ten minutes after her phone call, came straight over to my table and gave me a hug.

"How . . .?"

"My cousin Cathy called. She told me about your visit, and that you were planning on coming to St Andrews. I thought you'd still be in London. Imagine my surprise — and delight — to learn that you were here in town."

"It's mutual," I say, "the surprise and the delight." We both smile.

"Alec, my husband, is parked on a double yellow line across the street."

I look out of the window and see a man on the pavement opposite, leaning against a blue Citroën. He looks up and down the street, alert for any roving traffic wardens. He's shortish, slim, with long, greying hair tied back in a ponytail and is dressed all in black, right down to a pair of black suede ankle boots. He reminds me of Hugo Weaving as the Elf King in *The Lord of the Rings*.

"Why don't you come round to our house? It's about a mile out of town. We can have a good old catch up," Lucy says.

"Oka-ay," I say uncertainly.

"Quick then, before we get booked."

I follow her to the car. The king of the elves smiles at me. He's holding the back door open so I can climb in quickly.

On the way to her house, Lucy introduces us. "Ros, meet Alec, my husband of twenty-one years."

"Pleased to meet you, Ros," Alec says. I return his greeting.

Lucy cranes her neck round to speak to me. "I recognised you straight away, even though you look so different."

"You look different too." And she does. Her hair is silvery white, streaked with blue and cut in a swishy bob. She's wearing green lace-up ankle boots and black skinny jeans, with a long light-grey cardigan that looks soft enough to be cashmere.

"I hope so," Lucy comments. "I looked like a dog's dinner back in the day."

"You did have a style all of your own," I say. She grins.

"Here we are," she says, and Alec swings into a private road and pulls up outside the third house along.

Lucy ushers me inside while Alec puts the car in the garage. She shows me into a cosy sitting room and takes my coat.

"You have a lovely home," I say.

"Thanks. It's kind of big for the two of us, now that the twins have flown the nest, but Alec and I work from home so we feel the space is justified."

"It's good to see you, Luce . . . Good to see how your life has turned out. I've often wondered about you over the years. I was always sad we all lost touch." *After Moira was murdered.*

"My fault," Lucy says. "I left in a bit of a rush, didn't I? I was embarrassed about my state of mind. Back then it wasn't the thing to talk about feeling depressed, was it? And I wasn't exactly brilliant at keeping in touch."

"None of us were," I say.

"I moved around a lot in those first two years. Alec came out and joined me after the first six months. After a few more years, we moved to the States and lived there for eight years or so. Came home when the twins reached high— I mean, secondary school age."

"Sounds like you've had a more exciting life than me. What brought you back to St Andrews?"

"Alec's parents were getting older and their health was poor. They lived in Anstruther." I nod. Anstruther is a picturesque fishing village a few miles along the coast from St Andrews and not too far from Innes's cottage. "They're both gone now," she says with a hint of sadness. "My parents too."

"And mine." *And Doug*, I think to myself.

Alec appears with a bottle of red wine and asks if we'd like a drink. I feel I'm in need of one. After filling our glasses, he excuses himself, saying he's going to rustle up something to eat.

"Alec's a great cook."

"So is Lucy," he says immediately. "You should taste her salmon en croute." They exchange glances of genuine affection — no, love.

"I'm happy for you, Lucy. You seem so . . ."

"Happy?" She chuckles.

"Yes. Tell me about your family. Your cousin mentioned twins."

"We have two grown-up sons, twins. Ben and Ian. They both live and work in Edinburgh."

"Elspeth's in Edinburgh," I tell her. Lucy nods. She asks what Elspeth is doing but seems only mildly interested. When I mention Shona, on the other hand, her face lights up, and she seems delighted to hear that Shona has come out at last. "You knew?" I ask.

"Not for sure. I always suspected she was in love with Moira." We lock eyes for a moment, and then Lucy asks about my family.

"Well, I have a daughter," I say. "Izzy. She's been a student here since October." I tell her about Doug.

"I'm so sorry, Ros." There's a brief silence.

"It was a long time ago now. Not that time makes a difference." I'm relieved that she doesn't ask if there's been anyone since Doug.

"What you said about me being different now," Lucy says a little shyly. "Well, I am different. I was so immature in those days, emotionally that is. Sometimes, I wonder how I survived. Moving into the house on North Street with you all was a godsend. You, in particular, were so kind to me."

We are both silent for a moment. Moira's name has come up once and we skirted round it. Now that the house on North Street has been mentioned, it's inevitable what will follow. A shadow falls over Lucy's face.

"All ended in tragedy, didn't it?" she says.

"Yes. Is that why you left?"

"Yes. I was more affected by Moira's death than the rest of you, I think. It sent me into a downward spiral. I just couldn't go back to that house after the Easter holidays."

"You missed your final year. You could have taken a year off, and come back to complete your degree."

"That really wasn't an option. I just had to get as far away as possible from this place."

"Wasn't it hard, coming back here, given how you felt?"

Lucy sighs deeply. "It was a long time before I realised that it wasn't St Andrews I was trying to get away from. One of the first things I did when we moved into this house was go for a long walk along the East Sands and up to the cliff path, to where Moira's body was found."

"I did that too," I say, softly, "the day I brought Izzy here."

"So, you understand?"

"Yes. It's something that stays with you, wherever you go."

Lucy nods. "Yes. That's it, exactly."

We are disturbed by a loud beeping from the kitchen. A timer for whatever is in the oven. "Time to eat," Lucy says. We move to the kitchen.

Alec fills three plates with vegetable lasagne. There's warm garlic bread and salad to go with the meal. When we've finished eating, we go back to the sitting room, glasses replenished, and Alec joins us. Lucy and Alec talk about their time in Australia and the US, their return to Scotland and their sons. They are so easy-going and open that I find myself telling them about my own life over the past twenty-odd years.

"I worked for the Civil Service for a year but it really wasn't for me. I went back to school — art school, actually — in London. I taught art for years before going freelance. Now I make portraits of people's pets. You'd be amazed how much work I get."

By now the wine is taking effect and I find myself talking about Doug, the lonely years while Izzy was growing up. Lucy presses my arm and I'm reminded of how empathic she's always been. Maybe it's the wine, or maybe it's because I feel so at ease in her and Alec's company, but suddenly I feel it's an appropriate moment to talk about Innes and what he told me that day on the beach. My worry is that talking about that time in her past might upset Lucy.

"A funny thing happened the day I brought Izzy to St Andrews at the start of term."

"Oh?"

"Do you remember PC Innes Nevin, Lucy?"

"Yes, I do. He was the younger of the policemen who came to our house on North Street to tell us the terrible news about Moira." She looks at me, eyes alight with curiosity.

"This is going to sound a bit outlandish," I say. "But here goes. And, please, Lucy, if you feel uncomfortable hearing about this just say the word and I'll stop." Lucy and Alec exchange a look.

"Go on," Lucy says.

"As I said, after saying goodbye to Izzy at her hall of residence, I went for a walk on the beach . . ."

Lucy and Alec listen with increasing interest while I describe my chance encounter on the beach with Innes, how he told me about John Menzies going missing when he was out on his boat, and how his body was never recovered. When I get to the bit about a Canadian woman contacting Innes to say that Menzies had been living with her for years under an assumed identity, they both lean forward in their seats.

"I haven't even got to the interesting bit," I say. "Menzies died recently. He had dementia. Before his death, he told his wife that during his time with the Fife police, he planted evidence on a suspect in a murder investigation. The suspect's name was Stuart Brogan."

"I knew it!" Alec exclaims. His eyes flash with anger. Lucy clarifies.

"Alec never believed Stuart was guilty. He knew Stuart growing up — he was friends with Alec's older brother. Alec couldn't believe he was capable of doing such a thing." She pats his hand. "We knew about Menzies and his boating accident. Alec was still here at the time and he read about it in the local paper."

"I thought there was something funny about the fact that his body was never recovered," Alec says.

"You remember how my mind worked in those days?" Lucy asks me.

I nod. "You saw conspiracies in everything."

Lucy colours slightly. "I was a mixed-up individual back then. I know exactly who I am now. Writer of fantasy fiction, creative writing teacher, Labour Party member—"

Alec interrupts. "Loving wife and mother . . ."

"And conspiracy theorist." Lucy grins. "Some things never change. Anyway, when Alec described the circumstances to me, I thought it was a bit odd too. Menzies disappeared on a calm day, so there was no question of a rough sea or a strong wind knocking him off the boat."

"Menzies's life jacket wasn't on the boat," continues Alec, "suggesting that he'd been wearing it, so even if he'd suffered some sort of injury and fallen overboard, he would have stood a fighting chance of being found and rescued.

Then there's the fact that his body was never recovered. That was always a bit of a mystery."

Lucy shrugs. "Well, he isn't the first person to go missing at sea in mysterious circumstances and he won't be the last. Believe it or not, I did wonder if perhaps he'd faked his own death, maybe as some sort of insurance scam." She paused. "But there was no wife or kids to benefit. Then I wondered if maybe he'd had some pressing reason for needing to disappear. From what you've just told us, it sounds like he planted the evidence on poor Stuart Brogan to solve the case quickly — for who knows what reason. And then he panicked that someone would find out."

Lucy takes a sip of her wine. I lean back in my chair, impressed by her theory. But, if Innes and I are correct, she's not quite on the right track. I clear my throat. "We, that is, Innes and I, are considering another possibility alongside the ones you've just suggested. That someone might have paid Menzies to help frame Stuart for Moira's murder. According to his widow, Menzies — or Bob MacDonald as she knew him — had a substantial amount of money when he arrived in Canada. Much more than he could have saved on his police salary. It was enough to buy a house and set up a business."

"Wow," Lucy says. "Now look who's the conspiracy theorist."

But there's a dark side to all of this, which Lucy acknowledges. "If you're right, then Stuart really was innocent and Moira's actual killer was never caught."

"There's more," I say. "All the documentation relating to the investigation into Moira's murder was destroyed in a fire."

"Convenient," Alec murmurs.

"Innes Nevin worked the case with him," Lucy says. "He must remember some of the details."

"He was only a PC at the time. Inexperienced. His involvement was minimal. For instance, Menzies never told him about you being the last of our group to see Moira alive. Or that you'd given Menzies a description of the man you saw her talking with. The case has troubled Innes ever since.

As he gained experience, he began to question why the whole investigation was closed so quickly. Stuart's suicide seemed to confirm his guilt, but . . . what if it wasn't suicide at all?"

Lucy's eyes widen in horror. Alec's lips set in a tight, grim line. We are all silent for a few moments.

"But why kill Moira? Or Stuart? What possible motive could there have been for anyone? They were two innocent young people. Surely they weren't a threat to anyone?" Lucy says.

There doesn't need to be a reason, I think. In my mind I have a vision of a universe that is morally bankrupt, where money and the promise of a comfortable life outweigh the value of a single human life. It's like staring into an abyss. I think of Doug, kneeling on that dusty roadside with a gun to his head, his mind empty of hope. He'd been in the game long enough by then to appreciate that, for certain individuals, life is cheap — of less value than possessions or a fanatical ideal or . . . pretty much anything. Some people don't need a reason to kill.

But in Moira's case, I'm sure there was a motive.

"I for one am glad to hear that Menzies got a nasty disease and that he suffered. I just wish his mind hadn't disintegrated to the point where he probably forgot what an evil bastard he was." Alec is pitiless in his condemnation of Menzies.

"I wonder if somewhere in that splintered mind of his, he felt remorse. His wife told Innes that Menzies seemed tortured by the memory. Apparently it distressed him greatly to speak of it," I say.

Alec shakes his head. He doesn't want to be convinced. Lucy just looks sad. I hope this isn't going to rekindle those past negative feelings.

"I suppose that even if his wife agrees to give a statement to the police about what he told her, no one's going to believe that it wasn't just his dementia talking. His memories wouldn't have been reliable by that stage, just a jumble of the real and the half-imagined," Lucy comments astutely.

"People with dementia have moments of complete lucidity," I say. "Menzies's wife might be able to comment on what her husband's state of mind was like when he talked about this subject."

"Like she'd want to believe the man she'd lived with for twenty-odd years was a liar, a cheat and maybe something much worse," Alec says.

"She must have a conscience, or she wouldn't have contacted Innes in the first place," I point out.

"Do you think the man I saw talking to Moira that afternoon could have been her killer?" Lucy asks.

"We don't know. Obviously, it would be useful to identify him."

"Have you been able to find out anything at all about him? I remember thinking he was a bit too old to be a student, but could he have been staff?"

"Absolutely nothing. I thought maybe you could help with that. Give us a description, if you can remember what he looked like after all this time."

Lucy nods. "I can still picture his face. Probably because he was with Moira the last time I ever saw her alive, it's etched in my memory."

"Well, that's a start," I say.

"So, you and Innes Nevin are reinvestigating Moira's murder together?" Lucy asks. I guess this is a roundabout way of asking what else Innes is to me.

"I, er . . . we were, but it's . . . complicated now." I sigh. "Elspeth's just told me that Innes was accused of planting evidence on a suspect he was investigating in a case in Glasgow." I look at each of them in turn to gauge whether they see the significance in that. Their sombre faces tell me that they have grasped the irony. "It gets worse. The suspect died in mysterious circumstances before he could be brought to trial."

I'm not sure what I'm expecting — stunned silence? Incredulous stares? Exclamations of surprise at the parallels with Moira's case? Instead, Lucy bursts out laughing.

I feel a surge of irritation. How dare she laugh? These are serious allegations, and if they are true, they cast doubt on everything Innes has told me about Menzies, and Moira's murder. Surely, she can see that?

"I'm so sorry, Ros. It's just . . . that is such classic Elspeth. She always was a jealous, spiteful bitch. If anyone could dig up dirt on Innes Nevin to thwart any possibility of a relationship between you and him, Elspeth would be the one to unearth it."

"There is no relationship between Innes and me," I say, a little too quickly. "And Elspeth isn't jealous of my relationships. Well, maybe she was back then, but she's a grown-up now."

Even as I say it, I know that Elspeth might be grown-up, but she hasn't outgrown her jealous nature. It comes back to me how not long after I started seeing Doug, Elspeth called me to say that she'd just happened to bump into one of his old girlfriends, who'd told her what a shit he'd been when she became pregnant with their child, to the extent that she'd terminated the pregnancy.

When I confronted Doug, he told me the baby wasn't his. His girlfriend had been seeing his best mate behind his back for three months while Doug was out of the country. The dates confirmed that the baby was his friend's. Elspeth hadn't even bothered to check her facts.

"Well, Doug's ex didn't say that when she told me the story," was Elspeth's excuse when I confronted her over it.

"I know that you and Elspeth were — are — friends, Ros, but that woman could start a row in an empty room. She was always playing us off against each other. I wanted to be closer friends with you — Shona and Moira did too — but Elspeth always seemed to find a way to make sure you didn't have time for anyone but her. She was the one who shredded Moira's clothes that time, you know. We all knew it." *Except you.* Lucy's too polite to say it. "And all because Moira was screwing Andrew Kelso."

"It's just as well Moira's relationship with Kelso wasn't more widely known, or he might have been the one set up for Moira's murder," Alec comments. "I guess Stuart was an easier fall guy." From Alec's comment, I gather that Lucy has told him a lot about what went on in our house on North Street.

"More wine, anyone?" Alec asks.

"I should order a taxi back to my accommodation," I say, looking at the clock.

"Stay over," Lucy entreats me. "I'll make up a bed for you in the spare room."

I think of my cramped room at the guest house. It feels safe and cosy here with Lucy and Alec. "Thank you."

Alec refills my glass.

"So, the question is . . . what do we do next?" Lucy says.

"We?" I say, smiling.

"Alec and I will help in any way we can." She pauses before adding, "Perhaps you should ask Innes how he can use my description of the mystery man to find out who he is. That is, if you don't feel awkward contacting him again, Ros?"

This thing is bigger than my feelings about Innes Nevin. And, besides, after what Lucy's said, I feel I owe it to him to hear his account of what happened in Glasgow. "No problem," I say. *Sorry, Elspeth.*

CHAPTER TWENTY-TWO

Elspeth always seemed to have some excuse for not introducing us to Piers. If it hadn't been for Moira telling us he existed, I would have begun to wonder if he, like the elusive Gav from Edinburgh, was a figment of her imagination.

And then, one Friday morning in February, Elspeth drew me aside in the kitchen of our house on North Street and confided that Piers was arriving that evening. "Don't tell the others," she said.

"What others?" I said. "Shona's on a field trip, Lucy's gone home for the weekend and Moira's going away with Andrew this afternoon." No doubt this was precisely why Elspeth had chosen this particular weekend.

All that day I could barely concentrate on my work for wondering what Piers would be like. Elspeth had told me that he was twenty-four, a postgraduate student at Edinburgh University writing a thesis on some dry topic to do with the economics of the GDR.

She'd shown me a photo-booth picture of him, a washed-out image of a serious-looking young man with brown curly hair and a beard, wearing aviator-style glasses. He looked as if he'd had a bad case of acne in his teens, for his face was still pitted with scars which the beard couldn't quite disguise. I guessed that Elspeth had been attracted by his left-wing leanings more than his looks.

They were in bed when I returned home after my four o'clock lecture. I heard the bedsprings creaking as I reached the landing at the top of the stairs. I collected a few books and went down again. At seven in the evening, the pair of them joined me in the kitchen.

"Ros, Piers. Piers, Ros," Elspeth said. Her faced was flushed and she appeared to be too embarrassed to look at me.

"Hi, Piers. Nice to meet you." I couldn't resist adding, "At last." Piers raised one hand in a solemn wave and gave a brief smile. He was taller than I'd expected, and broader. He was also quite handsome in real life. The acne scars were less noticeable, and he'd dispensed with the glasses. Perhaps the photo-booth picture was a couple of years out of date.

"We're going for a curry, then down the pub," Elspeth said. "Want to come?"

"No thanks. I'm really tired. Think I'll just watch telly for a bit and have an early night." It wasn't as if they got a lot of time alone together, so I decided to leave them to it, much as I wanted to find out more about Piers.

On Saturday, I went off to the library first thing. Elspeth and Piers were still in bed. I had a feeling that they wouldn't be in a rush to get up. I was happy for Elspeth. Maybe now she was in a relationship, she'd get over her infatuation with the unattainable Andrew Kelso.

It was lunchtime when I returned to North Street. The smell of burnt toast told me that Elspeth and Piers must be having a late breakfast. I joined them in the kitchen, where they were eating beans on toast. We chatted for a while, and then they went out to do some shopping. They returned a couple of hours later and disappeared back up to Elspeth's bedroom for a while. Later, they announced that they planned to go to the cinema, and afterwards the pub. Again, I was invited along, and again, I declined.

Piers struck me as intelligent, and if not exactly dull — he knew a lot, especially about politics — he was a tad humourless for my taste. I could understand what Elspeth saw in him. He was after all, one of Kelso's protégés.

I had resigned myself to another quiet evening alone in the house, when around eight, the front door slammed shut. I ventured into the downstairs hall in time to see Moira hauling her weekend bag up the stairs, spitting oaths.

"What's up?" I asked. "Thought you weren't coming back till tomorrow."

"Bloody Cousin Hans is what's up. He only turned up at the hotel we were staying at in Edinburgh, so Andrew spent the morning in the bar with him. Then Andrew tells me Hans's wife's just left him and he's going through a bad patch, and he needs a bit of support — blah, blah, blah — so I might as well come back to St Andrews or be prepared to amuse myself for the rest of the weekend. Flipping cheek!"

"Hans? Hasn't he got any family or friends in Germany he could turn to?"

"You'd bloody think so, wouldn't you? He's closest to Andrew, apparently. To tell the truth, I got the impression he just wanted me out of the way."

Moira's ill-humour seemed to dissipate. She smiled at me. "Look, do you fancy going out? I can't face spending the evening moping around the house. Might as well have a bit of fun."

I agreed readily, glad to earn a reprieve from my lonely evening.

"Oh, sorry, were you planning on doing something with Elspeth?"

"No, er . . . Elspeth's out." Moira was sharp. She didn't miss the slight pause, and she knew that Elspeth rarely went out without me.

"Is Piers in town?" She was going to find out anyway, so I nodded. "Great. I can't wait to meet him. Give me twenty minutes to get changed and slap some make-up on."

My pleasure at the prospect of an unexpected night out was quickly superseded by worry about a collision between

Moira and Elspeth, so from the moment Moira and I left the house, I was on my guard. It didn't escape my notice that Moira was also watchful, but for an entirely different reason. Clearly, she relished the prospect of an encounter with Elspeth and Piers.

We spent a couple of hours in a pub on Market Street. Around eleven, we decided to go to the students' union disco. My sense of dread deepened as we walked into the darkened sports hall. Elspeth and Piers could be in here somewhere, so it was up to me to ensure that Moira didn't see them. It seemed an impossible task, even in a crowded hall.

I'd tried to stay sober, but my nerves had sent me to the bar repeatedly throughout the evening, and I could tell from the heightened effect that the music and lights were having on my senses that I was well on the way to being drunk. Already, I was swaying along to the music and gazing in wonder at the splinters of coloured light spilling across the floor from the disco ball.

There was always a good turnout on a Saturday night. Most people were tanked up on cheap pints of cider from the union bar or high on dope. Moira took my arm and propelled me through the throng of dancers towards the bottom end of the hall. She liked to be near the front, where she could get onto the stage to show off.

Sure enough, she immediately jumped up on the stage, leaving me to jiggle along to the music or stand at the side. I made my way to the side, dodging lighted fag-ends held in drunken fingers.

Please don't let Elspeth and Piers be here. The haze of cigarette smoke choking the atmosphere made my eyes sting. I rubbed them and looked about. There, about two feet away, was Elspeth, with Piers next to her, his eyes fixed on the stage. I didn't need to follow the line of his sight to know who he was looking at. Elspeth was furious.

"What the fuck is she doing here?" she mouthed with a nod at the stage. I shrugged, and shuffled over to her.

"She came back early. Andrew's cousin turned up again."

Elspeth's eyes narrowed. "Did you tell her Piers was coming this weekend?"

"No! How can you say that? I promised, didn't I?" Elspeth's eyes bored into me. I hoped she wouldn't turn around and see Piers ogling Moira. At that moment, the song ended. Next, was a slow dance.

Piers grabbed Elspeth, pulled her into his arms and led her onto the dance floor. I stood watching them with a feeling of impending disaster. Moira had already jumped from the stage and was making her way through the thinned-out crowds to join me. Elspeth scowled at me over Piers's shoulder. I felt trapped between two seismic forces about to clash.

When Moira reached me, I told her I wasn't feeling well. "Too much to drink, too quickly. Should have paced myself. Or had something proper to eat earlier."

Moira was dismissive. "Come on, Ros, we've only just got here. You're probably just dehydrated. Drink some water and let's have a boogie." Her hips swayed and she pulled me out onto the dance floor. *Here we go*, I thought. Sure enough, it didn't take long for her to spot Elspeth and Piers.

"Aw, just look at the lovebirds," she said in a loud voice.

"Moira, please . . ." Please what? Please don't spoil things for Elspeth? Please don't flirt with Piers? Please forgive Elspeth for ripping up your clothes and detesting you for being clever and for being with Andrew Kelso? It was too much of an ask. I wished the song would go on for ever. It was the Eagles — 'Take it to the Limit' — and Randy Meisner's voice became ever more strangulated as the song reached its climax.

Elspeth and Piers were soldered together. Piers's hands were clamped to her bottom, Elspeth's arms were around his neck and they were engaged in a deep, passionate kiss. As the music faded, their hold on each other loosened and they looked about the darkened hall, eyes glazed over with lust. In the heat of the moment, Elspeth had evidently forgotten all about Moira.

Moira stepped in front of me, waving. "Elspeth! Over here! Come and introduce me to your friend."

It would have looked bad for Elspeth in front of Piers if she'd ignored Moira.

"Hi, Moira. Piers, this is my flatmate, Moira Mackie. Moira, Piers Thornton."

Did Piers already know about Moira? Andrew Kelso had introduced Piers to Elspeth. Had he told him about his affair? It seemed unlikely. Andrew was a frequent visitor to our house on North Street but we'd all been sworn to secrecy about him and Moira. They were discreet about their affair around town.

Piers gave no indication that he'd heard Moira's name before. In fact, he said, "You never said that you had a fourth flatmate."

Elspeth feigned innocence. "Are you sure? I must have, and you forgot."

"Well, once known, never forgotten," Moira said. She smiled at Piers. His Adam's apple bobbed up and down.

"Piers and I were just leaving," Elspeth announced.

Piers looked surprised. "We were?"

"Oh, don't be so boring," Moira said. "Ros and I have just got here. Come and have a boogie with us. Piers?"

Piers peered at his watch. Looked at Elspeth. "It's not even midnight," he said.

For the next hour, Moira did her level best to charm Piers and enrage Elspeth. The four of us danced together but anyone watching would have concluded that Moira and Piers were the couple. Elspeth could only look on in silent rage as Moira bumped hips with Piers, danced around him seductively and even tried to grab him for a slow dance, saying to Elspeth, "You won't be jealous, will you?" Enough was enough. I grabbed her arm and pulled her away before Piers could respond.

"What do you think you're playing at, Moira?" I hissed, in the relative privacy of the toilets.

"I'm just having a bit of fun." Moira applied some scarlet lipstick and stood back to appraise herself in the mirror. She looked stunning.

"Well, your idea of fun is ruining Elspeth's evening — probably her whole weekend — with Piers."

"I can't help it if Piers is attracted to me."

"You're leading him on."

Moira looked from her reflection in the mirror to mine. Maybe it was the glass that made her gaze so chilly. "Then I'm doing Elspeth a favour. If Piers is so fickle that a little bit of flirting can lead him astray, then he's not going to be loyal to her for long, is he? Not that anyone would want to be with sourpuss Elspeth for long."

"That's unfair! And it's not as if you're the teeniest bit interested in Piers. You have Andrew. Or had you forgotten?"

"Look, Ros. Like I told you before, from the moment she set eyes on me, Elspeth Blair decided she hated me. Because I had Andrew and she didn't. Because I'm cleverer than she is. Because she thinks my liking for you might undermine her control over you. She's a jealous, twisted bitch. You can't see it because she marked you out as a friend she could manipulate and use at a time when you were vulnerable, and you've mistaken that for true friendship. But don't think you'll be spared her spite if you upset her."

"Stop it! Stop slagging her off! And you're wrong. I know Elspeth isn't perfect but—"

"She's your friend. I know." Moira's sigh was pitying rather than sarcastic. To my shame, I felt a tear trickle down my cheek. I hated confrontation.

"Okay, then. Let's go if it means so much to you."

We left the students' union without saying goodbye to Elspeth and Piers. We queued for chips on Market Street and ate them on the way back to North Street, warming our cold fingers on the greasy paper pokes. We didn't talk much. I kept going over in my head what Moira had said about Elspeth. One thing in particular gave me pause for thought. Once again, Moira had said she liked me, and that Elspeth resented it. It felt slightly uncomfortable to be caught between two such strong characters as Moira and Elspeth. For a moment I wondered if with friends like these, I wouldn't be better off with enemies.

CHAPTER TWENTY-THREE

I consider calling Innes, or texting him to arrange a meeting, but both options seem inadequate. Finally, I decide to speak with him in person. I track him down on the clifftop near his cottage, the afternoon after my reunion with Lucy. He cuts a lonely figure in his black jacket, collar upturned, silhouetted against the pewter tones of the stormy North Sea. Bronn is off his lead, head stuck down a rabbit hole, but he senses my presence and gives a muffled bark of welcome.

Alerted, Innes swings around to face me. His cheeks, stung by exposure to the salt wind, have a ruddy glow and his hair lifts in grey-white swirls, mimicking the foaming waves. His eyes gleam blue-black. A reflection of his recent thoughts, or displeasure at seeing me?

Bronn is at me now, weaving around my legs, licking my hands. Innes calls him to heel and the dog lurches back to his master and sits, watchful, by his side. But he's restless, doing that thing that dogs do when they've been told to keep still and can't quite manage it. He goes to rise, sits again, lowers and raises his head, looks from Innes to me, perhaps sensing the tension between us.

I risk stepping closer. When I am near enough to be heard over the pounding sea, I say, "I'm ready to hear your side of the story."

We walk back along the cliff path towards Innes's cottage, Bronn bounding ahead of us, joyous as a puppy. The sea booms around us but that's not the reason we walk in silence. There should be no distractions when Innes tells his story.

Once inside, Innes puts the kettle on and only when he's poured us both a mug of tea does he ask, "So, what made you change your mind?"

"Elspeth isn't entirely to be trusted. I can be a bit too . . . accommodating where she's concerned, because of our long-standing friendship." I want to tell him how much I want her story to be false, as I sense it must be, but I don't. Innes raises an eyebrow but doesn't comment. The awkwardness between us seems to grow. Bronn lopes over to Innes and licks his hand.

"What exactly did she tell you?"

"That you were accused of planting evidence on a suspect in an investigation you were involved with in Glasgow. That the suspect died in mysterious circumstances. You can see the similarities with the case we're investigating."

I await his response, conscious that what Elspeth has given me is the bare bones of a story. I really hope that when Innes fleshes it out, the details will exonerate him of all blame.

To my astonishment, he seems initially bemused. Then he smiles. "That's such a load of crap. It doesn't even make any sense. If I'd behaved in the way she suggests, I'd have been arrested and tried, not allowed to retire and walk off into the sunset on a full pension."

I feel myself flush. I was too quick to judge Innes, but at the same time, he is little more than a stranger to me. I've known Elspeth far longer. I think of Lucy's comments about Elspeth, and of what Moira said to me all that time ago. *Did it ever occur to you that she might have been feeling just as lonely and desperate as you?*

"I don't blame you for trusting your friend over me," Innes says, reading my thoughts. "You barely know me. Thankfully, the truth about the case Elspeth is referring to is much more prosaic. It was a drugs-related investigation. We were looking at a man called Rod Wisdom. Wisdom was a personal trainer at the gym in his local leisure centre. We suspected he was dealing to the kids who frequented the centre but we had nothing on him. Not until his locker was searched by his supervisor following a colleague's accusation that he'd stolen her purse. There was no purse, but the search did uncover a stash of cocaine."

"You were accused of planting the cocaine? But how? How would you get access to Wisdom's locker?"

Innes sighs. "This is where it gets slightly ridiculous. One of the pool attendants, a woman called Kristina, accused me of bribing her to plant the coke in Wisdom's locker."

"Why on earth would she do that?"

"Because Wisdom was her boyfriend, and the amount of coke he had stashed in his locker would have led to a hefty sentence."

"Wasn't it rather obvious that she was lying to protect him?"

"You'd think," Innes says with another sigh. "But she claimed that she wasn't seeing him anymore. No one believed the story but I had to distance myself from the case. I went on extended leave. Note, I was not suspended. My colleagues were able to prove without too much trouble that Kristina's allegation was completely false."

"What about Elspeth saying that your suspect died in mysterious circumstances?"

"Well, if driving into a brick wall at eighty miles an hour can be described as mysterious, your friend is correct."

"Suicide."

"That was the verdict. There were plenty of witnesses. An unusual method, but not overly mysterious. Not in my book, at any rate."

There's a silence while I absorb what Innes has told me. I can see now that Elspeth has been very selective in what she chose to tell me. Just as she was when she told me the story about Doug's ex-girlfriend.

"I'm sorry," I say, meeting Innes's eye, "for not having more faith in you."

"It's perfectly understandable. I'm impressed that your friend was able to ferret out this story and embellish it so damningly. Is she a journalist, used to raking through the minutiae of people's lives and putting her own spin on the details?" He's too polite to say 'digging up the dirt.'

"No, she's an accountant. So, you really did retire?"

"Yes. I really did retire. I decided that after thirty years, I wanted to do something different with my life."

We sit facing each other across the kitchen table. It seems vast, this small distance between us. I wonder if Innes feels it too.

"You've known Elspeth a long time, have you?" he asks.

"Yes."

"Hmm . . ." Here it comes, I think. Like everyone else, Innes is going to cast doubt on Elspeth's behaviour — and my loyalty to her. But he doesn't.

"Look, Ros. I hope my explanation clears this business up. I really enjoy your company and — I hope I'm not reading things wrongly here —I think you enjoy mine too."

My voice is a whisper. "You're not wrong." Innes nods, lets out a sigh that sounds like relief. He doesn't rise and come and take me in his arms, and I sit, frozen to my chair, but the atmosphere between us has undergone a shift. I hope it will continue. There's potential here for something good between us, something lasting. But not yet. First there is the matter of Moira's death to solve.

"Where have you been staying?" he asks.

"At Lucy's last night. A guest house the night before."

"Come back here," Innes urges. "I'll drive you into town. We can collect your things, then I'd like to take you out for a meal. How about the Old Course?"

I laugh. "Not the Old Course, please." Innes laughs too when I explain my reason for turning down his generous offer. Bronn, picking up on our amusement, gives a bark of approval.

As I wait for Innes to change, I call Lucy and tell her the news. "You were right about Elspeth." I decide to tell her how Elspeth tried to interfere in my relationship with Doug as well.

"Why am I not surprised?" is her only comment.

Bronn senses that we're about to go out without him. I'm sorry we have to leave him behind, so I suggest to Innes that we go to a dog-friendly pub instead of a fancy restaurant. Man and dog look grateful.

Innes chooses a pub that looks as though it will offer a better choice of food than the one close to his cottage, and a better atmosphere than the one near the hospital. Over our meal, I tell him about my evening with Lucy and Alec.

"Lucy is confident that she remembers the man's face well enough to describe it?" Innes's expression is sceptical.

"She said his face is 'etched on her memory,' because he was with Moira the last time she ever saw her alive. Only problem is, the image she has of him is years out of date."

"Hmm." Innes gives his habitual laconic response, which I now know means he is thinking.

I have an idea. "If Lucy can describe what the man looked like, maybe I could sketch him — or you could get one of those police artists to do it, and then age the likeness to give an idea of what he might look like now."

Innes smiles. "Now you're thinking like a detective."

Is this what drives people like Innes to become detectives? This feeling of elation when you sense you are getting closer to solving a mystery?

"That's a lot of 'ifs,'" he says, dampening my excitement.

Later, back at Innes's cottage, there's an awkwardness between us again, a sense that while we are where we were before Elspeth's interference, we haven't moved on. I say goodnight and turn towards the stairs.

"Ros." Innes says my name so softly it's almost a whisper. "It's good to have you back."

"It's good to be back."

* * *

The following day I contact Lucy about doing the sketch, and she invites me round for lunch, which she rustles up from the previous day's leftovers. After eating, we set to work. Her visual recall is impressive, but it still takes some time and a lot of erasing and redrawing before a likeness begins to emerge that satisfies her.

I hold the image of the man at arm's length, frowning. He is gingery-fair, with longish hair, a beard and large, black-rimmed glasses. Lucy thinks his eyes were blue, which his colouring would suggest. The image isn't entirely generic though. In her description, Lucy had emphasised the shape of his mouth.

"He does have distinctive lips," I say. "The top one is much fuller than the bottom and the bottom one is tight, and turns down at the corners. It gives him a sort of cruel, snarling look, don't you think?"

"Hmm," Lucy says, sounding like Innes. "I hope that'll help narrow it down. I'm sorry I can't be more precise about his age. He could have been in his or thirties or forties. With all that hair and the beard, it's difficult to say."

"I'll give this to Innes. Let's hope something comes of it."

CHAPTER TWENTY-FOUR

The same night that Moira returned, unexpectedly, from Edinburgh, and we encountered Elspeth and Piers at the students' union disco, an incident occurred that put all of Moira and Elspeth's previous clashes in the shade.

It was gone one in the morning. I was lying awake, worrying about what the repercussions of the evening would be, when I heard the door slam loudly downstairs. Guessing that it must be Elspeth and Piers, I lay, listening for the sound of voices. Hearing nothing, I began to grow anxious. Should I go downstairs? The memory of Moira and Andrew copulating on the sofa cautioned me to stay put.

I tossed and turned for a while longer, until tiredness and the alcohol I'd drunk earlier caught up with me, and I fell into a deep sleep. Sometime later, I was roused by the sound of a commotion coming from Moira's bedroom. Not screams exactly, but shrill cries of fear and panic.

I was out in the hallway in seconds. The door to Moira's room stood wide open. Elspeth was standing over Moira's bed, her back to me. Even in the semi-darkness, I could tell that something was wrong. Moira was cowering beneath her duvet.

"Elspeth!"

Elspeth swung around. In her right hand was a pair of large kitchen scissors. "Elspeth, what's going on?"

"That bitch spent the whole evening flirting with my boyfriend, that's what." I looked around for the missing Piers. "He's not here." Elspeth's voice shook with anger. It was too late for Piers to have gone back to Edinburgh.

"Where is he?"

"He can sleep on the beach and get hypothermia for all I care. Serve him right for ogling that cow all evening." She pointed the scissors menacingly at Moira, who was now looking a lot less terrified. Maybe she thought two to one was better odds.

Elspeth mimicked Piers's voice. "Hasn't your friend got beautiful hair? Like silk. So shiny . . ." As she spoke, she raised the scissors and cut the air menacingly. The snip-snipping sound set my nerves on edge.

Suddenly, I'd had enough. "For fuck's sake, Elspeth! Stop waving those bloody scissors around and give them to me before someone gets hurt. What were you planning to do? Murder Moira in her bed? Do you have any idea how crazy you look?"

Emboldened by my presence, Moira had now thrown her duvet aside. I hoped she'd have the sense to keep her mouth shut and not risk antagonising Elspeth any further. I held my hand out for the scissors and was slightly surprised when she surrendered them to me so readily.

"You're crazy, Elspeth Blair," Moira cried, as soon as the scissors were safely in my hand. "You need to see a bloody psychiatrist."

"I should have stabbed you while I had the chance," Elspeth retaliated.

I felt something snap. "Stop it! The pair of you! Elspeth, go to your room."

When Elspeth had skulked from the room, I turned to Moira. "She wouldn't have—"

Moira interrupted me. "You don't know that for sure, Ros, but you'll always defend her, won't you? She doesn't deserve a friend like you. I don't know what it would take to convince you that that woman is poison." With that, she lay down and pulled the duvet over her head.

"Lock your door," I said, and left her room.

It was cold. I was shaking, but mostly with nerves. Moira was right about one thing. Elspeth's behaviour had been crazy.

I stood outside Elspeth's bedroom door. From within came the sound of muffled sobbing. I knocked quietly, and it stopped.

"Go away," she called out.

"Elspeth, we need to talk. Can I come in?" At first, I thought she wasn't going to answer, but after a moment or two she came to the door.

"It's freezing in here." Elspeth gave a shrug, walked over to the heater and fed it twenty pence.

"Elspeth . . ."

"I know," she said, turning her white, tear-stained face towards me. "I went too far."

"Yes. You did."

Anger, and something I interpreted as fear, shone in her eyes. "If you hadn't come in . . ." I waited, needing to hear her say it. "I . . . I don't know what I might have done. I . . . was going to cut off her hair, but when I saw her lying there . . . I thought how easy it would be to . . . to . . ."

"Say it," I said.

"Hurt her." She buried her face in her hands. "Oh, Ros, what's wrong with me?"

There was no simple answer to that. We sat in silence for several moments. My legs were burnt in red stripes from the electric bar heater, but otherwise I still felt chilled to the bone.

Eventually, Elspeth said, "I wanted to hurt her, kill her. That's bad, isn't it?"

Surprised at her honesty, my eyes widened. "Yes."

"I don't even understand why I hate her so much. She just seems to bring out the worst in me. Is she right? Am I crazy?"

"I'm not a shrink, Elspeth. You need to talk to someone about all of this."

"I know. I . . . I will. I scared myself tonight."

"I suppose it's a good sign that you feel bad about it," I conceded.

Did she? She'd only said that she'd scared herself, not that she felt remorse.

"You think?" Elspeth asked. I repeated what I'd said about not being a shrink.

"I don't deserve a friend like you," she said, weirdly echoing Moira's words.

The following morning, Elspeth did something surprising. She apologised to Moira.

CHAPTER TWENTY-FIVE

"We need to speak with Andrew Kelso."

I'm standing in Innes's kitchen. He and Bronn have just returned from an early morning walk. It's wet outside, and Innes is busy wiping Bronn's paws. He looks up at me, water dripping from the tip of his nose.

"How much did you see of Kelso back then? What was he like?" he asks.

"He was practically part of our household for a time. He was vain. He loved to be flattered and made to feel important, which Moira was only too aware of. He was also ambitious. Determined to make a name for himself in academia."

I begin telling Innes about the time Andrew drew me into his study, just after he learned that Moira had been cheating on him with Stuart Brogan.

"He couldn't believe it." I shake my head, recalling his urgent questions about Moira, his *Who is she close to? Who does she confide in?* "I suppose he was trying to find out if she had any other lovers he didn't know about. Or maybe he wanted to know who she might have blabbed to about their affair. He was really anxious to keep it under wraps. Worried about his reputation, I suppose. But even back in the eighties, was it really such a big deal? I can't believe he'd have lost his job if news of an extramarital affair got out."

"Hmm . . ." I spoon coffee into the cafetière, allowing Innes time to think. He says, "Or perhaps it was the betrayal of trust that upset him the most. If Moira was capable of cheating on him with Stuart Brogan, maybe she was untrustworthy in other ways too?"

"What other ways? If you're implying he couldn't trust her to keep his confidences, I doubt he had anything worse than adultery to hide."

"It's an intriguing thought," Innes says, "that Moira might have known something about Andrew Kelso that he wouldn't have wanted her to disclose to anyone else."

"Not very likely, though, is it?" I say. "Unless it was something earth-shatteringly big, in which case I doubt he'd tell Moira about it."

"Perhaps he didn't tell her."

It takes a couple of moments for me to process what he means. "Oh! You mean Moira might have discovered something by accident? Again, it would have to have been a pretty big something, if we're speculating that he might have killed her to stop her talking about it."

"Hmm. I've been thinking about Kelso's politics." He pauses, as if to gauge my response. His next question seems to come from nowhere. "Did you ever watch that BBC documentary called *The Spying Game*?"

I frown, vaguely remembering. "I think so. Wasn't it about British people who'd been spies for the Stasi during the Cold War, or something?"

"That's right. After the fall of the Berlin Wall, the Stasi tried to destroy all the documents and files they'd amassed on their own and foreign citizens, but the people got wind of what they were up to and stormed their offices. Masses of files had already been destroyed, but many survived the shredders. After the reunification of Germany, there was a great deal of debate about what to do with the information that was rescued. Should the people be given access to it, or was it too sensitive, too inflammatory? The files were eventually declassified in 1992. One of the repercussions was that a number of UK citizens, academics included, were discovered to have been secretly working as informers."

I listen politely, wondering why he's telling me all this. Then, suddenly, I catch on. "Wait! Are you seriously suggesting Andrew killed Moira because she found out he was a spy?"

"Too far-fetched?" Innes says.

Yes! And yet, it does make me think again about Andrew's questions that afternoon, and his mood of general anxiety. "Wow. That would certainly meet the definition of something pretty big," I say.

A troubling thought occurs to me. I think back to the moment when Innes first asked us if Moira had a boyfriend. Andrew Kelso's name had been on my lips, but then Elspeth had glared at me and mentioned only Stuart Brogan's name. Surely Elspeth hadn't . . .? No, Elspeth was in love with Andrew. That was the only reason she'd been so protective of him at that moment, so keen to keep his name out of things.

"Well, it's only a thought. For now," Innes says. "A pretty outlandish one at that, but I like to cover all the bases." He smiles. "Your friend Lucy would be impressed."

While we've been talking, Bronn has been standing expectantly in front of the cupboard where Innes keeps his treats. He paws the floor and gives a little whine. "Sorry, pal." Innes opens the cupboard and extracts a box of doggie treats. He takes a couple out and gives them to Bronn, who chomps on them happily.

Meanwhile, my mind is working overtime. Could Andrew Kelso have killed Moira for the reason Innes is suggesting? Is it credible? If Stuart Brogan hadn't taken his own life and left that note of confession, Andrew would have been a prime suspect. Spy or no spy.

And what about the older man Lucy saw Moira with? Isn't he supposed to be our number one suspect? It's beginning to dawn on me just how complex conducting a criminal investigation can be, how the different possibilities can fan out in so many directions, and I hold Innes and his former profession in greater respect.

I pour the coffee. Innes has somehow conjured up warm croissants. I didn't even see him pop them in the oven. We sit opposite each other at the breakfast bar. I have a sudden, unwelcome thought. "What if Andrew's ex-wife contacted him after you questioned her about his alibi? If Andrew was aware you were asking questions again, he might have been watching you, which means he might have seen us together."

Innes understands my fear immediately. "You think he might have been behind the attack on Izzy? Kelso himself, or someone he hired to do his dirty work for him? To get you and Izzy away from St Andrews? Warn you off asking questions about the past?"

"Yes," I say in a weak voice. "Perhaps he meant to kill her. If Tom hadn't been nearby . . ." There's a silence as we both consider this possibility. Though the idea scares me half to death, I'm not put off. I repeat my earlier assertion. "We need to speak with Andrew Kelso," adding, "as well as John Menzies's widow."

Innes glowers at his croissant, which he is spreading thickly with strawberry jam.

"Even if all our efforts prove that Stuart Brogan was guilty after all, at least you'll know a proper investigation has finally been conducted," I say.

Innes stirs his coffee slowly. "It was my first year on the job, and the first serious crime I'd been involved with. Until then, it was your everyday petty crime — theft, drunk and disorderly behaviour, the odd indecent assault, by which I mean men exposing themselves. And then I saw Moira's body. It was a shocking thing for me to witness at that age. The image has never really left me. I prepared myself for a rigorous, protracted investigation. It didn't happen. Almost before we began, Stuart Brogan was dead. It felt wrong, you know? There were so many questions that were never asked, let alone answered, because it all happened so fast."

I put a hand on Innes's arm. "You couldn't have known your boss was crooked, or that he was involved in framing, perhaps even killing Stuart Brogan. Don't blame yourself."

Innes nods. "I contacted one of my ex-colleagues in Glasgow, Mark Mapleton. He's a friend as well as a colleague. Someone I trust. He's on holiday in Corfu but I've arranged to meet him when he gets back. I'll show him the sketches. He can run them through the databases, see if a match comes up."

"Oh." I can't keep the disappointment from my voice. I'd been hoping this ex-colleague would be available immediately. "Well, in the meantime, I can talk with Andrew Kelso." Innes looks troubled. "I'll be careful," I say, "maybe just sort of bump into him accidentally. Izzy's at the university. That's a good enough excuse for me to be here, isn't it? I'll engage him in conversation. Moira's name is bound to come up."

"Hmm."

"I'm not police. I can't just accost him in the street and demand an interview, or ask him to help with our enquiries. And you're not police anymore, so you can't do that either. And if you talked to him, it would arouse his suspicions."

I see regret flicker across Innes's face when I point out that he's no longer a police officer. His expression soon morphs into one of resignation. Retired or not, he switches to police mode.

"Okay. But if you're right about him being responsible for the attack on Izzy, we need to be careful. Kelso could be a very dangerous individual. We need to talk strategy. Plan how and when you'll approach him, and what you're going to say. And, it's probably best if you don't mention politics."

"Okay, boss."

We spend the rest of the morning contriving a plan. I look Andrew Kelso up on the university website and give an involuntary gasp, for he looks as though he's stepped out of a time warp. Surely, it's not possible for anyone to age so gracefully? He must be in his mid-fifties. His hair is greying and gravity has exerted its downward pull on his features, but he's instantly recognisable, and even in a head and shoulders snapshot, he exudes the same sexual allure that made him irresistible to so many female students.

"Silver fox." There's no hint of envy in Innes's tone.

"Distinguished." We both laugh.

"Clever bastard too," Innes says, his eyes travelling over Andrew's academic CV. "And prolific. Look at all those journals he's contributed to." He reads out a small selection of the titles. "*American Political Science Review*, *British Journal of Political Science*, *Comparative Political Studies*. And he's written a couple of books."

"Don't forget the prizes," I say, pointing to the accolades awarded to Andrew by various leading journals in the fields of politics and economic history. He's also served on numerous editorial boards and even on a US political committee in an advisory capacity. "He was a bit of a linguist too, if I remember rightly. Spoke fluent German and French, a bit of Spanish. At least one of his parents was German. They came over here after the war."

"It's a wonder he had any energy left for his sexual adventures," Innes says.

"He was less polished when I knew him. Twenty-nine years old. Not that much older than us really, though the age gap seemed bigger at the time. He was just starting out in the world of academia. He wore jeans and T-shirts, just like everyone else in those days. Looked slightly scruffy, in fact."

I think of Andrew, sneaking into the house on North Street under cover of darkness. Elspeth was jealous of his relationship with Moira, but it didn't stop her worshipping him. She had her own reasons for not talking about his and Moira's affair to anyone outside our house. It gave her power over Moira.

Innes and I spend the morning researching and preparing for my interview with Andrew. I phone his department and pretend I'm one of his students, so as to get an idea of where he's likely to be in the afternoon. The admin staff member I speak with is surprisingly helpful, and we are able to work out that Andrew is free after a departmental meeting at three o'clock. Otherwise, his schedule for the next few days is hectic.

"It's now or never," I say to Innes, who insists on preparing a script for my initial encounter with Andrew which, if all goes according to plan, will take place outside the library.

But the best laid plans 'gang aft agley,' as the poet said, and so it is with our plan for 'bumping into' Andrew. His meeting overruns, or he doesn't leave the building immediately after it finishes. I'm supposed to walk behind him, then come up alongside him and say, "Andrew Kelso? Is that really you?"

But he emerges from the building at the same time as a local primary school is disgorging its young charges onto the pavement in one great surge. Andrew niftily crosses the street to avoid them, leaving me stranded in a sea of excited, noisy children and their minders.

I dart after him, struggling to keep up with his lengthy strides. Out of breath and panting, I catch up with him at WHSmith.

A chance encounter in a shop seems like the next best thing to the library. I watch him browsing the journals for a moment or two before sidling up and picking out a copy of *Good Housekeeping* magazine. I take a breath and look up. "Andrew Kelso? Is that really you?" My words sound rehearsed, false. Andrew starts, peers at me, frowning. Recognition dawns.

"Ros Anderson?"

I'm beaming stupidly, glad that his response wasn't, "Do I know you?" Maybe the years have been kinder than I think. Or maybe he's been expecting me.

"Yes. It's been a while, hasn't it?" I give a forced laugh. "More years than I care to remember."

He smiles politely at the cliché. This must happen to him all the time. Former students he's forgotten or hardly remembers, hailing him like an old friend. He probably has a script for dealing with such encounters. A few gracious words that won't make his accosters feel inconsequential but will leave them in no doubt that he's too busy for small talk with virtual strangers. Do I have any more right to his time? I wasn't even a student of his. There is something that binds us, though, even after all these years.

"So terrible," I blurt out, "all that business about Moira." It's as if I've punched and winded him. The colour drains from his face, and instantly I'm looking at a much older man. I was supposed to ask him if he still works at the university, tell him I'm in town to visit my daughter who's a student here.

"Are you alright?" I ask. "I'm sorry, it's just . . . memories, you know." My voice trembles. My distress is genuine. Rehearsing the encounter with Innes hasn't adequately prepared me for the emotional impact of seeing Andrew Kelso in person. He recovers first.

"There's a café nearby. Shall we go there? I think we've both had a bit of a shock." I nod. We return our magazines to their shelves. I follow him outside, thinking that despite the script being abandoned, things are working according to plan.

He insists on queueing and paying for the drinks while I find us a table. As I wait for him to come over, I remind myself that we are equals now. Back then, I'd always felt like an awkward schoolgirl around him.

"You knocked me for six back there. It's years since Moira died, but hardly a day goes by without me thinking about her." The emotion seems genuine enough. I don't doubt for a nanosecond that he thinks of Moira often. It's what he thinks that bothers me.

"What happened to her shocked us all at the time, but I don't suppose any of us realised then that it would affect us for the rest of our lives. Her death — the way she died — it haunted me for years. I couldn't stop thinking about how scared she must have felt at the end," I gush.

"How do you think I felt," Andrew says, "unable to protect her from that monster Brogan?"

I've become so accustomed to discounting Stuart Brogan as Moira's killer that I'm taken aback when Andrew refers to him this way. We sit in silent contemplation for a few moments.

"What brings you to St Andrews?" It's an abrupt change of subject but of course, unlike me, Andrew isn't desperate to keep on topic.

"My daughter, Izzy. She's a student here."

"Congratulations. On having a daughter, I mean. Does Izzy have a brother, a sister . . .?"

"No. She's an only child. Her father died, and I didn't find anyone else I wanted to share our lives with." *Until now*, I think, picturing Innes's face. Andrew mutters his apologies. "How about you?" I ask.

"My first wife, Annie, left me shortly after Moira's murder. She knew I was seeing Moira but she was alright with it as long as no one else knew. When it all came out in the open, she couldn't cope. I've since remarried. Twice."

He says this with some regret. Moira always maintained that Andrew loved Annie. I don't ask how many other young female students he has slept with over the years. That's none of my business. He asks me about Elspeth and Shona. Lucy, he struggles to remember. He's probably seen her around town without recognising her.

"Elspeth's an accountant. She lives and works in Edinburgh. Shona's a geologist. She's worked abroad a lot, most recently in Australia and New Zealand. She and her partner are thinking of settling in Scotland, at least for part of the year."

"I knew Elspeth would do well. She had an enquiring mind. She was an . . . attractive young woman."

There's something about that pause. Our eyes meet. Immediately, I intuit that Andrew slept with Elspeth. It's a troubling thought. Elspeth's never mentioned it, and that worries me. She was jealous as hell of Moira's relationship with Andrew. Did she really stoop so low as to capitalise on her death?

I come straight out with it. "Did you and she sleep together before or after Moira's murder?"

To his credit, he doesn't lie or tell me to mind my own business. "After. She came to me one afternoon, distraught. I was at a particularly low ebb myself, and I suppose we sought comfort in each other's arms, so to speak."

I wince at the cliché. "How long did you 'comfort' each other for?" I know my hostility risks scuppering my chances of having a meaningful conversation with him, but I can't help myself. Knowing of their behaviour rankles.

"Most of that final term." Not a one-off then. For a moment, I'm lost for words.

"You didn't know?" he asks.

"No. Elspeth was my best friend. I'm surprised she didn't tell me."

"Well, I'm guessing you knew she hated Moira."

I stare at him in surprise. "Yes, but I find it hard to understand how you'd embark on an affair with her, knowing that."

"Moira had told me, of course. But Elspeth claimed she was really upset over the way she'd treated her. She was 'eaten up with remorse.' It took some time for me to realise that she was feigning her grief to get in my pants." He gives a bitter little smile, as if remembering the unpleasant taste of his own medicine.

"She was genuinely besotted with you, if that's any consolation."

"Besotted? That's not the word I'd use. There was something deeply disturbing about that young woman."

The memory of Elspeth standing over Moira, scissors in hand, flashes into my mind. Her denial that she'd cut Moira's clothes to shreds. Lucy's recent assertion that Elspeth was the culprit. The thing that bothers me most is the calm assurance with which Elspeth lied to all of us — even me, her closest friend. It makes me wonder what else she's lied about throughout our friendship. So, instead of contradicting Andrew, I find myself nodding in agreement.

"Can you believe she gouged out Moira's face from a photograph she found in a drawer in my office at the university? We all know what kind of person does that sort of thing, don't we?" Andrew lowers his voice to a whisper. "A psycho."

A little shiver runs through me. *Psycho.* That's not a word you want to hear in connection with a woman who has held your baby daughter in her arms, played with her and, worst of all, been left alone with her.

For a moment, I'm distracted, remembering an incident when my daughter was two years old, Elspeth left in charge of her for a short period of time, the tragedy that might have ensued . . . But now isn't the time to dwell on this. I need to stay focused on Andrew.

I want to believe he is being melodramatic, that all of this is sour grapes because he thinks Elspeth took advantage of his grief over Moira.

I take a sip of my coffee, feeling conflicted. Andrew's grief over Moira would have had to be genuine for him to be susceptible to Elspeth's deception, wouldn't it? Elspeth had preyed on his vulnerability. That made her a manipulative and scheming individual. But a psychopath? Hardly. Anyway, Andrew was an economist and a historian, not a psychologist.

A little voice whispers in my head. *There you go again, giving Elspeth the benefit of the doubt.*

I take another sip of my coffee. The alternative is that Andrew is lying to me. Leaving Innes's spy theory aside, what if he killed Moira by accident, in a lover's tiff? His grief would still be genuine, wouldn't it? I blow on my coffee, glance at him over the rim of my cup. He's looking at himself in a mirror hanging on the wall opposite. Andrew Kelso is a vain, self-centred man and a weak one. But is he also a murderer?

"I tell you what, if the police hadn't got to that Brogan character first, who knows . . ." His voice trails off. He shakes his head.

I'm already off script, so I clear my throat and ask him outright. "Have you ever considered that maybe it wasn't Stuart Brogan who killed Moira?"

His eyes narrow. I can almost feel the surge of blood in his veins, his elevated heart rate. He shrugs, as if to indicate that the thought has never occurred to him or that if it has, he dismissed it instantly. It's a good act, except his whole body has gone rigid with tension.

His recovery is swift. "The police got the right man. Brogan confessed, didn't he? And he had a motive. He was enraged when he found out Moira was seeing me. You were there that night when he came to your house on North Street. You saw him attack me."

This isn't the time to challenge him, but I do say, "Actually, no. That was Lucy. But I'm sure you're right. The police got their man."

"I cared about Moira, you know," Andrew says. There is the slightest pause. "More than she cared for me, I suspect. I don't say that just because she cheated on me with Brogan. She never asked more from me than I could give. And here's the thing . . ." He gazes wistfully into the mirror, seeing, perhaps, not the mawkish ageing man in the reflection, but the tragic victim of a doomed affair. "I loved her. If she'd asked, I would have given up the world for her. My career, my wife, my child. Everything."

Bullshit. I don't believe him for a nanosecond. Even if he didn't kill Moira, he's too self-centred for such an assertion to be true.

Again, spy theories aside, I can't think of any motive he might have had for killing Moira. Plus, how could he have afforded to pay Menzies off? Unless he'd had something on the man, but that seems unlikely, given that before Moira's murder they hadn't known each other from Adam. As a young man on the brink of a career in academia, Andrew Kelso would have lacked the resources to bribe anyone.

"Wasn't Elspeth seeing your friend Piers Thornton at the time when you were sleeping with her? Didn't you introduce them?"

Andrew fiddles with the fringe of his scarf. "Piers Thornton? Yes, he was one of my students. A gifted young man. And, yes, I remember introducing him to Elspeth Blair. I thought they would make a good match. They had a lot in common. Of course, I now suspect that Elspeth only agreed to go out with Piers as a means of getting closer to me."

"I wonder what Piers is doing now."

"He's a professor of history at Edinburgh University."

"You still see him, then?"

"He's a fellow academic. We tend to move in very small circles." He changes the subject. "What is your daughter studying here?"

Not your course, thank goodness.

"Geography."

"Ah. An all-encompassing subject these days. I hope she enjoys her time at St Andrews."

Watching his face closely for any reaction, I say, "Actually, something unpleasant happened to her recently. She was assaulted. Fortunately, it doesn't seem to have put her off studying here. Quite the opposite, in fact."

"I'm so sorry. I hope she wasn't hurt." He doesn't look guilty, but then if he'd arranged the attack or perpetrated it, he'd be expecting it to come up.

"Minor injuries. She was lucky that a passer-by frightened off her attacker, or who knows what might have happened."

Andrew shakes his head. "You must have been frantic with worry."

"Yes. The police are looking into it."

He nods, glances at his watch. Our coffee cups are empty. I can't draw out our conversation any longer without seeming suspicious.

"Thanks for the coffee," I say. We leave the café together. There's the inevitable awkwardness on the pavement outside. Moira's ghost hovers in the air, insubstantial yet forging a powerful connection between us. We make our clumsy goodbyes and walk off in opposite directions.

CHAPTER TWENTY-SIX

Innes is as surprised as I was to learn that Elspeth slept with Andrew after Moira's murder.

"Neither of them wasted much time, did they? It's almost funny that he and Elspeth turned to each other in their hour of need," he remarks dryly.

"I haven't really mentioned this before, Innes, but Elspeth and Moira didn't get on — to put it mildly."

I tell him about the tension in our household that arose from the animosity between Elspeth and Moira. I end with the night Moira flirted with Piers, and Elspeth standing over Moira, scissors in hand.

Innes looks pensive.

I'm quick to leap to Elspeth's defence. "Things were different after that night. Elspeth frightened herself. She actually apologised to Moira and got herself referred for help. It turned out that as a child she'd suffered abuse at the hands of an aunt who looked after her a lot when she was little, which is where her misdirected anger stemmed from. Apparently, Moira bore a strong resemblance to the aunt."

I'm not quite sure how to interpret the look Innes gives me. He clears his throat. "Don't take this the wrong way, Ros, but that doesn't sound very plausible."

"You think she lied to me? About the therapy? The aunt?"

"Again, don't take this the wrong way, but Elspeth doesn't seem like the sort of friend you can trust."

"Is this because of what she told me about the case in Glasgow?"

Innes doesn't answer for a moment. "Partly. But also because of the way she behaved towards Moira. Have there been other times when she's let you down?" I tell him the story Elspeth more or less invented about Doug's ex-girlfriend and the baby.

"You're not the first one to question my loyalty to Elspeth," I admit. "Doug didn't like her at all."

"That's not surprising," Innes says.

"Not just because of the baby thing." I give a sigh. "When Izzy was about two years old, Elspeth came to stay with Doug and me for a week. Doug didn't want her to come, but she'd just split up with her first husband and I couldn't turn her away. Two days after she arrived there was an . . . incident. Our house was burgled and a lot of Doug's photography equipment was destroyed. The police were called, but of course nothing came of their investigation."

"Doug suspected Elspeth?"

"Yes. The day it happened, he, Izzy and I had gone to see his sister. Elspeth was out too, visiting some museums in London."

"Didn't you think Doug's suspicions were justified?"

I think before I reply. "I suppose I wasn't ready to accept it."

"Do I sense there's more?"

"Something else happened." I hesitate, and Innes waits patiently. "The day before Elspeth was due to go home, she and I decided to go for a walk on the Thames path near my house."

Even now, it's hard for me to recount this story. It still leaves me with conflicting emotions, as well as a lingering sense of horror at what might have happened. But ever since Andrew told me about Elspeth cutting the face out of a photograph of Moira, it's been on my mind, demanding attention.

"I'd forgotten my gloves. I ran back to the house to look for them, leaving Elspeth with Izzy, who was in her stroller. When I caught up with them again, Izzy was missing. Elspeth was frantic. She told me I must have forgotten to strap Izzy in, and that she'd slipped out of her stroller and run off when someone stopped them to ask Elspeth for directions."

Innes's expression is solemn. "Did you remember strapping your daughter in?"

"I . . . I thought I had, but you do these things automatically, don't you? I couldn't swear to it. When I caught up with Elspeth, she was already at the path by the river. When I couldn't see Izzy, I thought . . . Well, I'm sure you can imagine what I thought. Thankfully, I was wrong. Izzy hadn't gone towards the river, she'd followed a woman with a dog, and the woman led her back to the path to find us."

"What did Doug say when you told him?"

"I . . . I didn't tell him. Elspeth had been beside herself with worry, she blamed herself . . ."

"I thought you just said she'd blamed you for forgetting to strap Izzy in?"

"Ye-es, but she still acknowledged that Izzy might have come to harm while she was in charge of her."

"Hmm."

"I didn't go out of my way to see Elspeth much after that. I think a seed of doubt had been sown. In fact, our friendship didn't really resume properly until after Doug's death."

"Who got back in touch with whom?" Innes asks.

"Elspeth called me when she heard. She was very supportive. I suppose I was grateful."

Innes doesn't comment. Instead, he says, "Talk me through Elspeth's movements again, the weekend Moira died."

"She was with me most of that weekend. You don't seriously suspect Elspeth? You said earlier that there was a sexual element to the crime that precluded the killer being a woman."

"There's such a thing as an accessory to murder." Innes sighs. I guess he's wondering why no one thought to mention all this at the time. I'm right. "Tell me about this Piers Thornton. How did he and Elspeth meet?"

"Andrew Kelso introduced them," I say.

"That's very interesting."

"It was a coincidence. They were all at some lecture or other. Piers asked Elspeth to go for a drink afterwards."

"What was the lecture about?"

"I've no idea. Does it matter?" Innes's frown reminds me of what I should know by now. In an investigation such as this, everything is relevant until proven otherwise.

"I don't know. Possibly something political to do with the GDR. That was Andrew and Piers's special area of interest back then." We exchange a look. If Innes is thinking about his spy theory, he doesn't mention it.

He rubs his chin. "How likely was it, do you think, that Moira might have acted on her attraction to Piers? Or he on his attraction to her?"

"Moira? Unlikely. She probably only flirted with Piers to upset Elspeth. Piers? I don't know. Are you thinking that Piers killed Moira now?"

"I'm thinking I wish I'd known that Piers existed twenty-odd years ago."

"I'm sorry. This must all be very frustrating for you. Someone should have thought to mention Piers at the time. One of the first things you and Menzies asked was whether we knew of anyone who might wish Moira harm. But, to be honest, Piers wouldn't have sprung to my mind. He'd only met her once."

When Innes doesn't comment, I add, "Piers wasn't the man Lucy saw Moira with that Friday afternoon. The sketch I made looked nothing like him."

Innes sighs. "If the investigation had lasted even a little longer than it did, all sorts of things would have come to light."

It's some consolation to hear this. "Andrew told me Piers is currently a professor of history at Edinburgh University."

Innes does a search on his phone. "Here we go." He shows me a picture. I stare at it, trying to connect it to Piers. The hair, or lack of it, puts me off at first. The man in the picture has a buzz cut, most likely to hide the fact that he's practically bald. I recognise him though, despite only having met him once.

"Yes, I'm confident that's him. Don't you think we should go to the police with all this?" I say, hoping Innes isn't offended by the suggestion. "With what we've managed to find out, wouldn't they reopen the investigation? Particularly when they learn that Menzies confessed to framing Stuart Brogan. They could question Andrew Kelso and Piers Thornton."

Innes is silent for a few moments. I suspect he wishes we were closer to finding out the truth ourselves. He sees this as his case, the one he never had the opportunity to solve because he was new at the job. It's the one blemish in an otherwise perfect professional record. But he's a civilian now. There are limitations to what he can hope to achieve.

"Hmm. I only have the Canadian wife's word that Menzies made any such confession. There is the documentation relating to his life in Scotland, but that doesn't prove anything other than that he wished to start a new life, leaving all the old baggage behind. True, a person's identity isn't usually thought of as baggage . . ."

Innes ponders a moment. "If there were another investigation, you and your friends would be questioned. Elspeth would be of particular interest, especially in light of what you've told me about her rather extreme behaviour towards Moira, and her relationship with Kelso. We should also bear in mind that Stuart Brogan may yet prove to be guilty."

"None of us would object to being questioned," I say. "Moira's death affected all our lives."

It is true. We were students. Our lives were carefree and uncomplicated but for the pressure of deadlines and exams.

We were young, and the future stretched ahead of us, distant and full of promise. Moira's death cast a long shadow over that future.

As we'd said that night at the Witchery, it signified the end of innocence. Long before Doug's senseless death, I had come to the realisation that safety is an illusion. What happened to Moira had already shown me that evil doesn't discriminate, and may reside as comfortably in this pretty seaside town as out in the wider world. I give an involuntary shudder.

"Okay?" Innes asks.

I nod, uncertainly. "Do you ever fear for your children, living in a world such as this?"

"All the time," he answers softly.

"You must have seen some terrible things in your professional career."

"Aye. I'd be lying if I said they hadn't affected me." He takes my hand. I feel a charge run through me. "But I've also seen the good in people, and that's what keeps me sane."

A simple philosophy, but there's no arguing with the sentiment.

I smile and step closer to him. Our first kiss is shy, hesitant, but heat flares between us, making us breathless and driving away any lingering doubts. Bronn is stretched out on the carpet near the log burner. He raises his head, lowers it again, yawns disinterestedly.

"Let's go upstairs," Innes suggests.

* * *

I am awakened by the jarring sound of my phone's ringtone. Startled, I look around at the unfamiliar surroundings. And then I remember where I am. In Innes's bedroom. We've had the most amazing sex and must have fallen asleep afterwards. The phone's urgent ringing denies me the satisfaction of luxuriating in the memory of it.

"It's Elspeth," I mouth to Innes, who's rotating his neck, perhaps to relieve a crick. Innes points a thumb at his mouth, miming drinking, and I nod. He goes downstairs to make coffee and, I hope, something to eat, because I realise I'm starving.

"Hi, Elspeth."

"Hi, Ros. I'm just calling to see if you're okay after your upset over Innes Nevin." *More than okay, no thanks to you.*

"I'm fine, thanks for your concern, Elspeth." I know she'll pick up on the edge of sarcasm in my voice, but I don't care.

"So, you're still in St Andrews then?" Elspeth texted me the day she went back to Edinburgh, inviting me to stay with her on my way back to London.

"As a matter of fact, I am."

"Oh." A short silence ensues. "Tell me you're not back with that man, Ros."

"If by 'that man,' you mean Innes Nevin, then, yes, we're together." Out of sheer devilment, I add, "In every sense of the word."

"Well, I hope you know what you're doing, Ros. I thought you'd be more circumspect in your dealings with him after what I told you."

"Which we both know to be a perversion of the truth."

"I might have heard the story second hand, but I believed it to be true at the time. You know I always have your best interests at heart, don't you, Ros?"

I decide not to pick a quarrel. It's just that Elspeth's way of looking out for my best interests often serves some end of her own.

"I bumped into Andrew Kelso this morning," I say, changing the subject. "He's a professor now."

"Yes, I was aware of that." Elspeth's tone is as dry as dust.

"Why did you never tell me you slept with him after Moira's death?"

There's a slight pause before she says, "Oh, so when you say you 'bumped into' Kelso, you mean you had a nice, cosy chat."

"Yes. We went for coffee. Had a bit of a catch-up. So, are you going to deny it?"

"It's not something I'm particularly proud of, but, yes, he and I had a fling. It didn't last long. I suppose you're going to ask how I could do such a thing after what happened to Moira?"

"I'm not judging you, Elspeth. I know you had a lot of issues to deal with at that time. But weren't you still seeing Piers Thornton? Sounds like Moira wasn't the only one with a complicated love life."

A heavy silence follows my words. Have I gone too far?

"I was still seeing Piers, but the relationship was going nowhere. I'd fancied Andrew for ages, but I did nothing about it because he was married. You remember how strait-laced I was back then? I was jealous of Moira because she refused to let moral scruples get in the way of her having an affair with him. Well, after her death, I decided that there was no reason why Andrew couldn't be mine after all. His wife had told him she wanted a divorce."

"And was he worth the wait?" I ask softly.

"As is usually the case, the things we want most seldom make us happy. Andrew Kelso was a vain, weak man. But I don't need to tell you that, Ros, do I? You always knew it." She gives a sigh. "I'm sorry for what I told you about Innes Nevin. I knew it was mostly hearsay and rumour, but I only checked him out because I care about you. I just have a funny way of showing it, as you know."

Elspeth has hurt me and apologised to me in equal measure so many times over the years that her words wash over me, leaving no impression at all.

"Regarding Piers," she says, "our relationship never really recovered after that time he responded to Moira's flirting. But it would have died a death anyway. He was due to go to the University of Leipzig for a year. And I was going abroad too. My feelings for him weren't strong enough for me to wait for him."

"Leipzig? Didn't Andrew spend a year there as an undergraduate? Don't you remember those heated discussions you used to have about all that? You were always droning on about how much you admired the GDR's model of communism — I guess to impress Andrew with your knowledge."

Elspeth is dismissive. "I can't really remember, Ros. It was a long time ago. Besides, I'm not that person any more. I've learned to embrace capitalism."

"Piers teaches at Edinburgh Uni now, you know. Haven't you ever run into him in all these years?"

"Never. Wouldn't want to either. Look, Ros, got to go. Work calls. Let me know if you'd like to visit on your way back to London."

The call ends. Something that Lucy said to me a long time ago pops into my head. *Elspeth's your friend now, but watch her when the wind changes direction.* I realise that the wind has been blowing from a different direction for a long time now. And even before it changed, I should have been warier of Elspeth Blair. I'm surprised to find that the thought that our friendship is adrift, at the mercy of the prevailing wind, no longer troubles me as it might once have done.

* * *

Innes has arranged to speak with Menzies's — Bob MacDonald's —widow via Skype. When her face materialises on the computer screen, there is someone else looking over her shoulder. Barbara MacDonald introduces the young woman as her niece, Amy, who's there to assist, as "Aunt Barb isn't very good with computers." Amy gives us a wave.

"Thank you for getting in touch with me, Mrs MacDonald," Innes begins, "and for agreeing to this interview. I know it must be difficult for you." I suspect that Innes hasn't told Barbara MacDonald that he is no longer a policeman.

"Please call me Barbara. Mrs MacDonald doesn't sound right anymore."

Barbara and Amy turn their eyes to me. "I'm helping with the investigation," I say. They seem satisfied with that.

Barbara, with her dyed blonde hair and plump, remarkably unlined face, looks too young to be Menzies's widow. There must have been a considerable age gap between them.

"I'll refer to my late husband as Bob, if you don't mind," Barbara says before Innes can begin, "because that's the name of the man I married. Though who he really was, I don't have a clue anymore." Amy presses her aunt's shoulder.

"I'm sorry you were deceived," Innes says.

Barbara sighs. "It's hard to know what to think. One part of me wants to grieve, the other wants revenge. He lied to me every day for years . . . but . . . he wasn't a bad husband." Her eyes shine with tears, and she dabs at them with a handkerchief. Beside her, Amy frowns. I wonder what she thinks of her Uncle Bob.

"You had no clue that he wasn't who he said he was?" Innes asks.

"None whatsoever. It was a complete shock when he started rambling on about his other life. Ditto when I found those documents relating to his life as John Menzies. Until then, I assumed he was muddled because of the dementia. You know, confusing fantasy with reality." Barbara frowns. "I used to think it was weird he never talked about his time back home in Scotland. He told me he had no family there, no friends he wanted to keep in touch with. And he never showed any interest in going back for a visit. Whenever I suggested going to Scotland for a holiday, he told me this was his home now and he had no desire to go back. I gave up suggesting it in the end."

Before Innes can ask another question, Barbara says, "He told me he was a widower. Was that true? Or did he leave a family behind in Scotland?"

She's worried Menzies might have been a bigamist. I can't imagine how it must feel to share half a lifetime with someone only to discover that you never really knew them at all.

Innes puts her mind at rest. "That was the truth. John Menzies's wife died two years before he disappeared. There were no children."

"That's something, then." Barbara's chest rises and falls in a sigh of relief.

"How did the two of you meet?" Innes asks.

"I managed a diner back then. Bob used to come in for breakfast maybe a couple times a week. We talked a lot. He was fifteen years older than me, but we got along real well. We started seeing each other and, pretty soon after, we got married. Bob started his own security business. I kept the accounts. It was a good life until . . . until he got Alzheimer's."

"What about money? Was Menz— Bob well off when you first met?"

"Uh-huh. He told me he'd sold his house and business in Scotland. I . . . I never thought to question it."

"Of course. Why would you?" Innes's voice is sympathetic. "Did you ever get the feeling that your husband was worried about anything? Did he seem like a secretive person?"

Barbara looks thoughtful. "Like he had something to hide? He had his moods like anyone else, but he got over them. Without drinking, I might add. In all the time I knew him, Bob never touched a drop."

Barbara seems proud of this aspect of her husband's character. Alcohol loosens the tongue, I think, cynically. Menzies's abstinence had been a virtue born of necessity.

"Did he ever go away on his own, or with friends, especially people you didn't know?" Barbara is silent for a few moments, her eyes focused on something beyond the computer screen. Amy follows her gaze. Barbara looks back at Innes.

"He went fishin'," she says. "There's a photograph on the wall just caught my eye. He'd take himself off to the lake and stay for three, five days at a time. Said he liked the peace and the time to reflect. I guess that's how he dealt with his moods. Far as I know, he was alone. Truth be told, my husband was a bit of a loner — wasn't he, Amy?" Amy nods.

"Did anyone ever come to visit him? Someone who'd known him back in Scotland, for instance?"

"No. Far as I know, no one called him either. I checked his emails after he died. I didn't find anything out of the ordinary."

I lean sideways so that I'm off screen and whisper to Innes, "Looks like he made a complete break with his past. We're not getting anything here, are we?"

Innes frowns and says to Barbara, "Would you mind showing us the picture that you referred to just now, Barbara?"

"Sure. Bring it over, would you, honey?" Amy goes off screen for a few moments. When she reappears, she has a large, framed picture in her hands which she brings to the screen to show us.

A middle-aged man is standing at the side of a lake, holding up his catch, a giant fish that Amy tells us is a walleye. By his side sits a German Shepherd dog. It looks like Bronn.

Innes nods. "That's the man I knew as John Menzies," he says. "Beautiful dog."

"He sure was. And so good-natured. Bob loved Hans like a child. First dog he got when he moved over here."

I frown, a memory stirring somewhere deep in my brain. Suddenly it comes to me. Beside me, Innes takes a breath, ready to ask another question. "Wait!" I say to Barbara, who looks surprised to hear me speak. "What did you say the dog's name was?"

"Hans," she says. "His name was Hans. Don't ask me why. Bob rambled on about him a lot in his last days."

I've been leaning into the screen, and now I sit back in my chair. I must look as unnerved as I feel, for Innes asks if I'm okay.

"Andrew Kelso had a German cousin called Hans," I say, quietly. "Moira met him. In Aviemore, and then in Edinburgh."

Innes inclines his head just enough to show he understands the significance of what I've told him. "Barbara, did your husband ever mention the name Moira Mackie to you?"

"I don't recall that he did." She frowns, shakes her head.

Amy stirs, looks at her aunt as if gauging whether she should speak. She says, "Once, when you were out and I was sitting with him, Uncle Bob called me Moira." Her aunt stiffens, as though dreading further revelations about her dead husband and his secret life. Perhaps to reassure her a little, Amy adds, "He was pretty confused at the time."

"What did he say?" Innes is sitting very still, as if moving will cause Amy to forget.

"He'd just woken up from a nap. He was pretty agitated. When he saw me, he stared at me like he didn't recognise me. Then he looked really scared and said something like, 'Moira? You're dead. I saw you.'"

Amy shakes her head. "I said, 'It's me, your niece, Amy.' He sort of cowered when I tried to get closer to him, like he was seeing a ghost. Then the fog must have lifted because he seemed to realise it really was me after all."

I can't help wishing she'd let him ramble on a little longer.

"Who is Moira?" Barbara bursts out.

Innes clears his throat. "Moira was a student at St Andrews University over twenty years ago. She was murdered. Your husband — then DI John Menzies — investigated her murder. When you contacted me, you said that your husband had confessed to framing someone by the name of Stuart Brogan for murder. Brogan hanged himself. A note of confession was found in his pocket, along with a ring belonging to Moira."

Barbara gasps and covers her mouth. "Did Bob kill this . . . this Moira?" Amy puts an arm around her shoulder.

"Honestly? We don't know. We think it's more likely that he was bribed to plant the evidence on Brogan."

"Money and a new identity, in exchange for letting that poor girl's killer go free," Amy says astutely.

"Yes."

"What kind of man did I marry?" Barbara asks.

There's no easy answer to that, so no one replies. It would be an insult to Barbara to suggest that Menzies somehow atoned for his past by living an unblemished life with her. If what Innes and I believe about him is true, Menzies paid for his comfortable new existence at the expense of at least two innocent lives.

"Is there anything else I can help you with?" Barbara asks.

"Not at the moment," Innes replies, no doubt appreciating that Barbara has had enough to cope with for now.

"Whatever you find out about my husband, promise you will tell me everything."

Innes promises. Barbara nods and gives a sad sort of wave as her image fades from the screen.

"Poor woman. She's going to struggle to reconcile her memories of 'Bob' with the reality of John Menzies's deception. I don't envy her," Innes says.

"So where are we now?" I ask.

"Well, we have a new suspect," Innes says. "What do you know about this Hans? Do we have a surname?"

"It could be a coincidence. The name, I mean. Hans was a German Shepherd dog. Maybe Menzies just thought it was amusing to give him a German name. Hans is probably one of the first German names that most people would think of."

"Hmm." Innes asks again, "What about Hans's surname?"

"I don't know. Even if Moira ever mentioned it, I wouldn't remember after all these years. I could ask the others — Elspeth, Shona, and Lucy. Or Andrew Kelso."

Andrew is the obvious one to ask but Innes cautions me. "Not Kelso. Not yet, at any rate. Perhaps the others, but if possible avoid saying why you want to know. Lucy excepted, of course, as she already knows about our investigation. What can you remember Moira saying about Hans?"

"I think she said he was older than Andrew. She found him boring. Very serious. Sorry, I don't know much about him, other than that Moira met him a couple of times. The first time was on a weekend trip to Aviemore. And again the weekend she flirted with Elspeth's boyfriend Piers. She'd gone to Edinburgh with Andrew but had to come home early because Hans turned up. If I remember rightly, she said Hans was having personal trouble and being his cousin, Andrew felt obliged to spend extra time with him."

"Why was Hans even in Edinburgh at the time? Surely, he wouldn't have flown to Edinburgh just to discuss his personal problems with Kelso? It's much more likely that he was in the country already. Was he a delegate at the conference too? Did he live in Scotland?"

"Sorry. No idea. I'm not being much help, am I?"

"On the contrary. You picked up on the coincidence of the dog's name. We have a new avenue of investigation to pursue. Another possible suspect." He pauses. "That's if we assume it's more than coincidence that Hans was known to Menzies as well as Kelso and Moira." Our eyes meet. I have one of my light-bulb moments.

"What if Hans is our mystery man? The one Lucy saw speaking with Moira the afternoon she disappeared?"

"Hmm." No doubt he was ahead of me with this.

"Is there some way to check Andrew's family background to find out the surname of the German branch of the family?" I ask. "The simplest way would probably be to ask his ex-wife, but she might blab to Andrew."

"She's Annie Calder these days. I'll contact her tomorrow, see if she'll agree to talk to us," Innes says. "And we need to speak with Piers Thornton." He looks thoughtful. "Did Thornton know Hans, I wonder? Given that they both knew Kelso, it's a possibility."

"I suppose it's possible, but I don't remember Moira saying that Hans was an academic. Piers was here in St Andrews with Elspeth the weekend Hans turned up in Edinburgh to discuss his so-called personal problems with

Andrew, so they didn't meet then. But you're right, it's very possible that they all knew one another."

"Where did Piers go after Elspeth rowed with him that evening?" Innes asks.

"I'd guess the Kelsos', even though Andrew was in Edinburgh. Piers had stayed with them before and I suppose Hans might have too. So, again, it's possible that they knew each other." I look at Innes. "Getting complicated, isn't it?" He doesn't answer.

"Who shall we tackle first?" I ask, mentally tossing a coin and coming up with Piers's face.

"Both Thornton and Calder live in Edinburgh, so we can do the two of them in a day. Assuming they're both willing to speak with us, that is."

"What can we say to get Piers to agree to see us?" I ask.

"Hmm. I have an idea about that. It involves borrowing your daughter for the day," he says.

CHAPTER TWENTY-SEVEN

Izzy is intrigued when I call to ask if she's free the following day. I explain that I'm making a trip to Edinburgh with a friend and that we'd like her to come along to help us with an important matter. I refuse to give her any more information over the phone, despite her pleas and attempts at blackmail.

"I won't come if you don't tell me. And who is this friend? Is it the one you're staying with? I'm picking up vibes that it's a man. Are you seeing him?" On and on she goes until out of exasperation, I confess.

"Yes, he's a male friend. His name is Innes Nevin and yes, we're sort of seeing each other." Her excited shrieks are deafening.

"I hope Izzy behaves herself," I say to Innes the following morning as we wait for her to come out of her lecture. "She's likely to bombard you with embarrassing questions."

Innes laughs. "I have a daughter too, remember? I'm up for it."

We wait by the car. Izzy arrives on time, backpack slung over her shoulder.

I feel a flutter of nerves as I introduce my daughter to Innes. I realise her opinion of him matters to me. Somewhat embarrassingly, she looks him up and down, before saying politely, "Nice to meet you, Mr Nevin."

"Nice to meet you too, Izzy. Please call me Innes. I've heard so much about you."

"All good, I hope."

Innes winks. Izzy smiles. I breathe a little easier. I think they're going to get along.

"So, what's going on? Why all the secrecy? You aren't going to announce your engagement or something, are you?"

"Izzy!" I feel myself redden. Out of the corner of my eye, I see Innes grinning.

"Well, it has to be something mega. You said you needed my help on an 'important matter.' I've tossed and turned half the night worrying what it could be, so I hope you feel guilty."

I doubt that. Izzy used to go out like a light at bedtime, and she was always hard to rouse in the morning. I'm sure she hasn't changed.

Innes and I have already discussed how much we ought to tell her. I take a deep breath and begin by explaining that when I lived on North Street, there was a fifth house sharer called Moira.

"Moira was murdered. Her body was found up on the cliff path. Soon afterwards, a local boy called Stuart Brogan took his own life, leaving behind a note confessing to her murder. Moira had had a short relationship with him and she'd two-timed him. He was very upset when he found out, and it seemed that he was upset enough to kill her. Innes was involved in the investigation into Moira's death when he was a young police constable."

For once, Izzy listens without asking loads of questions. I'm giving her the bare bones of the story. I don't mention Elspeth's behaviour towards Moira. I leave out any reference to Moira's affair with Andrew Kelso. I focus on Innes's recent communication from Barbara MacDonald, and the possibility that Stuart Brogan might have been innocent.

When I've finished, Izzy says that she can't understand why I've never mentioned Moira, or what happened to her, before now.

"I suppose we were all deeply affected by her death. We don't like to talk about it."

Is that the reason? Elspeth was the one who least liked to talk about Moira, allegedly because of her feelings of guilt over how she behaved towards her. She was always the one to steer the conversation in a different direction whenever Moira's name arose.

Doug once speculated that if Moira hadn't woken up that time when she crept into her room with the scissors, Elspeth might have been the one to harm Moira. Possibly I fed his imagination by telling him that Elspeth had all but confessed as much to me.

"You haven't told me why you need my help," Izzy says, touching my shoulder. Innes is driving. My daughter catches my eye in the mirror. "Am I right in guessing that ex-Detective Chief Inspector Innes Nevin and you are trying to uncover the truth about what happened to Moira?"

"Yes," I say. "We're interested in speaking with a man called Piers Thornton. He knew Moira. He's now a professor of history at Edinburgh University. We didn't want to arouse his suspicions by asking if he'd talk to us about Moira, so we thought perhaps you could pose as a prospective student. I emailed him yesterday. He agreed to meet us, but if you feel uncomfortable about it, we can pretend you weren't able to come along."

I feel slightly guilty about presenting our plan to her as a fait accompli, but there hasn't really been time to explain until now. Besides, I know my daughter. She loves a challenge and a mystery. Innes and I have discussed the possible risks to her from this venture. We won't be taking any.

"I never realised you could be so devious, Mum," she says, grinning. "Count me in. Innes, are you going to play Daddy?"

Innes laughs. "That's the plan."

"So, tell me what I need to say. Luckily I did history A level, so at least I can ask some convincing questions."

The rest of the journey is taken up with rehearsing our parts. Piers Thornton has arranged to meet us in the history department reception area at one, and will show us around. If we need additional information, he can give us a little extra time after the tour to answer our questions.

It is twelve fifty when we arrive. Izzy looks composed. She's not the type to be nervous. The bruises on her face have faded but are still visible. Innes has advised her to say that she was mugged if Thornton comments.

Innes and I have discussed the possibility of him recognising me. It's extremely unlikely, given that he met me only once in a darkened hall. Still, a tremor runs through me when he walks into the reception. He's a connection with Moira and the past. He might even be harbouring a sinister secret about what happened to her.

"Mr and Mrs Nevin, and Isabella?" he says, smiling, and shakes hands with each of us in turn. It's hard to resist staring at him, looking for any resemblance to the young man I met that night at the disco, but my memory of him is blurred and outdated. He looks like the man with the buzz cut in the picture Innes and I saw on the internet.

"We're very grateful to you for agreeing to show us around at such short notice," Innes says. "We can't make the open day, and Izzy has her heart set on coming here. She wants to apply as soon as she can."

"Not a problem," Thornton says at once. "I'm always delighted to meet prospective students and it's not often I have the time to do so. You've caught me on a day when my schedule is less hectic than usual. May I ask why you were keen to speak with me rather than one of my colleagues?"

Izzy is ready with her answer. "One of my history teachers is a bit of a fan of yours. She's always going on about your books and articles. When Dad said he was going to call and see if we could arrange an impromptu tour, I told him to ask for you. It's so cool that you're available."

Thornton smiles indulgently. He takes us through a door and into a corridor. There are offices on each side, all bearing the name of a department member. One is Thornton's. We walk past it and through a set of swing doors into a stairwell. We ascend some stairs and Thornton points out seminar rooms, the department library. Lastly, we look at the lecture theatres where first-year lectures are held. As we walk, Izzy, Innes and I ask the sort of questions that a prospective student and her parents might ask.

By the time we arrive back at Thornton's office, there's little else to find out, but when he asks if we'd like more time, we say yes. Izzy excuses herself, saying she has no more questions and she'd like to wander around on her own for a bit. Thornton looks a bit surprised. He wishes her all the best in making her application to the university.

"So what else can I help you with, Mr and Mrs Nevin?"

Innes asks about entrance qualifications, something we've covered already. Thornton explains again. I ask about academic and pastoral support.

Then, just as we are finishing up, I say, "Do you know, I think we've met before." Thornton stares at me as if he's hardly noticed me until now. I can almost hear his brain scratching through stray memories for a trace of the woman before him. He frowns, the search evidently having produced no results.

"I'm sorry . . ."

"Oh, no need to apologise. I didn't expect you to remember me. It's just that your name sounded a bit familiar. And I have a bit of a gift for remembering faces. As soon as I saw you, I had that déjà vu feeling, you know?"

Thornton nods uncertainly. He shifts in his chair. I've knocked him out of his comfort zone. Does he have a reason to be cagey about meeting people from his past?

"We met in St Andrews, I think. At a disco at the students' union. You were with my friend, Elspeth Blair. It was aeons ago — you probably won't remember. Oh, and I was Ros Anderson back then."

"I remember Elspeth," Thornton says coolly. "We dated for a couple of months."

"You met one of my other housemates too, I think. Moira Mackie?" I frown, pretending that I can't quite remember."

Thornton's eyes narrow ever so slightly. "Yes, I remember Moira, but only because of what happened to her. It was in the news. And of course, as we just said, I was with Elspeth at the time."

"Yes, it was a terrible tragedy."

Our eyes meet. Thornton's are dark with suspicion. "At least the police got their man. Must have been some consolation to the poor young woman's family." He picks up some papers from his desk, shuffles them, glances at the smartwatch on his wrist, indicating that we've overstayed our welcome. I plough on regardless.

"I worried when Elspeth came home alone after the disco. She was so angry with you for flirting with Moira that she didn't care where you stayed. It was far too late for you to go back to Edinburgh."

My words tumble out, apparently at random. I wonder what Thornton will make of this new direction the conversation has taken. "I assumed you stayed with Andrew Kelso. You were his student once, weren't you?"

"Er . . . yes. I spent the night at the Kelsos', though Andrew wasn't there. Away at a conference, I don't doubt. As I recall, the baby was sick with croup or whatever babies get. Cried half the night. I returned to Edinburgh the following day."

"Did you ever see Moira again after that night?"

"Why on earth would I? I wasn't interested in Moira, as I kept telling Elspeth. If she hadn't been so blinded by jealousy, she might have seen that." He looks at his watch, less subtly this time. "No offence, but I have to get on."

"I'm sorry. I got carried away with the past. I suppose I've just always wondered what really happened to Moira."

Thornton freezes. "We know what happened. That local boy she was seeing lost his temper when he found out about her and Andrew."

I nod. Thornton's patience has run out. And I think he guesses at the real reason for our visit. He's going to be even more put out by my next question, coming out of context and after he's as good as told us to get out. "Did you ever meet Andrew Kelso's German cousin, Hans?"

Thornton bristles. "Andrew never mentioned a German cousin to me. Look, I appreciate you were affected by your friend's death but I hardly knew her, and I really don't have time to chat."

I shrug. "Moira met him. In Aviemore, and in Edinburgh. I just thought you might have met him too, given your friendship with Andrew."

A vein on Thornton's forehead throbs. "No. I'm sure I didn't."

Innes tugs at my sleeve. "You'll have to excuse my wife, Professor. She's been haunted all these years by what happened to her friend. It's become a bit of an obsession, to the point that she's convinced herself that the police never caught the true killer. I've told her it's ridiculous. The police don't make mistakes like that."

Innes gives me a patronising look. I have to remind myself he's playing a role. "Come on, love. We've taken up enough of the professor's time already. And Izzy's probably wondering why we're taking so long."

We thank Thornton again. I feel his eyes on my back all the way along the corridor from his office.

"I overdid it, didn't I?" I say to Innes anxiously, as soon as we're out of earshot. "That question about Hans was way out of context. He'll either think I'm crazy or it'll make him suspicious."

"It was a bit out of left field," Innes agrees. "But if he had nothing to do with Moira's death, he'll have no reason to be suspicious. At least the questions sounded more convincing coming from you. I'd have sounded like the policeman I am . . . was."

"Did we learn anything?" I ask. "Anything that we didn't know already, I mean."

"There's one thing I picked up on," Innes says, turning to look back up the stairwell. He steers me to the exit. "The Kelsos claimed that their baby had croup the weekend Moira vanished. I find it hard to believe he was struck down with the same ailment two weeks before that, when Thornton turned up looking for a bed for the night."

I stare at Innes, impressed. "Meaning that the Kelsos lied about their alibi?"

"It's easier to lie convincingly if you stick to a partial truth. I don't doubt they were telling the truth about their son's illness . . ."

"They just switched around the weekend he was sick."

Innes shrugs. "It's a possibility."

"If so, then Annie Kelso lied for Andrew. Is still lying for him. Why would she do that now, when she owes him nothing, and he could be a murderer?"

"Perhaps she knows her husband didn't kill Moira, but that he was up to something that weekend, and it was something she wouldn't want to become common knowledge."

"So, it could be something that would bring shame on her as well as Andrew?"

I take a while to imagine the moment when Annie Kelso demanded that her husband tell her the truth about his whereabouts at the time of Moira's murder. What had he told her?

Innes looks as puzzled as I feel. "Of course," he points out, "it could be that Kelso convinced his wife of his innocence and she lied to save him having to answer a lot of awkward questions when the police came to call. And of course, we can't discount the possibility that Annie Kelso might have known that her husband killed Moira, and lied to protect him, or to spare their son from ever knowing that his father was a murderer."

I give a sigh. "So many possibilities. How do you begin to find the truth amidst so much clutter?"

"Good solid police work, plus a certain amount of guesswork." Innes gives a wry smile. "And sometimes a bit of luck."

CHAPTER TWENTY-EIGHT

"So how did I do?"

We meet up with Izzy in a café near the history department. She looks at us over a cone-shaped blob of cream floating atop a tall glass. She claims it's a coffee but it looks more like a dessert.

"You were a star," Innes says.

"Great performance. Thanks, Izzy."

"How did it go after I left? Did you get the information you needed from Professor Thornton?" She lowers her voice. "Is he a killer?"

"We had an interesting conversation," I say, putting my finger to my lips.

"Okay, so you don't want to talk about it here, right? I get it," Izzy says.

"Time for a quick lunch before we speak with Annie Calder?" Innes asks. He had contacted Kelso's ex-wife the previous day. She'd been reluctant to meet with him again, but he'd managed to persuade her it was important.

Izzy, who's already eaten, says, "If you don't need me this afternoon, I think I'll go shopping for a couple of hours. There's a shop on Rose Street that a friend told me about."

We agree to call her when we are finished speaking with Annie Kelso.

"What about Elspeth?" Izzy asks as she's shrugging into her coat. "Did you find out if she's free this evening?"

On the drive over, Izzy had expressed a wish to see Elspeth while we were in Edinburgh. To be honest, I wasn't keen on Elspeth meeting Innes again, but he suggested that it might be useful for him to question her, subtly, about the past.

"Oh, yes. I almost forgot to tell you. Elspeth's invited us to eat at her place. I suggested we go out, but she insisted on Duncan cooking for us. Apparently he's one of these people who can rustle up a feast out of leftovers."

"Well, if it's as good as the lasagne he cooked for us last time, I'll need thirds," Izzy says. She kisses me on the cheek. "Hope your next interrogation goes well. Laters."

She breezes off, leaving Innes and I alone. As soon as Izzy is out of sight, he takes my hand. At his touch, my entire body tingles with desire and happiness. I sense he feels it too. Our eyes meet and we smile shyly, like a pair of teenagers discovering the wonder of love and sexual attraction for the first time. I'd like nothing more than to leave the café, go somewhere private and make love all afternoon.

"What you're thinking," Innes says, with a twinkle in his eye, "that's what I'd like to do too."

The waitress hovers near the table with our order. I feel slightly embarrassed, as though Innes and I must be very obviously oozing sex.

"One ciabatta with brie and cranberry, one with ham and cheese. I'll be back with your drinks."

We're just another middle-aged couple to her. Probably look like we've been married for years. As I take a bite of my ciabatta, I contemplate how it might be, spending the rest of my life with this man. Would Doug approve? I think he'd give me his blessing.

"Penny for them," Innes says. He reaches across the table and tucks a stray strand of hair behind my ear. His hand lingers on my cheek.

"Just . . . memories," I say, knowing he'll understand. He's a widower, after all.

"They'd want us to be happy."

"Yes." I press his hand against my cheek and put it to my lips. I haven't felt like this about any man since Doug. It's like waking in wonder after a long sleep.

* * *

Annie Calder, as she is now, lives in a modern house in the New Town.

"You're late," she says by way of welcome.

"Sorry. We've walked quite a distance to get here. It seemed the better option, given the traffic," I say.

"I've no idea why you've come," Annie says, addressing Innes. We are still standing on the doorstep. I didn't expect to be met with open arms, but this reception is borderline rude. Innes doesn't introduce me and, to my relief, she doesn't seem interested in knowing who I am. "You'd better come in. But I'd be grateful if you'd be quick. I have things to do."

The door leads into a wide hallway with a parquet floor. We follow Annie into a tastefully furnished living room filled with light. The décor is neutral, restrained and lacking in personality. Annie sits down but doesn't invite us to do the same. We sit anyway. There's no way she's going to offer us a cup of tea.

"So, how can I help you this time, Inspector?"

Innes doesn't correct her. "Well, to begin with, I'd like you to confirm again that Andrew Kelso, your then husband, spent the weekend of Moira Mackie's murder at home with you and your sick child."

"How many times do I need to repeat myself? Yes. Andrew was at home with me and Karl all that weekend. Karl had croup. We took turns walking the floor with him. It was exhausting."

"How long had your son been sick?" Innes asks.

"Since the day before. He had a fever and a bad cough."

"Am I right in saying that croup generally doesn't last longer than forty-eight hours?"

"As long as there are no complications, which there weren't with Karl. I used to be a nurse. I knew the signs to look out for. He was feverish and grizzly but his symptoms were mild. I told the police about this at the time. I couldn't have coped without Andrew."

"Was there anyone else staying at your house that weekend, Mrs Calder?" Innes asks.

"No. It was just the three of us."

"You're quite sure about that?"

"Yes."

Innes leans forward. "What about two weekends prior to that one? Anyone stay with you on the Saturday night?"

Annie appears to be thinking. After a few moments, she says, "Not that I remember. It was a long time ago. The weekend we're talking about only stands out because it was the weekend Moira Mackie was murdered, and the police questioned us about what we'd been doing."

"So, Andrew's friend, Piers Thornton, didn't stay with you two weeks prior to the weekend Moira was murdered?"

A wary look creeps into Annie's eyes. "Piers? No." She hesitates. "Then again, he might have done. Piers did stay with us from time to time when he came over from Edinburgh. It's too long ago for me to remember one way or the other. Why do you ask? Have you been speaking with Piers?"

"Yes. We spoke with him just this morning. He distinctly remembers staying with you two weeks before Moira was murdered. He remembers that weekend particularly because he'd rowed with his girlfriend and missed the last train back to Edinburgh. He claims that he spent that Saturday night with you, and that Andrew was in Edinburgh. He remembers your baby being sick and crying a lot. You were floor-walking him half the night and he distinctly remembers you telling him he had croup. Seems unlikely that Karl had croup both weekends, since as you said, it's usually a short-term illness. And you also said that Karl's was a mild case."

The intensity of Annie's frown brings her eyebrows together into a single line.

"Piers must be mistaken," she says. "Karl didn't have croup that weekend. It was the weekend Moira Mackie was murdered, as I've said already. Piers didn't have any experience of young children. Perhaps he heard Karl crying a couple of times in the night and thought he'd been crying for longer than he really was." She again reminds us that we are talking about events that occurred a very long time ago.

"Do you mind if I ask you about your ex-husband's cousin, Hans?" Innes asks abruptly.

"Cousin?" She frowns again. Has she even heard of Hans?

"Andrew's parents were German, weren't they?" Innes says. "He had German relatives, I believe."

I take out my sketch of the man Lucy saw speaking with Moira the day she disappeared, and show it to Annie.

She shakes her head. "Er . . . I never actually met him." She looks down, rubs at the arm of her chair as though trying to remove a stain.

"Hans never came to visit when he was in Scotland?" Innes asks.

"No. Andrew tended to meet his cousin in Germany, or . . . or somewhere else when Hans was over here. Which wasn't that often."

"What was Hans's surname?"

Annie Calder seems to recoil. "I . . . I don't remember."

"You don't remember your own relative's surname?" Innes injects a liberal dose of incredulity into his tone.

"Ex-relative's. And I've already told you, I never met Hans. All that was in another lifetime as far as I'm concerned. Andrew and I were only married four years, for Christ's sake. I've been married to my present husband for twenty."

I've been studying Annie Calder and her reactions. Initially hostile, she's become increasingly on her guard. Now she looks defeated, almost as though she's finally breaking under the weight of a long-held burden.

Then again, perhaps her account of that weekend is the truth and she is right about Piers exaggerating the baby's distress on the night when he stayed with them. If so, her discomfort might just be a symptom of her reluctance to revisit this unhappy time in her past. I begin to doubt that we will ever know the truth about what happened to Moira.

"What did you think of Andrew's politics, Mrs Calder?" Innes asks.

Annie Calder gives a start. "What have Andrew's politics got to do with anything? He was left wing. He still is. That's not a crime. What is this? Some kind of witch hunt?"

It's intriguing that this question agitates her so much. I think of Andrew in the house on North Street, arguing with Elspeth about communism. How he'd claim his views had been modified by his time in East Germany in the late seventies. There, he'd witnessed first-hand the effects of living under a repressive regime.

"Of course not. My apologies," Innes says. Annie looks at me. I see a different emotion in her eyes now. Suspicion.

"Who are you, exactly?" she asks me, before demanding of Nevin, "What's going on here? Are you even police? Show me some identification."

Innes raises his hands, but Annie Calder is past placating. "I'd like you both to leave. Now."

I stand and head for the hallway. Innes follows. We leave Annie Calder calling that she will report us to the real police.

Out on the street, I ask Innes what he told Annie Calder about his present professional status.

"When I called her to arrange this meeting, I introduced myself as plain Innes Nevin. I said I'd worked on the Moira Mackie case and was following up on some new information that had come to light. She assumed, and . . ."

"You didn't bother to correct her. Couldn't you be in a lot of trouble if she reports this?"

Innes shrugs. "Do you think that's likely?"

He's right. "No. I get the impression that Annie Calder doesn't want the police — real or otherwise — poking their noses into certain aspects of her past."

"Hmm," Innes responds. "That was my impression too."

"It panicked her when you mentioned Andrew's politics, and Hans in particular." Innes nods, but says nothing. I sense we're on the same wavelength.

* * *

Not long after leaving Annie Calder's house, I receive a text from Izzy. She's making her own way to Elspeth's place and will see us there.

Innes and I walk arm-in-arm through Princes Street Gardens. We pause for a few moments at the floral clock, waiting for the cuckoo to sound the hour. I feel a childish delight when it pops out, remembering years gone by when I stood here with my parents, and later with Doug and Izzy.

Looking back usually makes me sad, but not this evening. For the first time in ages, I feel that this later stage of my life need not be a gradual descent into lonely old age. Part of that is because when I contemplate the future now, I see Innes at my side. But it's more than that. I know that my house in London will soon be sold, and I feel more in control of my life than I have in years.

Innes slips his arm around my waist, draws me into an embrace and we kiss. I am weak and dizzy with desire. So much for being in control of my life — I can't even control my body! A group of young people walks past, sniggering. One of them calls back, "Get a room!"

"Impudent pup," Innes says. "Shame we can't follow his advice. Right now."

We collect Innes's car and drive to Morningside. Izzy has arrived ahead of us and is curled up on Elspeth's sofa sipping a glass of white wine. Duncan, who was there to show us in, asks us what we'd like to drink.

"Elspeth's not home from work yet," Izzy explains. "Duncan says she'll be back any minute."

"Sorry, I should have said something when I answered the door," Duncan calls from the hall. His head appears around the door. "One of her clients requested a meeting at short notice." He hands each of us a glass of wine. "Elspeth is too accommodating sometimes." He looks at Innes. I wonder what Elspeth has told her husband about him.

"Izzy's been telling me about her terrible experience," Duncan says.

"Yes, it was terrible," I say.

"Have the police got anywhere with finding out who was responsible?"

"No. Not yet. We're just all glad she's recovering well."

"That's the most important thing," Duncan says. After the slightest pause, he adds, "Izzy's safety."

I feel a prickling sensation in my spine. There's nothing sinister about his words, or the way he said them. Duncan is only saying what anyone would say. It's difficult not to resort to platitudes in these instances. So why do his words provoke a sense of unease in me?

The door slams suddenly. Not loudly, but enough to make me jump.

"Sorry I'm late, everyone," Elspeth calls from the hall. "Bloody client," she says, appearing at the door. "Wasn't even anything urgent. It could easily have waited until tomorrow."

Duncan pours her a glass of wine. She puts it down immediately and comes over to embrace me and then Izzy. Finally, she turns to Innes. I cringe inwardly.

"It's a pleasure to meet you again, Innes." Elspeth smiles and I relax a little. She's opted to act as though their last meeting never happened. It's a talent she has, airbrushing out elements of the past that don't fit with the present.

"Pleasure to meet you again too, Elspeth." Innes is politeness personified.

Duncan asks if we are ready to eat. Izzy instantly jumps to her feet, making noises of approval. Elspeth disappears upstairs. She returns minutes later, having discarded her suit in favour of jeans and a pale blue cashmere sweater that softens her features.

Duncan says, "So, Ros, Elspeth tells me you two met on the beach the day you dropped Izzy off at St Andrews, but that you knew each other years ago while you were a student at the university." I glance at Elspeth, who is holding her glass of wine aloft, swirling the contents. I catch her eye. It appears distorted through the wine glass.

"Yes," I reply hesitantly.

"I've told Duncan that Innes worked on the investigation into Moira's murder when he was a young PC," Elspeth says, clearing up any uncertainty.

"I can't believe you guys never mentioned your housemate Moira before. It's such a huge thing to happen." I decide to let Elspeth comment on Izzy's remark.

"I think we were all just relieved that Moira's killer was caught quickly. We just wanted to put it all behind us and focus on the future." She turns to Innes. "The police did a tremendous job in solving the case so rapidly. They're to be congratulated." She holds her glass aloft in a toast to Innes. He gives a little bow, which brings a smile to my lips. I peer at Elspeth over the rim of my glass. Is she mocking us?

Izzy glances at me. I'm glad she doesn't ask any more questions about Moira. I've spoken to her about not mentioning the real reason for our trip to Edinburgh, or Innes's communication with Barbara MacDonald. I know she's eager to know more and I will fill her in later, at a more appropriate time.

So I'm unprepared for Izzy's next comment. It's not her fault. With everything else that's been going on, I've forgotten to ask her not to mention Lucy.

"So, when are you coming across to St Andrews to see your long-lost friend, Lucy?" She asks Elspeth. Elspeth freezes, fork in hand, and looks at me. Heat prickles over my face and neck.

"Lucy is in St Andrews?"

"Yes. I was going to tell you, Elspeth. I just haven't had a chance."

"How . . .?"

"She settled there a few years ago. She'd lived abroad before that. We bumped into each other in a coffee shop. She's like a different person, so much more confident. It's lovely to see."

"Did she mention why she never bothered to keep in touch?" Elspeth asks.

I skirt round the question. "She lived abroad for years — Australia, New Zealand, more recently the States. She has a husband and grown-up twin sons."

"Good for her." Elspeth's undisguised sarcasm causes Izzy to give me a questioning look. I glare at her. Duncan looks a bit embarrassed. I wonder how well he really knows Elspeth.

"Didn't you like Lucy, then?" he asks.

"I didn't much like that she couldn't be bothered to keep in touch with her best friends."

"Lucy quit university after Moira's death. It affected her much than the rest of us," I explain. "It brought on a bout of depression. She couldn't face coming back for her final year."

"I seem to remember Shona being cut up over Moira too, but she managed to hold herself together and get a good degree," Elspeth says.

"Well, Lucy didn't have Shona's inner resources at the time. The only way she knew how to cope was by getting away."

"A complete break with her past," Izzy comments.

I'd like to tell Elspeth that Lucy would love to see her, but Lucy has admitted that she never truly liked Elspeth. Her willingness to get on with Elspeth in the past had sprung not from genuine affection, but from insecurity and her anxiousness to fit into the cliques within our household. She'd also feared that crossing Elspeth would have cost her my friendship. Lucy had always been the odd one out.

"Well, here's to Lucy." Elspeth raises her glass. I can't tell if her tone is mocking or not. We join her in toasting Lucy. After that, to my relief, the subject is dropped.

The meal over, Duncan and Innes retreat to the kitchen to wash up. I can hear Duncan telling Innes about his work for the Scottish parliament. Izzy is upstairs, texting her friends and, I suspect, calling Tom. She's had too much to drink and will probably fall asleep. Elspeth and I are left together.

"Innes seems charming," Elspeth says. "I'm pleased for you."

I steer clear of mentioning her attempt at sabotaging my relationship with him. Maybe Moira and, more recently, Lucy were right. I do go to great lengths to avoid confrontations with Elspeth. I've always believed it's because I knew her better than anyone else in the house on North Street and understood what motivated her. Now I wonder if I've been seeing her through a glass darkly, as they say. Misinterpreting her all along.

"We seem to get along well," I say.

"You seem to have been bumping into a lot of old ghosts lately — Innes, Andrew Kelso. And now Lucy."

"Yes, I suppose it does look that way."

"And all chance meetings. Quite the coincidence." Her eyes are narrow.

I shrug. "St Andrews is a small town."

"Must have been awkward seeing Andrew after all that happened. God, that man was vain."

"You didn't think so at the time," I say.

Elspeth's lip curls in distaste. "I suppose I was infatuated. What can I say? I was a naïve young thing back then."

Young, yes, I think, but it's a stretch to believe that Elspeth has ever been naïve.

"So, you hooked up with him after Moira's death?" I say.

"I told you when you called me, remember?" Elspeth gives a sigh. "I suppose I should have told you back then but I knew you wouldn't have approved. And Shona would have freaked out, so . . ." Elspeth waves her arms in the air. "All water under the bridge now, isn't it?" Her eyes slide slowly over my face. It feels like I'm being carefully scrutinised for the slightest hint of disagreement.

I swallow. Clear my throat. "No, not really."

Elspeth's eyes are slits. "What do you mean? Surely you don't hold it against me after all these years?"

I'm glad she's misinterpreted me. She's assumed I was referring solely to her affair with Andrew. For a moment, I'd been tempted to blurt out everything, and demand to know whether there's anything else she's been keeping from me about that time. I feel a sudden urge to antagonise her, so I say, "Andrew told me he loved Moira. Got quite misty-eyed about her."

Irritatingly, Elspeth just snorts, "In what world do you think I care about that now? For fuck's sake, Ros, Moira's been pushing up daisies for a quarter of a century. And I am so over Andrew Kelso."

From the kitchen comes the sound of laughter. Innes and Duncan seem to be bonding. Elspeth's words shock me somehow, for they seem to suggest that Moira's murder meant nothing to her. I look for explanation for her lack of empathy and, as usual, I find one. Of course. The wicked aunt. Elspeth suffered as a child. She learned early on that you had to draw a line under the past, otherwise it might consume you. Then Innes's words about this story probably being apocryphal ring in my ears, and the more I think about it, the more I agree with him.

"I'm sorry, Elspeth," I say. How often have our disagreements ended with me apologising? But this time, my words are ambiguous. I'm not really saying I'm sorry *to* Elspeth, I'm sorry *for* her. It's as though the wicked aunt has been banished to the fairy-tale realm where she belongs, allowing me to see that there really is something not quite right about Elspeth.

"Haven't 'bumped into' Piers Thornton as well, have you?" Elspeth asks suddenly.

"What? No. Why do you ask?"

"Oh, come on, Ros. It's kind of obvious you and your ex-policeman boyfriend are interested in Moira's murder and are asking questions like a pair of bloody amateur detectives."

Maybe I've underestimated her. She always was as sharp as splintered glass. Maybe asking her about Piers when we spoke on the phone was too much.

"It's probably because Moira's death is a common element in all our pasts, that's all."

"So why did you want to know if I'd kept in touch with Piers?" she asks.

I don't remember saying that exactly. I think I only asked if she'd bumped into Piers in Edinburgh. It's not the biggest city, after all. Elspeth's question seems laden with menace.

"I just thought maybe your paths had crossed, given that you both live here. Meeting Innes, bumping into Andrew, it's set me thinking about the past, I suppose. We don't talk about it much, do we?"

"Well, our paths haven't crossed. I believe J.K. Rowling lives in Edinburgh but I've never bumped into her either."

"We should have told the police about Piers Thornton," I say.

"Told them what? There was nothing to tell."

"Well, we could have said that he and Moira knew each other. Didn't you ever wonder whether Piers acted on his obvious . . . attraction to her?" Elspeth flinches when I mention this. Not all water under the bridge, then. "The police never had a chance to question him."

Elspeth frowns. "I'm not sure where you're going with this, Ros. The police didn't need to speak to Piers, or anyone else for that matter. Stuart Brogan killed Moira. End of story." She gives me one of her penetrating looks. "Is it Innes Nevin who's got you in a tizz about all this? He was only a PC when he worked on Moira's case. What the hell did he know about anything?"

It's not what Innes knew then but what he knows now that concerns me. Out loud I say, "What if Stuart Brogan was innocent?"

"Ros, that's . . . ridiculous!"

"Why is it? He hanged himself before the case could be properly investigated. Forensic science was in its infancy in those days. Think how differently a case like that would be investigated now."

Elspeth is shaking her head. The look she gives me is condescending.

"And you probably don't know this, but all the notes and evidence relating to the original investigation into Moira's death were later destroyed in a fire."

Now Elspeth laughs out loud. It makes me want to shake her. "You really have been talking to Lucy, haven't you? That's just the sort of nonsense she would have spouted. Seeing conspiracies where there are none. I'm surprised at you, Ros."

"I don't think Piers killed Moira," I tell her, "but the police should have been made aware of him as a potential suspect."

"So, who else do you suspect? Andrew Kelso? Me?"

"Ros?" Innes is standing in the doorway. The sound of his voice makes me start. I wonder if he can sense the tension between Elspeth and me. "It's getting late," he adds. "Time to go?"

"I'll tell Izzy."

I go upstairs to the spare bedroom, the one Izzy and I slept in the last time we stayed. As I suspected, she has fallen asleep on one of the beds. It seems a shame to wake her but I'm angry at Elspeth, and I don't want my daughter spending another night under her roof. I don't want to stay in this house a moment longer.

"Izzy." I give her a shake. "Wake up. It's time to go. We're driving back to St Andrews, remember?"

Izzy stirs and groans. "Okay," she says, yawning. I wait while she goes to the bathroom. The door to Elspeth and Duncan's bedroom is ajar. I can hear Elspeth talking downstairs. I think again of the time I woke in the night and found Elspeth in Moira's room, brandishing a pair of scissors like a weapon. The memory makes me shudder.

We go downstairs. Elspeth, Duncan and Innes are still talking in the kitchen, so I go to collect our coats from the cupboard in the hall, where Elspeth usually hangs them when we visit. I put mine on and stick my hand in the pocket, searching for the lip balm I keep in there, but instead my fingers close around an unfamiliar object. Puzzled, I pull it out. It's a pen. There's some writing on the side.

Edinburgh University — Department of History.

I'm wearing Elspeth's coat. And she's lied to me about Piers.

* * *

"It doesn't necessarily mean she's been in touch with Thornton," Innes says when I tell him about the pen. It's one in the morning and we are back at Innes's cottage. All the way back to Edinburgh, I'd been itching to tell him what I'd found in Elspeth's coat pocket, but I couldn't talk about it in front of Izzy. We dropped her off at her hall an hour ago, collected Bronn from a friend of Innes's who'd been looking after him and driven here.

"I know, but I saw some just like it in a desk-tidy on Thornton's desk this afternoon," I say. "That client she claimed kept her late at work? What if it was Piers? He could have contacted her after our visit and asked her to come and see him."

"It's one of those pens they give out free at open days and the like. She could have picked it up anywhere."

"Yes, I know. But — department of history? It has to be more than a coincidence."

"Hmm."

Why am I so eager for the pen to have originated in Piers's office? Wouldn't that suggest that Elspeth was mixed up in Moira's death somehow? Surely this isn't an outcome I'm hoping for? But is it becoming one that's unavoidable?

I recall all the times when Elspeth has steered the conversation away from the subject of Moira. I'd always assumed it was out of guilt over the way she'd treated Moira when she was alive. But what if she had a vested interest in ensuring that no one dwelt on the events of that time for long? *There's such a thing as an accessory to murder.* Innes's words seem to have a particular resonance now.

Innes's laconic reply is slightly exasperating, but it's been a long day and there is something else to attend to right now.

I lead Innes upstairs.

CHAPTER TWENTY-NINE

In the morning, I wake to the aroma of freshly made coffee. Innes appears at the bedroom door, tray in hand. He's dressed, and his cheeks are ruddy. He's already taken Bronn for his morning walk. It must be later than I think.

"Just had a text from Mapleton. He's got some information for me on the identity of the man in your sketch but he doesn't want to discuss it over the phone. I said I'd drive over to Glasgow this morning and meet him. It's probably best if I see him alone but you're welcome to come along for the ride."

The thought of four hours in a car after driving to Edinburgh and back only yesterday isn't appealing. "No, it's okay. If you don't mind, I'll stay home — I mean, I'll stay here. Do some catching up. Take Bronn for a nice long walk."

"I don't mind," Innes says, kissing me on the cheek. He pulls away, beaming. Though he doesn't comment on my slip, I can tell he's delighted that I've referred to his cottage as home.

When he's gone, I sip my coffee and think of my house in Chiswick. It's never completely quiet there. I wake every morning to the noise of traffic that's barely muffled by the double glazing. I eat breakfast accompanied by a cacophony of blaring car horns and sirens. I paint with the noise of machinery a near-constant screech in my head. On my street, someone is always having something done. Conservatories, orangeries, new windows, kitchens, bathrooms, extensions . . . Some days the constant noise and activity drives me crazy. Other days it's a comfort, a reminder that there's a vibrant, living city on my doorstep.

Here, it's so still and quiet that I can hear my own heartbeat, the sound of Bronn's velvety paws padding across the carpet in the downstairs hall. Is Innes's little cottage too quiet for me? Too isolated? I realise that I'm picturing myself living here. Waking day after day to stillness and quiet. Stillness and quiet. I think I can live with that.

I take a shower and go downstairs. Bronn is ecstatic to see me. I slip him a few treats from his special cupboard, though I'm not supposed to. "You'll get fat if I move in with Innes," I warn him. He whines at the mention of Innes's name, and I soothe him by ruffling the thick fur of his nape and letting him lick my face — just this once.

After breakfast, I take him for a walk along the cliff path and down to the beach where the path levels out. It's a cold day but not gloomy, as it so often is in winter. The forecast is for unsettled weather later. Now, though, the grey of the sea is daubed with splashes of blue and white. Bronn flirts with the waves at the water's edge. I look for smooth stones to skim, and laugh at his attempts to catch them. Innes must have done this for him countless times, but Bronn still seems newly astonished when the stones skip over the waves one, two, three times or more — before sinking with a splash.

My thoughts turn to the previous day's interviews with Piers Thornton and Annie Calder. I consider the threads connecting Moira, Andrew, Piers and Elspeth. I recall asking Innes why he wished to know what the conference Andrew attended was about. It had seemed irrelevant, a minor detail. It occurs to me now that these conferences and talks were a stage, the place where all these players met and interacted, with Andrew in the lead role. They were never just background.

Moira often went away with Andrew, sometimes just for a day but occasionally overnight and, more rarely, for a weekend. Like the time they'd gone to Aviemore and Andrew had spent time with his cousin Hans. Moira had been put out, as she had been on that other occasion when he spent time with Hans in Edinburgh. She'd been excluded. Evidently, whatever Andrew and Hans had to discuss did not concern Moira. Nothing odd about that really. It was most likely family matters. Or so Moira had assumed.

Moira had described Hans as dull and boring. Serious. Old. German. *You'd have liked him,* she'd said to Elspeth. The implication being that Elspeth was boring and serious. But what if Moira had been suggesting that Elspeth would get along with Hans for another reason? Because of their political views? I have no idea what Hans's politics were, and I'd just assumed he was from West Germany but perhaps he'd lived in the GDR.

A jumble of thoughts and images rattle through my head. Amidst all the ideas about what might have happened to Moira, Innes's odd theory about the Stasi keeps rising to the top. Moira's lack of interest in politics had always infuriated Elspeth. She simply couldn't accept that Andrew could be infatuated with someone who not only failed to share his political views but even occasionally mocked them. Andrew had introduced Elspeth to Piers assuming they would get along because of their similar political views.

Bronn's whine makes me realise that I have been standing deep in thought for several minutes, paying him no attention. I pick up a piece of driftwood and toss it into the air. He races after it.

I picture Elspeth in the small sitting room of our house on North Street holding forth on Marx and Engels, the evils of western capitalism. Moira suppressing a yawn. Andrew sitting in the corner of the room, listening, adding the occasional appropriate remark. Reining Elspeth in whenever she expressed an opinion that was too extreme. He had lived in the GDR for a year, and the experience had moderated his views.

Or so he'd claimed.

But what if that wasn't so? What if, instead of modifying his views, his time in the GDR had reinforced them? And what if Hans hadn't been his cousin at all?

I call to Bronn and put him on his lead. We make our way back along the beach and up the cliff path, heading home.

Back at the cottage, I sip tea and mull over my thoughts. I feel like a person who's trying to remember a past that was lived in partial darkness but is slowly becoming brighter. There are things I feel I know but I still don't understand how they all connect. Or why Moira had to die.

My brain won't rest. I sit down to do some research on my laptop. I read a series of articles published in the late nineties about how the Stasi's Hauptverwaltung Aufklärung, or HVA, had recruited British academics as informers. Some were approached while on exchange programmes in the GDR. My heart sinks as I think of Andrew Kelso and his year in Leipzig. Of Elspeth, who also intended to study there but was forced to change her plans by the cataclysmic events leading up to the fall of the Berlin Wall.

I pull up more articles. Read how faculty staff at UK universities informed on visiting academics from the GDR, putting them and their families at risk when they returned home. How they identified students likely to be sympathetic to the GDR and encouraged them to apply for places on exchange schemes. Particularly those students who might end up working in sensitive areas of the government, or the military, or in scientific institutions. Those who would have access to important research materials and maybe even be able to influence policy.

At first, it is hard to envision Andrew Kelso involving himself in such activities. Then, as I read more about the personalities of the individuals who had been seduced by the HVA, I realise that he was exactly the sort of person who would have fallen under their spell. Vain. Susceptible to flattery. He would have enjoyed the importance of being singled out from his peers.

Had Moira found him out? If so, had Andrew killed her and left her on that lonely cliff path because he feared that she might go to the police? It would have meant the end of his career, or worse, a charge of treason. I think of him gazing in the mirror in the café, telling me how he'd loved Moira so much that he would have sacrificed everything for her. In more ways than one, I'd been right in concluding that it was all bullshit.

I consider calling Innes. He'll be in Glasgow now.

My phone rings.

Izzy.

"Hi, Mum."

"Hi, sweetheart. Is everything okay? You sound a bit groggy. Have you been drinking?"

"No. I'm sooo sleepy."

"Izzy?"

"Your daughter is unharmed." A man's voice. Piers Thornton. "Whether she remains so is up to you."

"Piers! Where are you? What have you done with my daughter? Let me speak with her."

"I'll be in touch," Piers says. "Your daughter is fine. No harm will come to her so long as you do exactly as I say. Firstly, no police. Secondly, I want an assurance from you and your boyfriend that you will desist from asking questions about Moira Mackie's death. Do you understand?"

There's no time for deliberation. Piers isn't messing about. Izzy's life might depend on my answer. "Yes. No police. Stop asking questions about Moira's death," I say robotically.

"Good. I'll be in touch."

"Wait! You can't just—" I'm talking to myself.

I need to stay calm. I call Innes and am overwhelmed with relief when he answers. He's no longer a policeman, so technically I'm not going against Thornton's directive.

"Innes? Oh, thank goodness. Innes, I think Piers Thornton's kidnapped Izzy."

"What? Jesus! Are you sure?" I explain about the call. My voice breaks. I take in great gulps of air.

"Ros." Innes's voice is calm, measured. "I need you to be calm."

I give an edgy laugh. I remember reading somewhere about studies proving that telling someone to be calm has the opposite effect. Maybe so, but Innes's tone, if not his words, help quell my turbulent thoughts.

"Okay. Sorry, sorry. I completely lost it there. I'm okay now. What do we do? We can't go to the police."

"I'm coming back. Right now," Innes says.

"No. You have to keep your appointment with your colleague, especially now. The information he gives you might help us find out if the mystery man is Hans, and just who this Hans truly is. And it might help Izzy." There's no basis for believing this, but Innes's silence suggests that he agrees. "Okay, but, Ros . . . You have to contact the police. Whatever Thornton said, you must."

"No! Not yet! You're police. You can work out what to do."

"No, Ros, listen to me—"

"No! We have to wait. At least until Thornton contacts me again. He needs to know he can trust me. Please, Innes, don't tell anyone yet. I've lost so many people in my life — I can't lose Izzy."

Reluctantly, Innes agrees to give it a few hours. "You shouldn't be alone at a time like this."

"I'll call Lucy."

"Alright. One more thing."

"Yes?"

"Don't do anything rash, Ros."

"I won't. I . . . promise."

We say goodbye. I'm not concerned about breaking my promise to Innes. What I intend to do next isn't rash, and it isn't stupid. It's necessary. I can't just wait around doing nothing. Not when my daughter's life is at risk.

I grab my coat, telling Bronn I won't be long. He regards me with mournful eyes. Time has no meaning for him, he only knows absence.

Outside, the weather has changed. The sky is heavy and overcast. As I walk towards my car, it begins to rain.

I don't have much of a plan. I don't even know where Andrew Kelso's office is exactly, but he's a professor in the department of history. It shouldn't be difficult to track him down.

I park outside the School of History. It's midday now and there are students about. I ask one of them where to find Professor Kelso's office. There's scant likelihood of him being there but when I knock on his door, I hear him say, "Come in."

Andrew looks up from his PC. He doesn't seem surprised to see me, which causes me a moment's concern. Surely, I should be one of the last people he'd expect to see standing in his doorway this morning? His greeting makes me more uneasy. "I've been expecting to see you again."

He doesn't invite me in, but I enter anyway and close the door behind me. "Oh. Why's that?"

"You weren't exactly subtle when you *bumped* into me the other day. It was obvious you had some hidden agenda. And I heard from my ex-wife again last night."

Again. So, Annie did contact him after Innes spoke with her the first time. It sickens me to think that the man before me could be the person responsible for the attack on my daughter.

"It seems that you and *ex*-Detective Nevin have been harassing her."

"That's not the word I'd use. But that's not why I'm here. Piers Thornton has my daughter. I expect you know that already though, don't you?" Andrew stares at me. His surprise seems genuine.

"Alright," I say. "It's time to stop playing games. This is to do with Moira's murder. I believe you know more than you've ever admitted about what happened to Moira Mackie. And there are facts that have come to light recently that no one could have guessed at during the original investigation."

Andrew doesn't speak. He's waiting to hear how I can back this up.

"*Detective* John Menzies," I say, surprised to hear that I'm whispering, as though I'm the one who needs to be discreet. I watch Andrew closely because I know he's probably been telling himself not to react, whatever I might say. But I see immediately, in the slight narrowing of his eyes, that Menzies's name is not what he was expecting to hear.

"Who?"

I give a heavy sigh. "You know perfectly well who John Menzies is — or was. What you probably don't know is that he died a couple of months ago. In Canada. His widow was kind enough to contact Innes Nevin to tell him that Menzies — or the man she knew as Bob MacDonald — confessed on his deathbed that he helped frame Stuart Brogan for murder."

I leave out the part about Menzies's dementia. I also fail to mention the fact that Menzies never disclosed who bribed him for his secrecy. Even so, my announcement clearly resonates with Andrew. His self-assurance seems to waver, just a little.

"So," I continue, "what you and your ex-wife interpret as *harassment*, I call investigating the truth about who really killed Moira. Your alibi was always dependent on your wife's word. It wouldn't have stood up if a rigorous investigation had been conducted. You weren't home the weekend Moira was killed."

"Annie told me you had some crazy theory about my alibi. But you're wrong."

"Your son had croup the weekend Piers stayed at your house. Two weeks before Moira's murder. You weren't at home that weekend either."

"Is that all you're pinning your hopes on here? A sick child? You have a daughter. You must know that kids can be sick for more than one weekend in a row. Karl was forever coming down with some bug or other in his first couple of years. It would be more surprising if Thornton remembered him being hale and hearty."

He makes me doubt myself but I'm not giving up. "Where were you, really, that weekend? You must realise that the truth is going to come out. This case has preyed on Innes Nevin's mind for more than twenty years. He's not going to let it go now. Right this minute, he's talking to a former colleague in Glasgow about your *cousin*, Hans. Is that who you were with the weekend Moira died?"

At the mention of Hans's name, a little more of Andrew's composure leaks into the air around him and I know I'm right.

"It doesn't matter where I was the weekend Moira Mackie died. It doesn't change anything."

"Change isn't the issue. Surely you can see that?"

In a sudden gesture of defeat, he covers his face with his hands. "My reputation."

Whatever gravitas and accolades he's accrued from his academic success can't mask the fact that he's essentially a weak, vain individual. Disgust wells up inside me.

"You say you cared for Moira. I suspect you cared for yourself and your precious career more."

I look at Andrew Kelso. He's in a world of his own, hardly aware of my presence. Just like that time before, when he questioned me about Moira.

"I didn't kill Moira Mackie," he says at last.

I believe him. He's a despicable coward, possibly a traitor, and his faults are too many to enumerate, but a killer? I just don't see it. "Then who did? Was it Piers Thornton? Your *cousin,* Hans?" He looks at me sharply. "Hans wasn't really your cousin, was he?"

"No." Kelso gives a nervous laugh. "I don't even know if Hans was his real name."

"So, he got you involved, did he?"

"Yes, for my sins," Andrew says in a quiet voice.

"And, Moira? Did she find out what you were all up to? Is that why Hans killed her?"

"Hans didn't kill Moira." He looks slightly surprised. I wonder if I've made a wrong assumption, if my theory is pure fantasy after all.

"Then it was Piers." Last man standing.

"Yes. Piers killed her."

"And you knew? At the time, I mean?"

Andrew looks stricken. He stares at his hands. "I . . . I loved her . . . Moira," he says. "I didn't want Piers to get away with what he did but there was nothing I could do."

"You could have told the police."

Andrew shakes his head. "My academic career would have been over. The scandal, if it had all come out . . . what I had been involved in. I thought I'd go to prison for the rest of my life."

"So, you let Piers get away with murder for the sake of your pathetic career?" I'm so angry I don't care how much I provoke him. "Did you know that Moira was beaten? Raped?" Andrew flinches. "You must be so proud of yourself, letting a man who'd done something so monstrous walk away scot-free."

"He said he didn't mean to do it. He was contrite . . . said he'd make amends. I . . . I believed him. Piers was valuable to . . . to them. He was a brilliant student. He was destined for a career in government, or the military. Whatever he chose. He would have been an invaluable resource." After a slight pause, he adds, "That's another reason why I said nothing. I . . . we . . . we had beliefs. There was a cause, a greater good. But . . ." He falters. "It was all for nothing because then—"

"Then the Wall came down?"

"Yes," he says bitterly. "Because then the Wall came down, and everything changed."

* * *

My head reels. I reach for the edge of Andrew's desk and stand, swaying. He is out of his chair in an instant, diving around his desk in time to catch me as I pitch forward. For a moment or two I'm disoriented.

"I think you should sit down," he says. He helps me to a chair, pours me some water.

As I recover, I'm aware of the irony of Andrew's apparent concern. I look up at him. "You attacked Izzy. Your ex-wife contacted you after Innes Nevin questioned her about your alibi. You saw Innes with me, and you panicked. You were worried I'd help Innes find out about Piers and . . . and Hans. You thought you could scare Izzy into leaving St Andrews and that would get rid of me too."

Andrew hangs his head. "I told that idiot I hired not to hurt her, just to give her a good scare. I just wanted to give you a warning, before you started asking questions of the wrong people."

"You mean Piers? Elspeth?" I know I'm right about Elspeth, but my heart sinks when he nods.

"Where would he have taken my daughter?" Andrew looks conflicted. My patience is at an end. "For fuck's sake. You already have two deaths on your conscience, do you really want a third?"

He flinches. "I . . . I don't know. I'm sorry. Unless . . ." He furrows his brow. "There's a place on the outskirts of town, a house that's sometimes used by visiting academics. It belongs to a retired professor who lives in one of the fishing villages. Piers might have gone there."

"On the outskirts of town? You mean here, in St Andrews?"

"Yes."

"Do you know this professor? Can you contact him and find out if Piers is using his house?"

Andrew nods. He pulls out his mobile, taps the screen. "Hello? Gordon? Andrew Kelso here. I was just wondering if your flat is free tonight? A colleague from Edinburgh needs somewhere . . . Oh, you've got someone there this evening already, have you? Never mind. It's not Piers Thornton, is it? I know he was planning to come over this week. It is? Well, no doubt I'll be seeing him soon . . . Yes, yes, it has been a while. We must get together . . . I'm . . . rather pressed at the moment. I'll call you. Give my love to Sarah, won't you?"

I wait impatiently for Andrew to finish. "He's there?"

"Yes. He collected the keys from Gordon this morning."

I stand up. "We'll take your car," I say.

Andrew stares at me in disbelief. "If you don't mind my asking," he says, "what exactly do you intend to do when we get there?"

"I do mind you asking." I spit out the words and he backs off, raising his hands. He retreats behind his desk and sits down, looking dejected. He must know that the truth is going to come out now.

But he's right. There's nothing to be gained from acting recklessly. Arriving at the flat without a plan isn't going to help Izzy. I think of PC Nadia Fraser and how kind she was at the hospital after the attack on Izzy, and I have half a mind to call her now. It's what Innes wants me to do, and now I have information on Izzy's possible whereabouts, which must be an advantage.

No police, Piers cautioned. He asked me to wait for further instructions. I look at my watch. That was two hours ago now, and he still hasn't been in touch.

I look at Andrew. "You know him better than me. What do you think he plans to do next?"

Andrew says nothing. My mobile rings. Innes.

"Ros. I've spoken with Mapleton. He's identified 'Hans.' His real name was Kurt Berger. He was an active member of the Stasi in the seventies and eighties. It's likely he acted as Kelso's handler. It's looking like our spy theory isn't the stuff of fantasy after all."

"Andrew, Piers — they were both involved," I say quietly. "And Elspeth." *Let's not forget Elspeth.*

"I'm sorry, Ros."

"Don't be. Innes, I think Piers Thornton killed Moira. His motive isn't clear yet but I think Hans covered up the murder because of Piers's potential usefulness. Piers killed Moira, and now he has my daughter."

"I'm already on my way back," Innes says. "Any word from him?"

"No."

"Where are you, Ros? You're not with Lucy, are you?"

"I'm with Andrew Kelso. He's worked out where Thornton is holding Izzy. There's a house on the outskirts of town owned by a retired professor. Kelso just spoke with him, and he confirmed that Thornton's there."

I can hear Innes's displeasure in the silence before he says, "It's time to involve the police, Ros." I don't answer. "Ros?"

"Yes, yes. I know. Can you call them? They'll listen to you." Innes says he will. I get the address from Andrew and give it to Innes, who wants me to promise I won't go anywhere near the house before the police arrive. "I think we need to wait — until Thornton contacts you again. Find out what he wants from you. From us. He doesn't know about Menzies's confession, or what else we've discovered."

"He's desperate," I say. "Why else would he kidnap Izzy? He's hoping he can bargain with us. Izzy's safety in return for us dropping the whole thing. He's hoping we haven't involved anyone else yet. What will he do to Izzy when he finds out it's all over for him?"

Innes tries to reassure me. "It wouldn't be in his interest to add hurting Izzy to his other crimes."

By 'hurting,' I assume he means killing.

* * *

Andrew's car, a red Audi, is parked in the staff parking area a short walk from his office. I opt to drive. I'm nervous and I stall the car before I even get it going properly. The weather is atrocious now. Though it's only mid-afternoon, it's already almost dark.

The rain picks up force, pounding against the windscreen. Even at full speed, the wipers can't cope. The noise they make slashing to and fro sets my nerves on edge.

On the way, Andrew blubbers out his story. "Piers met Moira on the F . . . Friday evening. I was with Hans. Hans was my handler." Andrew glances at me and I nod to show that I know what he means. "He took her to a caravan and . . . and they had sex."

I'm so angry I can barely control the car. "Stop saying that! He raped her, and you know it."

"No. They had rough sex," he insists.

"Seriously? Was Moira ever into that with you? Did she ask you to beat her? Because he did beat her, Andrew. Amongst other things. Innes Nevin could have shown you the photos if they hadn't conveniently gone up in flames."

He's crying openly now, but I can't summon up any sympathy. I wait for him to continue. "Piers contacted Hans and told him he'd k . . . killed Moira by accident. He asked him for help." He stutters between sobs. "Hans agreed. He had big plans for Piers."

It's sickening to hear him relate all this, knowing that he's kept quiet about it for all these years. "And what happened to Stuart Brogan? Was Hans responsible for his death?"

"I . . . I don't know. I didn't ask." He pauses. "I assume so. Oh God. It's all my fault. If only I'd never introduced Elspeth to Piers . . ."

"Shut up! Which house is it?" I ask.

The rain and the dark are making it difficult for Andrew to see where we are. He leans forward and squints through the windscreen. "Slow down. It's on the left, just up here." I brake too hard, jerking us both forwards in our seats, then sideways as I veer into the kerb. Now that we are here, I feel a renewed sense of urgency. I glance at Andrew. He points to a window on the second floor.

I turn to Andrew. "If Piers is up there, he'll let you in. He knows you."

"No! He'll be suspicious of me turning up here of all places. And out of the blue. He'll know you're behind it."

I know what he says is true but I can't stand the thought of just waiting and doing nothing.

I remember the question I asked him earlier, before we were interrupted by Innes's phone call.

"What do you think Piers's next move is likely to be? Do you think he's buying time? But why take Izzy? If he thought everything was about to collapse around him, why didn't he just take flight instead of coming all the way to St Andrews? He's evaded being brought to justice for more than twenty years. Why would he make a stupid mistake now?"

It's partly my nerves, making me think aloud. Andrew's gloomy silence is oppressive. I wonder if he feels a shred of sympathy for Izzy or me, or whether he's brooding on the imminent demise of his reputation.

"I'm sorry," he says eventually. "I can't second-guess him. Never could. It was a shock to me to learn what he'd done to Moira. Piers Thornton killed the only woman I truly loved. I despise him."

"For fuck's sake, get over yourself," I say. "You've had more than twenty years to do something about it, to ensure that he was brought to justice. All you cared about was the damage it could've done to your career if the truth came out — the truth of what you were all up to."

He has the decency to hang his head in apparent shame. I glance at his face. I'm slightly disgusted to see that he's weeping.

"I don't know what Moira ever saw in you."

Andrew runs his hand through his hair. "I . . . I honestly don't know what Piers will do next, but I do know enough about him to know that he believes what *they* believed. That everyone is corruptible."

I look at him. "Like John Menzies?"

"Yes. Piers believes everyone can be bought for the right price. For some, it's money. For others kudos. Or power. Or position."

"And Izzy is my price?"

He is too cowardly to say it aloud, but he nods.

My thoughts start racing again. If I can persuade Innes to remain silent about John Menzies's confession, give up his quest for justice, and let discovering the truth about Moira's murder be enough, then Izzy will be saved. Everything would return to how it was before Barbara MacDonald contacted him and no one would be any the wiser.

It's tempting. I think of Stuart Brogan, wrongly accused but long dead. What good can the truth do him now? There's his sister, Isla, who would never see justice for her dead brother, but she'd never allowed herself to hope for that until Innes and I came knocking on her door. I think of her plea to us, to let her know what we found out. We are her last, her only hope.

Then I think of Moira. She, too, is long dead. Her parents. I know she had siblings, but they are nameless and faceless to me. Moira hardly spoke about them. As far as they know, justice for their sister's death was served the day Stuart Brogan took his own life.

Lastly, I think of Doug. His killers will never be brought to justice, but his is a wholly different story.

Andrew fumbles in his pocket and produces a handkerchief, which he offers to me. I didn't even realise I was crying. The handkerchief is white linen and smells freshly laundered. I bury my face in its folds, hiding my thoughts from the man beside me.

I hand the handkerchief back to him and open the car door.

"What are you going to do?" he asks.

"Isn't it obvious?" I say. "I'm going to speak with Piers."

* * *

The professor's flat is on the second floor. I press the button on the intercom, grin for the camera. The door releases with a click. I climb the two flights of stairs and stand outside on the landing, staring at the big brass number five on the door. It's hanging slightly askew.

I'd expected him to be waiting for me, but Piers makes me knock. Takes his time to answer.

"You were supposed to wait until I called. I take it you tracked me down through Andrew Kelso."

"I want to see my daughter."

"Then you'd better come in." Piers steps out from behind the door and I see he's holding a gun. I gasp.

"Breathe," he says. "Where's Nevin?"

"At home, waiting for me to call. I thought it would be better if I came alone. He disagreed, but I insisted. We haven't spoken to the police. All we care about is Izzy. If you hand her over safely, we'll stop asking questions about the past."

We're in a small, square hallway. Piers points to one of three doors.

"Open it. Your daughter's inside. But you won't find her very responsive. I've given her something to make her sleep."

It's as he says. Izzy is slumbering peacefully on a double divan. He's even covered her with a plaid blanket.

"Can we talk?" I ask. Piers nods towards one of the other doors. It leads into a compact, open-plan kitchen and living area.

"Take a seat," he says. He moves to the window, pulls back the vertical blind slightly and looks down at the street, where Andrew's car is parked.

"I see you've brought company."

"Only Andrew Kelso. He helped me find you."

"I expect he's hoping I can persuade you to keep quiet." When I say nothing, he adds, "Can I?"

"All I want is to keep Izzy safe."

"Tell me what you know," he says.

I tell him most of it, including how I believe Hans bribed Menzies to help frame Stuart Brogan for Moira's murder. But I don't mention Menzies's deathbed confession. To my surprise, Piers seems to relax slightly.

"You have no proof," he says when I've finished. "Kelso will never talk about his activities back then. And there's absolutely no evidence of our hypothetical involvement in what you allege. You have nothing."

I wonder if he's thinking that he's made a huge mistake, and his need for self-preservation has led him into a situation he might have avoided. I'm confused. Have Innes and I missed something? I sense that Piers is surprised at how little, not how much we know. There's a part of the puzzle still missing, I think, with frustration and panic.

I feel a surge of anger. At the risk of provoking him, I say, "Andrew Kelso's convinced himself that his 'activities,' as you call them, did no one any harm. He assured me he never hurt anyone. That's debatable, but not in your case. You raped and murdered a young woman and for that, you deserve to be brought to justice." I rein my emotions in then, speak more calmly. "Even so, Izzy's more important to me than making you pay for what you did to Moira."

Piers strides up and down the room. Weighing his options, I suppose. I sit completely still, willing myself not to glance towards the window. If Piers sees me look, he'll know instantly that I'm expecting back-up. Will the police announce their arrival, I wonder? Piers might panic if he hears a siren or catches a glimpse of a flashing blue light through the blinds. I wonder if the Fife constabulary has much experience of hostage situations. I'll just have to trust them to know their job.

Piers continues to pace.

"Let my daughter go, Piers. Innes and I will keep your secret. The past will stay buried."

My thoughts race. How can Piers take a risk like that? He must know that as soon as Izzy is safe, nothing will prevent Innes and me from going straight to the police. Why should he trust us? My breath catches in my throat. The price Piers wants for Izzy's safety is not our silence.

My gasp gets his attention. Our eyes meet. He understands that I have caught on at last.

"How will you cover up your mess this time, Piers?" I say in desperation. "You're of no value to anyone anymore. It'll all be on you. Explaining away three corpses in a flat you've been staying in won't be easy. There'll be no one to come along and clean up after you now."

I don't care if I'm repeating myself. I hardly know what I'm saying.

Piers stops pacing. "Call your boyfriend. Tell him where we are and tell him to get here fast. No police. Do as I say and Izzy lives. She'll sleepwalk right out of here and back into her comfortable life." He shrugs. "Motherless, but that's the price."

I know he's lying. Izzy has met him. He can't afford to take a chance and let her live. I do as he instructs. It's good to hear Innes's voice. It would be even better to hear some reassurance that the police have a plan. But of course, Innes can't risk Piers overhearing.

As soon as the call ends, Piers resumes his pacing. Ten minutes later, a knock on the door makes us both jump.

"Don't move!" Piers backs into the hallway. I suffer agonies of indecision. Do I disobey Piers, risk taking a bullet so that Innes can use the distraction to overpower him?

There's no time to think. I watch as Piers struggles with the lock. He leans sideways so that he can watch me while he angles the gun at the door.

My whole body starts to shake. Blood pounds in my ears. Adrenalin, I realise. Urging my body to act.

The door opens inwards. In a flash, I'm out of the chair. Just before I duck, I see Piers swivel around, gun raised. A shot rings out, hits the window. Shards of glass explode across the room. I shield my face, crying out as the splinters embed themselves in my hands and fingers.

Blinking through a lattice of blood and slivers of glass, I see not Innes but Andrew Kelso standing on the threshold. He and Piers are staring, mesmerised, at the gaping window, as though it's a portal to another dimension.

They seem to stare forever, but it's only a split second before Andrew lunges at Piers, grabbing his wrist. The two men wrestle ineffectually for a few moments, Andrew struggling to get hold of the gun.

But Piers is the stronger of the two. He knees Andrew in the groin, and he goes down, clutching his balls, face contorted in agony. Piers silences him with a pistol whip to the head. He stands up, staggering, thrown off balance by the encounter.

He's forgotten I'm here. No sooner does the thought flash into my mind than Piers recovers his senses. He steps over Andrew's prone body and levels the gun at me.

This is it. This is how it was for Doug, I think bleakly, squeezing my eyes shut.

"Mum!"

Piers freezes. He swivels to see Izzy, dazed and confused, emerging from the bedroom. Adrenalin courses through me a second time. One moment there's a dagger-sized splinter of glass at my feet, the next it's lodged in Piers Thornton's neck.

* * *

And now the cavalry arrives. They don't herald their presence with blaring trumpets but nevertheless, the noise they make is enough to wake the dead. A seeming horde of uniformed officers storm through the open door in a burst of shouts and controlled chaos.

And close behind them is Innes Nevin, looking older than I've ever seen him — until he spots Izzy and I clinging to each other. Then his smile transforms him, briefly, into the shy young constable I first met more than a quarter of a century ago.

"That's an arterial bleed," someone exclaims, and yells, "Medic!"

Do I care if Piers Thornton bleeds to death? Not at this moment, but I'm somehow relieved to see two paramedics rushing to his aid.

"Come on. Come away," Innes urges. "Let them save the murderous bastard."

CHAPTER THIRTY

"So, what you're saying is that Andrew Kelso and Piers Thornton were spies for the East German secret police? The Stasi?"

Lucy's expression of incredulity is mirrored in her husband's face. They are having trouble taking in all that Innes has just told them. For Izzy, who grew up long after the Cold War and is only dimly aware that a wall once divided Germany, this must seem a bit surreal.

It's two weeks since Piers Thornton was arrested and charged with abducting Izzy and threatening to kill me. The police are in the process of assessing whether there is enough evidence to charge him with the murder of Moira Mackie. Andrew Kelso is showing himself to be only too willing to talk at last. One theory is that Berger instructed Piers to kill Moira because he considered her relationship with Andrew Kelso a threat.

We're all gathered together in Innes's kitchen to discuss recent — and distant — events. Shona is here too, and she is as astonished as Lucy and Alec.

"I know it's a lot to take in," Innes says. "Lucy, your description of the man you saw talking to Moira that fateful Friday afternoon proved invaluable in unravelling the intricacies of this whole affair. The sketch Ros produced from your description enabled my colleague in Glasgow to identify Hans as Kurt Berger. Berger recruited Kelso in 1979 when he was studying at the University of Leipzig."

"It's hard to believe that people would do that, isn't it?" Shona comments. "Inform on their fellow academics. Pretend to take them into their confidence and then betray them as soon as their backs are turned. And from what you've just told us, the Stasi singled out people who would be attracted by the excitement of it all. The glamour, even." She shakes her head.

"In Kelso's case, Berger's initial lure was a promise to arrange visa permits for Kelso to visit the GDR after his exchange year was up." Innes looks at me, "But from what Ros has told me about his personality, I'd guess he also succumbed to flattery."

"Do you think the Stasi files on Kelso will ever be recovered? Like the ones on the people we already know about, whose files turned up after the Wall came down?" Alec asks.

"Who knows? They haven't come to light yet. It's more than likely they were amongst those destroyed," Innes says. "Then again, it's difficult to comprehend the sheer scale of the information the Stasi gathered on its own citizens at home and abroad." He shrugs.

I think of what it must be like for ordinary citizens of the former GDR to read their files and discover that people they'd believed to be their friends and neighbours had been secretly informing on them. It makes me shudder to think of the tentacles of this sinister repressive regime reaching out as far as our little house on North Street and contributing to the death of our friend.

I look at Innes. His eyes no longer have that blue-black gleam denoting extreme emotion, but I know that recent revelations have shaken him to the core. As all the pieces of the puzzle begin to fall into place, it is becoming clear that Piers's confidence that he would be protected, back then, and even now, stemmed from layers of corruption going all the way to the top. Through Berger, he had access to a whole network of sympathetic comrades all over the UK. Men and women in high places who could make any trouble disappear.

My heart goes out to Innes. It strikes at the very heart of everything that he believed in when he took his oath as a police officer. As a young, inexperienced police constable, he put his trust in the integrity of the criminal justice system, and in those who sought to uphold what it stood for — from his fellow officers and his superiors, all the way to the top. Only to be betrayed.

I know he's bitter about all this. It is something he will just have to live with. That is, knowing that people he worked for perverted the course of justice for Moira and Stuart in order to further the interests of a regime that routinely betrayed and tortured its citizens. But I am certain that in the coming months he will do his utmost to ensure that this time around, justice is served.

Now Innes looks around the room, taking in the dazed expressions. "I think we could all do with a drink," he says. He leaves the room and returns with a bottle of scotch and five glasses and pours everyone a generous measure.

Izzy, who's just swigged back half her scotch, interrupts. "I have left-wing leanings. You do too, Mum."

Lucy smiles. "You'd be hard-pressed to find anyone in this room who votes Tory, Izzy. But none of us would support a regime that viciously represses its own people."

"Just winding you up," Izzy says, a mischievous gleam in her eye.

"Maybe you should go easy on the scotch," I say.

"Hey, I was kidnapped by a murderer two weeks ago. My nerves need soothing." As a joke, it's on the dark side. Izzy seems to have recovered from her ordeal remarkably well, helped, no doubt, by the fact that she slept through most of it.

Piers had lain in wait for her outside her hall of residence and injected her with a sedative before bundling her into his car. The last and only thing she really remembers before waking up, confused, in the professor's flat, is being surprised to see Piers Thornton so soon after meeting him in Edinburgh. Lucky for both of us that he underestimated the dosage required to keep her under.

I smile at my daughter and I don't object when Innes tops up her drink. I pick up my scotch and swirl the liquid around in the glass, before swallowing it in one gulp. Izzy crosses the room to sit beside me. She puts her head on my shoulder, her mischievous mood gone. "How much did Aunt Elspeth know?" she asks me.

"She's not your aunt," I say sharply. I am aware that all eyes in the room are on me now. Elspeth's friend. Her unfailing supporter. The one person she could always rely upon to find the good in her. I think of the first time we met, her calling to me across that packed and seemingly hostile lecture theatre. She'd offered me the lifeline of friendship at a time when I was at my lowest ebb and my gratitude had blinkered me to her true nature. But I'm no longer that person. I realise she's been gone for a long time.

"Everything," I say. "She knew that Piers Thornton murdered Moira, and she knew Stuart Brogan was innocent. As far as she was concerned, Piers did her a favour. With Moira dead and Annie Kelso asking for a divorce, she got what she wanted at last. The great Andrew Kelso."

"But not for long," Lucy said.

"No. Elspeth told me he was less of a prize than she'd imagined. But I think what he told me is closer to the truth. He saw quite quickly what Elspeth was, and wanted nothing to do with her."

There's an irony in that, I think, considering how long I dragged my feet over acknowledging Elspeth's true nature. I'm grateful that neither Shona nor Lucy comments.

"As soon as she discovered I was in touch with Innes, she became suspicious, contacted Andrew and asked him if I'd approached him. That was before I'd spoken with Andrew, but of course, Annie Calder had already mentioned to him that Innes had been asking her about his alibi. Elspeth must have panicked when he told her about that. She told me that stupid story about Innes to stall me and give her time to think what to do. She also contacted Piers Thornton."

No one speaks for a few moments. Finally, Lucy says, "Two innocent young lives sacrificed, and the man responsible walked free — for what? In the end it was all for nothing, wasn't it?"

"Because then the Wall came down, and everything changed," I say quietly, remembering Andrew's words.

"What will happen to Kelso, Thornton and Elspeth?" Izzy asks. "I mean, they were sort of . . . traitors, weren't they?"

"It will be for the court to decide what part each one of them played in Moira and Stuart Brogan's murders," Innes says. "As for their involvement with the Stasi, possibly nothing more than being shamed publicly for their activities, if history is anything to go by."

Lucy, who has been nodding throughout, says, "To answer your question, Izzy, some of the people named in the late nineties were investigated by British Intelligence. Some were suspended from their posts only to be reinstated later. Many remain in post to this day as heads of university departments, researchers, politicians. Most of them still maintain that their activities were harmless and that they didn't hurt anyone."

A hush falls on the room.

"Tell that to all the people who were locked up or exiled from their own country as a result of information passed on by people like Kelso," Alec says quietly.

"Tell it to their families who suffered hardship and fear when their loved ones were taken in the middle of the night," Shona adds.

"Tell it to Stuart Brogan's sister, and Moira's siblings," I say. "And to their parents, though it's too late for any of them to hear."

* * *

It's late in the evening. Everyone has gone home, leaving Innes and I alone with Bronn, who is in need of a night time walk.

"Alright?" Innes asks, as he hands me my coat.

"I will be. It's just . . . so much has happened since that day we met on the beach. So many terrible truths have come to light."

"Maybe it's time to look forwards, not backwards," Innes says.

"Yes." Our eyes meet. Neither of us has to say it aloud. *There's a lot to look forward to. Now that we have each other.*

THE END

OTHER BOOKS BY JANICE FROST

NEAL & MERRY
Book 1: DEAD SECRET
Book 2: DARK SECRET
Book 3: HER HUSBAND'S SECRET
Book 4: THEIR FATAL SECRETS
Book 5: DIRTY SECRETS

Please join our mailing list for free Kindle crime thriller, detective, mystery, and romance books and new releases, as well as news on Janice's next book!
http://www.joffebooks.com/contact/

FREE KINDLE BOOKS AND OFFERS

Please join our mailing list for free Kindle crime thriller, detective, mystery, and romance books and new releases, as well as news on Janice's next book!
http://www.joffebooks.com/contact/

Thank you for reading this book. If you enjoyed it please leave feedback on Amazon, and if there is anything we missed or you have a question about then please get in touch. The author and publishing team appreciate your feedback and time reading this book.

Our email is office@joffebooks.com

http://joffebooks.com

Follow us on Facebook www.facebook.com/joffebooks

We hate typos too but sometimes they slip through.
Please send any errors you find to
corrections@joffebooks.com
We'll get them fixed ASAP. We're very grateful to
eagle-eyed readers who take the time to contact us.

Printed in Great Britain
by Amazon

34562410R00166